# THE SWIM

## A NOVEL ABOUT FRIENDSHIP AND THE LONGEST SWIM IN THE WORLD

### BY JENS F. COLTING

THE SWIM
A Novel About Friendship and the Longest Swim in the World
by Jens F. Colting

Published by Moppet Books
Los Angeles, California

ISBN: 978-0-9988205-3-8

Cover art and book design by Melissa Medina

*Special thanks to:*
Laura X, Melody Foster

Printed in China

**MOPPET BOOKS**

www.moppetbookspublishing.com

*for Melissa, Merci & Jonas*

53.2707° N, 9.0568° W, Galway, Ireland

11:44 AM, Monday, April 17, 1988

"You've got the squash headed turtle that swims over 3000 miles every year just to get back to the beach where it was born. And on the left, folks, are a herd of grey moose, the largest species of moose in the world, weighing as much as 2000 pounds. And right above them we have a flock of colorful pearl toucans with beaks so strong they can crack open an oyster. And over by..."

"Who are you talking to?"

Goliath turns from the bus window, where drab looking concrete blockhouses and parking lots pass as if on an urban assembly line. The girl, who is pretty with a perfect nose that curves up just a hint at the tip (this means she's inquisitive, or as her brother would say, annoying) probes him again.

"Are you talking to yourself or something?"

Goliath looks at her through his round glasses. He wonders if he should bother explaining. And it is a bother. Sometimes people just don't get it. Most people look out the window and see a gas station with little red flags sitting sadly on the canopy when it's pretty obvious that it's a family of white-horned rhinos.

And when most people look at the bus stop with the line of pensioners wearing tweed coats and hats, even though it's the middle of spring, because that's just the kind of place Galway, Ireland is, they don't notice the emperor penguins standing about in groups, chit-chatting about the weather, which is usually different types of water: there's the summer rain which wouldn't be so bad would it just not happen all summer, the winter storm rain that sometimes turns into a mushy snow, the from-the-side and upwards rain that happens during fall and gets you if you have an umbrella or not, and of course, the most common one type of water: plain, old drizzle.

And when most people see a cracker factory with a red brick chimney that pours out white smoke every day of the year, except Christmas, (no crackers need to be made on Christmas- it's for eating them), they don't see the giraffe or the cluster of spider monkeys that swing from its neck. In his twelve years of life it's become apparent to Goliath that most people don't see the forest for the trees. Or in this case, they don't see the animals in the trees.

The girl proves her nose right. She *is* inquisitive.

"Because my gran talks to herself but she's got Allshammers."

The bus comes to a stop in front of a flat concrete building. An old iron fence runs along the entire perimeter, and from the outside you might think you've landed in that movie with dinosaurs on an island, but as you enter in the middle, through the long, black bars that open up and make it look like they're from the mouth of a giant whale, all you can really think of is the story of Jonah and the whale. Not that Goliath would mind much.

Caught in the belly of a whale, traveling the world. Now that is an adventure he'd sign up for.

There is an old ticket window that is the only point of entry, and above it a rusty sign that reads "Municipal Pool". Further in, behind the ticket booth and the changing rooms, is a corner of a flat, light blue surface. The entire complex is sort of like a reverse castle, with the moat on the inside instead of around it.

Goliath releases the handbrake on his wheelchair and maneuvers it down the bus aisle. At the door, he pivots his chair as if he's done it a million times before, which he has, because he's been in a wheelchair since like forever. He presses the button for the hydraulic lift and peers at the girl with a deadpan expression, as the ramp lowers him to the ground with a steady hum.

"The mustached puff bird inhabitates the jungles of Colombia and Venezuela, but sometimes you spot them on a bus in Galway."

Goliath sees the girl staring at him through the window as the bus pulls away. Through the pinkish cloud of fumes he sees her mouthing what looks to be the word "weirdo." The world is blind, and *he's* the weirdo?

Sometimes people just don't get it.

———————

Goliath was named after Goliath, the giant in the Bible who was beat up by the much smaller David. It's an ironic name, considering Goliath's size. He rolls up to the ticket window and has to stretch his head up, like a flamingo, just to be able to see above the edge. His thin arms strain to lift his upper body, while his legs dangle lifeless below him. Nothing but overcooked noodles strapped to a wheelchair. Strapped. Like they would go anywhere.

"My little sparrow", his mom, Susy, used to call him when he was little.

What she should have called him is David. That would have made a heck of a bunch more sense. Parents should wait a few years to name their kids so they can come with some input. But Goliath isn't complaining - having the name of a giant is pretty cool. He could do without the sparrow part, though. He's twelve. He may still be little, but he's nobody's sparrow.

"Class is cancelled," Bill says, not looking up from his newspaper.

"Yesterday's copy", Goliath thinks, because Bill is a real cheapskate. That's why he mans the ticket window himself, even though he's the pool complex manager. He doesn't trust anyone else with money. He doesn't trust anyone else with anything. In fact, he doesn't even *like* anyone. And that's why nobody really likes Bill. Plus he's always muttering and swearing under his breath, suspecting that people sneak into the pool to swim without paying the fare. That's what he says, *fare*. As if swimming is a ride.

His full name is Bill Buskly but people always refer to him as Bill Bruskly.

"That's OK Mr. Buskly, I'll go in anyway." Goliath flashes his pass.

"Kids don't go to school these days?" It's not so much a question as a statement.

It doesn't faze Goliath though. Not much does. When you're in a wheelchair you sort of become less afraid of the things other people are afraid of. It's like there's one less thing that could happen to you, and that makes a difference.

"It's Saturday, Mr. Buskly, there's no school."

Bill mutters something under his breath as Goliath rolls through the gate, and into the pool area.

It happens ever so often that Goliath's swim class is cancelled. Miss Jones, his instructor, is as reliable as their old car, his mom says. And their car breaks down just about every week. But Goliath doesn't mind. He prefers being at the pool by himself. Not so much for the swimming - he *has* to do the swimming, Doctor Gupta says, in order to keep the little muscle he has from completely shriveling up and disappearing. Swimming, or rather, the water exercises that Miss Jones takes him through are really the only form of movement Goliath can do, except pushing his wheelchair around. He's done it ever since Doctor Gupta told them he had to, last year. Only one problem: Goliath doesn't like getting wet.

But he does like being by the pool, and being by the pool without getting wet is a rare thing. And rare things are moments that make life feel special, like watching TV outside, or eating ice cream for breakfast. And that's why Goliath is happy his class is canceled.

He looks around. The pool is completely deserted. The surface is still and unbroken like a huge mirror, reflecting the mass of grey clouds slowly floating above. He spies across the grass and the benches but Goliath can't spot one other person, even though, in the middle of the day, there are usually at least a couple of old folks doing their laps in slow-motion. Watching them swim is like watching sloths move down a branch.

From the other side of town the air brings cheers that seem to come from a thousand people. A soccer game. That explains the deserted pool. Everyone in Galway is crazy about soccer. But not Goliath. He's never been able to get excited about tiny people dressed in the same colored shirts, running across a field, chasing a small ball. Running in general is pretty silly, Goliath thinks.

Around the pool is a ledge about two feet wide and a couple of inches high. Goliath positions his wheelchair against it and carefully applies pressure on the wheels with his arms. He's trying to get his wheelchair onto the ledge but has to control how fast he climbs over it, or he'll risk rolling right into the water.

He pushes down on the front of the wheel, the rubber grabbing the stone ledge. Like a digger climbing through a steep construction site, he inches the chair onto the ledge. As soon as he breaks free from gravity and begins rolling forward towards the pool, he pulls back on the rubber and comes to a stop.

Africa, or more precisely Lake Victoria. Goliath is right at the edge of the famous watershed that was the end destination of so many expeditions. It was here that explorers were forever lost in the thick and thorny jungle that surrounds it, walking aimlessly for days, months and years. Others—the lucky ones—

were eaten by cannibals. Either way, the explorers were never heard of again.

Goliath looks into the muddy water that provides perfect cover to the mysterious Nile perch. One of the largest fresh water fish in the world, with a length of six feet and a weight of up to 500lb, its mouth is big enough to swallow an unsuspecting child.

For days his expedition has forged torrid deserts and steep mountains to get close to this dinosaur of a fish, a fish only a few handful of people have actually seen.

There! Something huge has disturbed the surface, creating ripples that roll across the water. Whatever it is, it's moving along shore, probably looking for a kid to eat.

Goliath lifts himself up from his seat and cranes his neck, out over the edge, as far as he can. A Nile perch!

The fish is swimming closer, and it's a terrifying and beautiful sight. Terrifying, because it's like a silvery torpedo coming right at you, but oh what a beauty she is!

It's right below him now. Goliath nudges the wheelchair closer, and leans forward a few more inches. You see, an explorer has to be in the heart of things, come face to face with danger.

The Nile perch is longer than he is, the scales of hardened, copper plates overlapping one another like a knight's armor. It's intelligence superior to any other fish. This particular one lifts its ancient looking head out of the water and looks right at Goliath. It has lips that seem to be made of an old, chewed up, leather sole, but those eyes...those eyes are filled with the deep intelligence of nature.

Goliath is mesmerized by the round, black pools of wisdom, and he feels like he might be sucked into them at any moment. And suddenly he is.

From one moment to the next the world is turned upside down. The sky turns into the ground and the ground opens up beneath him, as the jaws of the giant Nile perch swallows Goliath whole.

For a moment, the surface of the pool is wild and broken. But after only a few seconds it has mended itself back together to one, solid mirror again.

Goliath is just sitting there. The swimming pool stretches out before him, the blue haze making it seem the whole world is covered in water. He opens his mouth and tiny bubbles race for the surface. Watching them go, small balloons of air, has him so fascinated that for a moment he doesn't know what is going on. Then suddenly it hits him. The world is covered in water! He's at the bottom of the pool.

He immediately beings struggling with the seat belt. As soon as he gets that off he will float to the surface, just like the air bubbles. But something doesn't work. The belt clasp has slid under the hem of his pants, and is caught there, in a jumble of fabric. Water fills his eyes and makes it hard to see where the clasp is in all that mess, and then there's the sound. It's like something is covering his ears, while at the same time he hears every itty-bitty sound. There's water sloshing against the side of the pool and there's a steady drone of what must be a pump in the distance. It's all so unreal, as if it's not actually happening. And in this dream everything is heavy and light at the same time, as well as loud and subdued, but it's oddly pleasant to feel the slight pressure against every part of your body, as if the air was suddenly thick and creamy. It's only when Goliath feels the burning sensation in his lungs, as they demand a new breath, that he gets scared.

---

Tiny holds the ladder while Kurt climbs up and starts cleaning the gutter. He holds it with both hands because that's how Kurt has told him to do it, even though he can keep it steady with just one. As a matter of fact, Tiny can lift the entire ladder, straight off the ground, with just one hand. Not that he ever would. And there have been plenty of people in Tiny's life that have wanted him to lift things up from one spot and put it down in another, just to prove a point. Tiny is strong. He's strong *and* big. In fact, even though he's only 14, he is *gigantic*. At 7 feet tall his hands are the size of dinner plates, and not the small plates on which you eat salad, but the big ones that can hold an entire pizza. His chest is seemingly molded from a wine barrel, the way it makes every t-shirt he wears sit snugly around his body like a crumpled up sock, and then there's his shoulders: so wide they have to turn sideways just to fit through a door!

But despite his size Tiny has never been a show off. Tiny, the giant boy, is incurably shy. He's so shy that people think there's something wrong with him. Granted, he's always been a bit slow. Slow to learn, slow to speak, slow to think on his feet.

Half of that is probably just from the fact that he is so shy.

Kurt drops a wad of dead leaves from above.

"Damn squirrels," he mutters.

With a weathered face where lines cut deep canyons in his leathery skin, and a beard so white it lights up the night, Kurt looks just like what he is: an old sailor. He's got tattoos of mermaids and island girls on his forearms to prove it. When he works the wrench on the old water pump that breaks down at least once a week, his muscles flex and suddenly the island girls seem to be doing the hula dance. And the stories that keep boh him and Tiny up late at night, stories about exotic locations where sly customs officers won't let you into the harbor without a bribe, or the big, thundery storms that threaten to tear the mast clean out of its bracket and off the deck, come from a life lived at sea. Kurt is as salty as they come.

Although the only sailing Kurt does these days is on dry land. His boat, Bertha, no longer rocks to the rhythm of the ocean, but sits stranded on piles of wooden pallets behind the pump house. They retired together, the captain and his boat.

It's a little sad to see a boat on dry land but Kurt could never sell her. Not after all they've been through together. She's part of him, and he's part of her. That's just the way it is. Kurt is certain that she has feelings and sometimes, when he lies awake at night, they speak to each other, in hushed voices. He's never told anyone about it. Not even Tiny. Kurt and Bertha love each other.

He reaches out for another wad of dead leaves, stretching as far as his old body will go. Tiny takes a firm grip of the ladder.

He doesn't want Kurt to fall down and hurt himself.

Kurt took him in, gave him a place to live and this job assisting him at the pool. He treats Tiny with respect and kindness, as if Tiny mattered. As if what he feels and thinks actually means something. Nobody had ever done that before. During the dark times Tiny never felt safe. But when he met Kurt he felt like a real person for the first time. He would do anything for the old man, and as much as Kurt takes care of Tiny, Tiny tries to take care of Kurt. Like now, when he's holding the ladder.

Kurt tries to reach the very end of the gutter. There's a wad of leaves there that sits tauntingly just out of reach. Tiny carefully lifts the entire ladder, with Kurt on it, and moves it closer.

"Whoa there, lad," Kurt cries.

Tiny likes how he calls him lad. He's been called freak, giant and even retard by people, including his own father. Although that wasn't why he ran away. It was mostly because of the beatings.

There's a splash behind Tiny, and he turns his head to scan the pool. There's not a single soul there. Strange.

"Strong as an ox," Kurt says, chuckling. "Couldn't do it without you, lad. Probably fall down and break my back, clumsy as I am."

P-u-m-p H-o-u-s-e. Tiny looks at the sign on the wall in front of him. They try to practice reading after dinner in the evenings, but other things often seem to come in the way. Like TV, or Kurt's stories of the sea.

It's not that Tiny is dumb. Things just take a little longer for him, and before Kurt nobody ever seemed to have the extra time to spend on him.

"Just one more pile and we're done."

Kurt leans to grab the last pile of leaves. And when he does, he feels the ladder tip to one side, and disappear from under him.

"Whoa!"

He manages to grab the rain gutter and holds on for dear life. When he looks down, he sees the ladder lying on the ground. There's no sign of Tiny. He's disappeared. And here he was, trusting the lad to keep him from falling.

Facing the wall, Kurt can't see Tiny running as fast as he can towards the pool, and he can't see how he doesn't slow down when he gets to the edge and just throws himself in the water. He doesn't see the big splash that reaches as high as the rain gutter, and he doesn't see Tiny disappear under the surface, his big body suddenly gone, as if he too had been swallowed whole by Goliath's giant Nile perch. All he sees is the wall.

———————

Goliath struggles with the belt. He feels panic hammer his chest from the inside as he claws at the clasp, the same chest that *should* be filled with air but is now screaming for help. Screaming, Goliath thinks. He opens his mouth and lets out a shriek.

A league of bubbles race towards the surface, as if the bubbles themselves couldn't wait another second to draw a breath.

Goliath hears his own voice through the water. But it's subdued and weak, like he's leaning his entire face into a wall of Jell-O, trying to scream through to the other side. His voice doesn't carry. It just hits the wall of water and falls to the tiles on the bottom.

What's worse, there are no more bubbles now. And the clasp still refuses to move. Why doesn't it come off? He's used that clasp thousands of times before, several times a day for years, releasing and securing the seat belt. It's almost like a friend, just like the rubber on the wheels, and the padding under his butt. These are the things he touches day in and day out. They are family. You'd expect a little...loyalty.

He tries again to pull it apart. Come on, my friend, Goliath thinks. But the seat belt that's meant to keep him safe, and keep him from falling out of his wheelchair hurting himself, is now doing a great job of drowning him.

He thinks about his mom. He imagines her at the kitchen table, sitting all alone. There's an empty plate because she still forgets that he is gone. Or maybe she remembers, but does it out of habit. As if she does it enough times perhaps he'll come back. Who will get the mail now? Goliath always gets the mail. He knows when Ben the mailman will come around the corner and he knows that Tuesdays are the mail heavy days because of the coupons. Once they even got a letter from Argentina. It was from the Watfords who used to live around the corner but one day old Mister Watford scratched a lottery ticket on his coffee break at the cracker factory and won half a million. They moved to Argentina a few weeks after that because they both loved the tango. They only got the one letter and then Goliath's mom heard Mr. Watford passed away. She never said how he died but Goliath always pictured him in dying in the middle of the dance floor, with a rose in his mouth, and Mrs. Watford kneeling by his side.

Dead. That's what he would be too. He'd be with old Mr. Watford while his mom would be all alone with nobody to take in the mail, setting out places for a ghost.

Goliath's tears mix with the chlorinated water. It stings, but he doesn't care. He hears his own heart beat, louder and louder, as if his skin was tight like a drum and his heart banging harder and harder from inside, demanding air.

Suddenly a shadow appears from nowhere, blocking the light from above. So, this is it, Goliath thinks. I'm officially drowning. It's over. The end of the road. They're closing the lid on me and soon everything will be completely dark. Soon it will be me and old Mr. Watford.

Then something strange happens. He suddenly feels very light. Even inside the darkness he feels light. He feels light because he's no longer afraid. If I'm not afraid I can't die, Goliath thinks.

As if on cue, the shadow of death descends upon him, saying, *I'll give you something to be afraid of.* And Death puts its arms around him, and picks him up. All of the sudden Goliath feels terribly heavy. Death shakes him, hoisting him up and down, doing his damndest to scare him. Goliath can't see a thing anymore. A complete darkness has settled before his eyes, and the grips of death feel so strong, so strong. He simply gives up. He's tired of resisting. He decides that opening his mouth and letting the water in isn't the worst that could happen. He just wants Death to leave him alone so he can rest. He tells his jaws to let go, and he tells his lips to relax. Neither of them put up much of a fight.

"You want to come in here, water? The door is open. How about I even help you?" Goliath draws a big breath, though he knows it will be his last. It's strange. It doesn't feel as bad as he thought it would. He draws another deep breath. It feels even better.

Right outside of the darkness, behind his eyelids, he hears footsteps. Then someone is breathing hard into his mouth, as if they'd just run a mile and now they want to tell him about it, but they want to tell it straight to his mouth instead of his ear. And there's a voice too. It sounds like it's coming from far, far away, booming over a long distance.

"Is he OK? What happened?"

Now there are hands on his body, and suddenly he is released from the stubborn belt and up he floats. "I'm going to heaven", Goliath thinks. There's a part of him aware enough to feel lucky, because he's read about hell in Sunday school and if you had a choice you'd much rather go to heaven. That's the thing. You never really know until it is your time. But the upwards motion can only mean one thing, because even though Goliath wasn't the best at bible study, at least he learned the directions of Heaven and Hell.

Although, this particular angel must be new on the job, because it's a very bumpy ride. And he'd always imagined heaven as a quiet place, but this angel is screaming at the top of his lungs.

"Ambulance! Call an ambulance!"

When he finally arrives in Heaven everything becomes still and quiet. He is wrapped in something warm and soft, a heavenly blanket, and only now does he realize how cold he was. It's time to take it in. Heaven, his new home. He takes a deep breath, or whatever they call it here, and opens his eyes. The first thing he sees is a giant towering above him. The giant's hair is long and golden, the sun bouncing off it, making it sparkle. He looks at Goliath with big, friendly eyes.

"Hello, God," Goliath says.

God looks confused, and Goliath suddenly realizes that he doesn't know his name. "Hello, God". That's like saying "hello, police", or "hello, baker". He feels stupid, but God doesn't seem to care.

"You fell," God says, and points at something behind them. Drops of gold fall from his hair and it rains over Goliath. He's on his way now, into a deep, slumbering darkness. But before sleep takes over he needs to know.

"What's your name?" He asks.

And then the darkness arrives. It spirals around and around, overtaking him, and before he hits the bottom and his eyes are completely shut, he hears the word, "Tiny".

"That's a strange name for a giant God", Goliath thinks, before everything turns black.

---

Susy has her hands full of pancakes and coffee when the call comes in.

"Is for you," Antoine, the chef, calls out, reaching the receiver out through the hatch where he normally slides plates full of food. His other hand is moving around hash browns on the griddle. Nobody likes burned hash browns; Antoine knows this, even though he only learned about hash browns when he moved to Ireland from France less than a year ago.

Susy navigates the diner expertly, with the tray held up high, just like in the movies, except she's not wearing roller blades but a beige and brown uniform with a hat that seems to be made out of paper. She cruises past tables towards an expectant family of four that follows her every step with hungry eyes. Antoine calls out again, now flipping eggs with his other hand. Eggs he knows. In France they are experts on eggs.

"You better take right away. Is on Goliath."

Antoine can't really hear the woman on the other end of the line, with the fan going and the eggs frying. Besides, his English isn't that good yet. But he is sure he did hear the woman say Goliath. She says other things, too, but the bacon needs to be taken out and five pancakes are on order. What was that last word? Horsepetal?

"Something about a horse!" He shouts out through the hatch.

Susy is just about to put the plates on the table. The family seems mesmerized by the sight of food, as if they haven't eaten in days. They don't speak but hold their forks and knives in ready position. They are just waiting for the start signal. In the kitchen Antoine has put down the phone, flipping pancakes with one hand. In France they call them crepes but here they are just pancakes. He flips sausages with the other hand when it hits him. Horsepetal... it's a very strange word he's never heard. Like a flower petal on a horse? Ah, but they must mean...

Hi picks up the phone and asks the lady on the other end of the line.

"Hopital?"

She tells him yes, and to hurry up and get Susy. The pancakes are burning and the eggs are well overdone, but Antoine doesn't care because one thing they have that are exactly the same in France as in Ireland are children.

"Susy, rapidement, is from hopital!"

Someone might as well have poured a glass of ice water down Susy's back because as soon as she hears the word she feels a chill run down her spine. She turns around and hurries to the kitchen counter, taking the tray with her. Antoine looks embarrassed as he hands her the receiver. Behind him black smoke rises from a piece of burned toast.

"Hello?" Susy listens to the nurse speak and feels like she's floating outside of her own body.

The father at the table of the hungry family looks as if he's been robbed.

"Uhm...Ma'am? Excuse me, ma'am… is that our order?"

Susy doesn't even realize she's holding the tray until she tries to get in the car and it hits the doorframe and falls to the ground.

Goliath lies tucked into a hospital bed when Susy races into the room. He seems to be in a good mood. He has a jelly sandwich in one hand and the remote in the other.

"Hi, Mom." He flips through the channels and takes a big bite of the sandwich.

Without slowing down, Susy comes at him like a rugby player. She drops her bag on the floor and collides with Goliath. The sandwich flies out of his hand and lands, face down, on the floor.

"Mom, my sandwich!"

Susy could care less about a jelly sandwich right now. She wraps her arms around him so tight that Goliath has trouble breathing.

"It's OK, Mom. I'm OK."

She looks at him. Finally she lets go. Now that he's safe in her arms, she can let go. Tears well in her eyes.

"Please don't cry, mom."

She hugs him again, but less violent this time, and Goliath pats her shoulder while glancing at the TV behind her back, wishing nobody comes into the room and sees him like this.

"You could have drowned," She says once she's calmed down enough to speak.

She wipes her tears and smudges the already smudged mascara even more.

"There, and there," Goliath says, pointing to the spots on her face.

She looks like a raccoon but he feels this isn't the right time to mention it.

She uses her uniform to clean her face.

"Thank god for lifeguards."

Goliath's expression changes. How does he tell her? It wasn't a lifeguard, it was...

She sees his mind working.

"What?"

Goliath looks around the room to make sure no one is listening, which isn't necessary since he's got his own room, but you can never be too careful. He leans forward, and puts his lips close to her ear.

"It wasn't a lifeguard," he whispers.

Susy looks surprised.

"It wasn't? Then...who saved you?"

Goliath looks at her with the most serious face in the history of serious faces. He is not kidding, is what this face means.

"It was a giant."

A doctor in a white coat walks into the room. "

How we doing?", he says.

He glances quickly at a clipboard as if it held some sort of answer, because that's just what doctors do even though the patient is usually right there in front of them, and they could just ask.

"Hey Dr. Gupta," Goliath says, annoyed that his secret story was interrupted, but kind of relieved that he didn't have to explain it.

Dr. Gupta puts his hand on Goliath's forehead.

"How is he?" Susy asks, still worried.

"Strong as an ox," Dr. Gupta says.

"So, I can go home?" Goliath asks, longing for his own bed in his own room with his own stuff.

"Sure thing. We just have to make sure your wheelchair is ready. They sent it to the garage for a tune up.

The garage. Goliath's been there a couple of times. It's a pretty cool place. The best part is the prosthetics corner, where legs, hands and arms sit on a shelf along the wall. The robot corner, Goliath calls it.

Susy follows Dr. Gupta to the door.

"Thanks."

"No problem. He's a strong kid."

He seems to think twice, before adding

"Considering his condition, of course."

"Will this have any effect on his health?"

"Not at all. He'll recover fully."

Goliath is leaning out of bed, one hand holding on to the metal railing, trying to reach the jelly sandwich on the floor.

"If he hasn't already," Dr. Gupta says and winks.

"Thanks, Doctor." Susy, says, and is finally relaxing.

"We do still see a development in his muscular dystrophy, like we spoke of the last time."

"What about that new treatment I've been reading about?" Susy says.

"It's still years from being approved. Putting him on a low stress, low impact rest program, with medication when necessary, is in his best interest."

There's something about his reply that rubs her the wrong way. She knows Dr. Gupta is just trying to help, but sometimes doctors don't seem to understand that they are dealing with real people, with real lives, and real feelings. She's also tired and her words come out snappy.

"Doing nothing is in his best interest?"

Dr. Gupta has dealt with emotional patients and loved ones before, and his voice is as calm as ever.

"Susy, it's the only way we know how to prolong his life. His heart is a muscle and it deteriorates for..."

"I'm sorry. It's just that he needs to live like other children, not sit cooped up and wait to...And that article said they are already treating people in the US."

"It's a pilot program that is not covered by health care, so even if you were chosen to participate, it is extremely expensive."

"I see."

All Susy wants is to go home with Goliath. They've spent enough time in hospitals through the years.

"Don't worry. For now, let's be happy that he came out of this incident without a scratch. We can talk more about our options at our next meeting."

He squeezes Susy's shoulder and continues on his rounds.

"See you later, Goliath."

Dr. Gupta is not the bad guy, Susy tells herself.

"Schee you, Dr. Gupchta," Goliath says through a mouthful of jelly sandwich.

He sits in bed, his lifeless legs dangling from the edge.

"Let's go home, mom."

Susy thinks she's never heard a better idea in her entire life.

---

Kurt flips burgers on the bbq, in the stern of the boat. Lanterns cast a gentle glow into the surrounding night, from each of the four corners of the deck. Tiny is busy hanging multi-colored Tiki torches across the deck, without using a ladder. Below and around them the pool area is empty and still. The crickets and the sizzling burgers are the only sounds heard.

Suddenly a voice cuts through the darkness.

"Hello? Is anyone here?"

Kurt spies through the rising smoke. It's coming from the entrance.

"Hello?"

"Probably someone forgot their goggles," Kurt mumbles, and puts down the spatula.

He starts descending the roped ladder that hangs off the side of the boat, making the hula girls on his arms dance back and forth.

"Keep an eye on those burgers, will ya?" Kurt calls through the darkness as he walks across the cool evening grass towards the gate.

Susy is pushing her head against the black metal bars. She looks as if she's trying to squeeze right through them. Goliath is sitting next to her, and he's holding a big, square cake with green frosting, and they both spy towards the pool.

"It looks empty," Goliath says.

It does look empty. Then, from a distance, they see a shadowy figure, as if cut from the rest of the darkness, moving towards them. When it gets close the shadow speaks with a thunderous voice, dark as the night itself, but not all unfriendly.

"Lost and found is open during the day. We're closed now."

"Oh. Are you Kurt?" Susy asks.

There's a moment of silence before an answer.

"Depends. Who's asking?"

"I'm Goliath's mom. We just wanted to stop by and thank you for what you did."

"Hi," Goliath says, because it feels weird to just say thank you to a shadow.

The shadow moves closer. The first thing they see is a white beard, floating by itself, before the contours of an old man appear.

"We brought cake," Susy adds, pointing at it.

Kurt winks at them through the gate.

"I know someone who will be happy to see you," Kurt says to Goliath, and jiggles a key in the lock.

As they approach the boat Goliath is in awe.

"Wow, you live on a boat?!"

"Sure do," Kurt says.

"That's so cool."

"You're welcome to come on board," Kurt says, before he catches himself. He looks at Susy, and adds, "If it's OK with you?"

"It would be OK," Susy says, and scratches her head. "But like I said, we just wanted to..."

Goliath interrupts her.

"Yes!"

Now it's Kurt's turn to scratch his head. He looks first at the boat, then at Goliath's wheelchair, while Susy tries to calm Goliath down.

"It's awfully high, honey and there's no way up there."

Kurt feels pretty bad for offering the kid to come up on the boat without thinking it through.

"You know what? I can get some rope and pulleys. I won't be but a moment," And he scurries up the ladder with more agility than you'd guess a man his age would have.

Goliath and Susy wait on the ground.

"Honey," Susy says gently. "There's no way up but this ladder."

Goliath doesn't say anything and keeps his head lifted towards the sky, and they both listen to Kurt rummaging around deck.

"Tiny, where are the pulleys? Tiny?"

Susy shrugs because she knows there's no way of talking Goliath out of it. When he gets that look in his eyes (a glazed over expression) she knows there's nothing she can say to change his mind. He's a stone-headed boy. And it makes her so proud that her heart aches. Despite his handicap Goliath won't let anything get in his way.

Kurt pops his head over the ledge.

"Susy? Can you give me a hand? I don't know where that lad went."

"Sure thing," Susy says, and without thinking why she's trying to scale a stranded boat propped up on rickety wooden pallets, at the public swimming pool, and in pitch darkness, she begins climbing up the ladder.

Goliath listens to the two of them rummaging through what sounds like boxes filled with tools. He sits right outside the ring of shadow cast by the hull of the boat. In the corner of his eye, Goliath suddenly sees the shadow moving. The first thing that comes to his mind is that the wild rummaging has set the old boat in motion, and now it's falling over. Instinctively he puts his hands on the tires and begins rolling backwards. But the boat isn't really moving. Instead it is the big, hulking figure, half hidden next to the hull, that creates a shadow nearly as big. Goliath peers at it, more curious than afraid. After a moment's silence (which for Goliath is a waste of precious time since he likes talking), he says,

"Did you know that the Arctic tern flies 44000 miles a year, which in a lifetime is equal to three times to the moon and back?"

The figure doesn't move, so Goliath continues.

"What about the moose? Did you know that the Yukon moose is the largest animal in North America?"

The figure still doesn't come out of the shadows. It only stands there, as if waiting for a more interesting fact.

"OK, then. What about the Goliath frog, also called the giant slippery frog? It's the largest frog in the world and it can weigh up to..."

Tiny steps into a ball of light cast from one of the lanterns.

"I like frogs," He says shyly.

Goliath looks at him. His face is chiseled, with thick bones that make up his chin, cheeks and forehead, sort of like on one of those Picasso paintings made from just angles. His hair is long, like it's never been cut once in his life, reaching to his lower back. And his frame is impressive, to say the least. In fact, Goliath has never seen such a big person before. He really is a giant, Goliath thinks, gazing at Tiny with the same kind of interest he gazes at the exotic animals in his books with.

Tiny feels Goliath's gaze and doesn't know where to rest his eyes. He's never liked people looking at him, but there's nowhere to go. He lets his eyes move from his feet to the boy in a wheelchair, then back to his feet. Back and forth, and what he sees when he looks up is this small kid with glasses and curious, lively eyes peering at him. His legs are like sticks and his arms and upper body are just marginally larger. More than anything he reminds Tiny of a grasshopper. A very confident grasshopper.

"Then we'll get along just fine," Goliath says.

---

On deck Kurt and Susy are putting together a contraption with rope and pulleys that were once used to hoist equipment onto deck. It's been a long time since Kurt used it last and he's is trying to remember how to assemble it.

"Hmm... pass me the middle coil, please," Kurt says, holding a steel rod in each hand.

"OK...the middle coil." Susy is confused as she looks at a bunch of coils on the deck in front of her. "Is that the middle coil?"

"Uhm...I think it's this one," Kurt says, pointing to a different coil as he lets go of one of the steel rods to pick it up.

The rod falls against the deck with a thud. He looks at the coil but doesn't seem to be sure either. He sighs.

"The lad usually does this, " he says

"Where is he?" Susy looks around, but the deck is empty but for the two of them.

"Tiny? Oh, he's so shy he's afraid of his own shadow. He'll come out when he's ready."

They continue to sort through the mess of coils.

"Is he your son?"

"Naw, it's complicated. I met him in the harbor."

"In the harbor?"

"Caught him in my net."

Susy doesn't have to feign surprise.

"You caught him in your net?"

Kurt stops working for a second, as if the burden of searching for the right coil and explaining himself at the same time is too much.

"It's not as strange as it sounds."

He pauses, gazes for a moment into the distance, and continues.

"Actually, it *was* pretty strange. I was out in the harbor refolding my net, because it's easier to do in the water than on dry land, especially by yourself. Anyway, when I went to pull it in I felt this weight. It was something very heavy, so I put it on the winch and began to haul. When the bulk of it had been gathered by the side of the boat, I looked down, and there he was. All tangled up, squirming like a fish."

Susy seems to think that the story should explain not only the what, but also the how. As in, how on earth did Tiny end up in a fishing net?

"But what was Tiny doing swimming in the harbor? Isn't that dangerous?"

"He wasn't swimming in the harbor. He came in that way when he had finished," Kurt says as if he thinks it is the most natural explanation in the world.

"Finished with what?"

"Swimming in the ocean."

Kurt sees Susy's skeptical look. In fact, if he could draw a question mark above her head it would perfectly match her face.

"Tiny feels more at home in the water than on land," Kurt tries to explain.

"And why is that?"

Kurt looks around the deck and even though nobody is

there he lowers his voice.

"The lad had a pretty rough childhood. His dad was a drunk. Beat him up because he's slow and big and a bit… different, you know? Kids called him a freak and all that goes away in the water. That's what I gather from what he's told me. In the water he feels free. Free and safe."

Kurt finally finds the right coil and inserts it in one of the steel rods.

"Ah, there. I think we're ready to go."

"Are you sure that this will hold?"

"Don't you worry, this will pull up a whale if it had to."

Susy looks down over edge.

"Honey, you ready?"

But there's nobody there.

"Goliath?"

Kurt looks over the edge too.

"Now where did he go? Lads disappear at a faster rate than ice melts here…"

Behind them, on the other side of the boat, Goliath pops his head over the railing. He's still sitting in his wheelchair, and he's still holding the cake.

"Can someone please take this?"

Kurt and Susy spin around.

"Where on earth did you come from?" Susy hurries over.

Kurt grabs the wheelchair with two hands and gently lifts it onboard.

"I found an elevator."

Behind him Tiny comes climbing up, without a roped ladder or anything. He just uses the side of the boat, and in a couple of movements he is standing on deck. All seven feet of him.

He glances at Susy, and then looks down at his feet, as if he's a dog that's done something wrong. But he hasn't done anything wrong. As far as Susy is concerned Tiny has done everything right.

She grabs his big hand, and hers look puny in comparison. With her other hand she lifts up his chin until their eyes meet. Tiny's big, brown eyes aren't sure where to rest. Susy doesn't seem to notice. She looks at him lovingly, the way only a mother can, and her voice is filled with gratitude.

"Thank you for saving my son."

She embraces Tiny, her arms unable to reach all the way around him, and Tiny looks like he's never been hugged before in his life, the way he stands with his arms straight down.

Susy keeps the hug going for a long time. Tiny looks over at Kurt, who smiles and gives him a thumbs up. Underneath the awkwardness, deep inside his giant ribcage, Tiny feels something stirring. It's an unfamiliar feeling, something he can't ever remember feeling before. It's like he feels...warm and nervous at the same time and he knows he didn't do anything wrong. He's pretty sure he did something important. And the longer

Susy hugs him the more he feels it. He did good. He feels something he can't ever remember feeling. He feels...proud.

"Rats!" Kurt rushes over to the bbq and starts fanning the smoky burgers that by now have been turned into lumps of coal.

"Forgot all about the burgers."

He opens a trashcan with his foot and uses his spatula to drop the lumps into it.

"Sorry, we'll have to start over."

Susy isn't fazed. She lets go of Tiny, and winks at him. Tiny can't help but smile. He didn't plan to but it's like Susy's wink is connected to the side of his mouth.

She picks up the cake from Goliath's lap and puts it on the table.

"Dinner is served."

Kurt is the first one to laugh. The entire situation is pretty funny. Not long after Goliath joins him, and when Susy herself lets out pearly laughter, Tiny can't help but start laughing too.

---

Goliath's room is filled with two things: posters and books. The posters depict all sorts of animals, but mostly moose. And the books are all books about animals, including moose.

"I like animals," Goliath says, as if there was a need to explain it.

Tiny nods. He sits on the floor, thumbing through a book about New Zealand with his giant hands, listening to Goliath speak. And speak he does, as if he weren't in a bedroom on a second story house with a slight lean, but at Oxford University, lecturing about biology.

"I've seen fifty-two animals so far. You want to hear them?"

"OK," Tiny says, looking expectantly at his new friend. Not that it would have mattered if he said yes or no, because Goliath is on a roll. He begins counting them off.

"Porcupine, badger, elephant, tiger, lion, water buffalo, seagull, seal, chicken, zebra, raccoon, fox, rabbit, crow, eagle, coyote, pig, cow, horse, goat, cat, dog, adder, frog, rat, giraffe....," He counts them off on his fingers as he speaks. The list just keeps going. "Skunk, cod, bear, seagull, bat, squirrel, beetle, penguin, dolphin, orangutan and...," Suddenly he spots something on Tiny's hands that makes him forget all about counting animals.

"What happened to your wrists?"

Tiny tries to hide his hands by sitting on them, but it's too late. Goliath's keen eyes have already picked up on the scars. Long, white, pinkish cuts that go across Tiny's wrists.

"My dad," Tiny says quietly, "tried to cut them off."

Goliath can't believe his ears.

"He tried to cut your hands off?!"

Even though they've only been friends for a day Tiny already knows there's no way to stop Goliath's questions once he gets going. So he relents.

"He said he would sell them. Make some money."

Tiny keeps sitting on his hands, keeping the scars out of sight. "Because my hands aren't normal," he adds.

Goliath seems to think about what Tiny just told him for a second, and then he unbuckles his belt and begins pushing his pants down.

"Wh..what are you doing?"

Goliath doesn't answer. He works hard to get his pants lower and lower, until they are so far down they dangle from his feet. His bare legs are thin like twigs. He uses his hands to lift one leg up.

"It's called muscular dystrophy. Nobody knows for sure why you get it, but I have it. It makes all your muscles really weak. Your heart, too. Eventually they disappear. That's why I can't use my legs."

Tiny looks at Goliath's thin, white legs. They look more like cooked noodles than legs, but that's not what makes them so interesting. Right in front of him is another person with something wrong with him. An abnormality. Some call them freaks, but Tiny hates that word. He knows how much it hurts.

"For how long?"

"For always. Well, I remember running towards my dad once when I was real little but that could just be a dream. He isn't around anymore."

"My dad is gone too."

"That's a good thing, right?"

Tiny nods.

"My dad was OK. I think anyway. I hardly remember him."

Talking about his father seems to have put Goliath in a bit of a somber mood. Tiny wiggles his hands free and sets them carefully in his lap. Goliath follows his every move, and Tiny slowly open his palms.

"Spread your fingers".

Tiny does and between the base of each of his fingers is a web of skin that connects them all together, just like on a frog's foot. Goliath carefully reaches out and touches the web. No one's ever done that before. Normally Tiny would never let anyone see them, let alone touch them, but somehow it's different with Goliath. Maybe it's his noodle legs.

"Does it hurt?"

"No," Tiny says, because it's really just skin. He waits for the verdict. Freak or...?

"It's so cool!" Goliath exclaims. "You're like a superhero!"

Tiny holds up a palm and studies his own hand, as if there is something about it that he's missed.

"Yeah?"

"Yeah!" Goliath is excited. "Like Aquaman! I wish I had something like that, instead of these." He taps his skinny legs. "Although my dad never tried to cut them off to sell them. I don't know, maybe he would have if I had frog legs."

"Professor X," Tiny says.

"Huh?"

"He's a superhero like you, in a chair, with a smart mind. I wish I had a smart mind."

Tiny picks up a book, holding it as a person who doesn't know how to read. It's Goliath's turn to notice that Tiny's mood has darkened. He thinks on his feet. Well, in his wheelchair.

"Hey, you know what makes the X-Men so great?"

Tiny shakes his head.

"They work together, one superpower combined with another."

Tiny seems to think about it. He's always felt dumb because he can't read and because other people have told him he is, well...dumb. Maybe they've all been wrong. Perhaps all he needed was...another superhero friend! He nods and smiles at Goliath.

"Hold your fist like this," Goliath says. Tiny forms a giant fist and holds it in front of himself. It's almost as big as Goliath's head. Goliath's tiny fist meets it head on. Bump. He even says it out loud.

"Bump."

Then, with an earnest look, he adds,

"Now we're superheroes."

---

Dracula glides down the street. It's like he's hovering, never even touching the ground. Next to him, Frankenstein lunges forward, stiff legged and gigantic, with screws sticking out from the side of his mouth.

"Where are we going again?" Tiny asks, and one of the screws drops to the ground as he opens his mouth.

Goliath doesn't slow down and Tiny hurries to pick up the screw.

"I want to show you something," Goliath says, and keeps his wheels spinning.

They pass a couple of other kids, dressed as wizards and princesses. All along the street are glowing, grinning pumpkins guarding the doors to every other house. It's All Hallows Eve.

At an intersection they cross the street and continue around the block.

"Here we are," Goliath says, his breath a bit short, as he stops in front of a building with large windows filled with cobwebs and skulls. Tiny looks up and slowly reads the sign that sits on the wall. Big, black letters form the word H-O-T-E-L.

Goliath presses his face against the window. "What do you think?"

Tiny looks at the skeleton that is about to crawl out of a coffin.

"Spooky", he says, and he means it.

"No, up there!" Goliath points past the window display, at the wall above the bar inside. Over the shelf that holds a selection of bottles hangs a giant moose head. It solemnly looks down over the bar, as if watching over its kingdom.

"That's a grey moose," Goliath says. "Well, part of one," He adds.

It looks strange to Tiny. "Where is the rest?"

"It's on the other side of the wall."

Tiny looks bewildered.

"How..." He begins, and then he sees Goliath's smile.

"Kidding! It's just the moose head; I don't know where the body is. But I think that's a very..." Suddenly something comes flying right between them, fast as a meteorite, and it explodes against the window. SPLATCH!

"Whoa, what was that?" Goliath looks around.

The next egg hits Tiny right in the back of his head. SPLOTCH! Laughter erupts from the other side of the street as the sticky egg slowly runs down Tiny's neck.

"Happy Halloween, freak!" More laughter.

Billy Buffoon. His real name is Boffin, but everyone calls him Billy Buffoon because he has this wild laughter that makes his entire body shake, almost like he's doing a silly dance. Just like a buffoon. Which could be cute, except Billy Buffoon never laughs *with* you, he always laughs *at* you. He's a big kid, 15 years old and his number one hobby is picking on other kids.

Billy straddles his moped, nicknamed by kids in the neighborhood *The Black Death*, because it's spray-painted black, but there's also a rumor that Billy once tied a fourth grader to the back of it and did wheelies until he threw up. His two sidekicks straddle their own mopeds, one on each side of Billy's. They look like a gang of robbers from a Western.

They stare at Tiny and Goliath, holding an egg in each hand.

"You out scaring kids again?" Billy says, taunting Tiny.

"Who are they?" Goliath asks, but Tiny doesn't answer and turns to start walking back up the street, away from Billy Buffoon and his gang.

"Let's just go," he says, wiping egg off his shoulder.

Goliath won't have it. He turns his chair around and looks across the street.

"Who are you dressed as? The chicken gang?"

Tiny hushes him, pulling on the cape, willing him to leave.

"Let's just go home, OK?"

It's too late. Billy's heard him.

"What did you say?"

He gives Goliath a menacing stare. His accomplices straighten in attention, like well-trained dogs.

Goliath seems totally oblivious of the danger, and keeps talking.

"I was just wondering how you decided to make eggs your superpower. I mean, I have wheels and Frankenstein here has superpower hands, but it seems that you guys are just a bunch of..."

"Don't say it," Tiny pleads.

But Goliath either doesn't hear him, or doesn't care.

"...Chickens."

He starts making chicken sounds.

"Bwaaak! Bwaaak! Bwaaaaaaaak!"

For a moment Billy hesitates, as if he can't believe someone would actually talk to him like that. He's not letting this kid in a wheelchair ridicule them.

"Bwaaak! Bwaaak! Bwaaaaaaaak!"

He is going tie him to the Black Death and tow him around town until he begs for mommy.

Billy Buffoon screams out the order, spit flying from his pimpled face.

"Get 'em!"

His gang stands up, viciously kick-starting their old mopeds.

Tiny grabs the wheelchair and begins running down the street with it. Eggs rain down on them, some hitting Tiny in the back. Others get Goliath's cape and stain it with sticky, yellow splotches.

Tiny keeps running, and behind them the moped engines scream as Billy and his gang accelerate to catch up with them.

Despite being chased Goliath keeps taunting them, until an egg hits him square in the back of his head. That shuts him up long enough for Tiny to use his long legs, and clamber down the street far enough that Goliath's chicken sounds won't give their position away.

Finally, Tiny turns a corner, crosses a street, turns another corner, and runs to the end of that street before he dares cast a glance behind him. It's empty. They got away.

"I think they're gone," Tiny says, breathing hard.

They take a moment to survey the damage. They're a real mess. Their costumes are covered in sticky egg, and bits of eggshell hang from their hair. Goliath can't help but laugh at how silly they look. Soon Tiny starts laughing too, and together they laugh so hard that an old lady walking her dog crosses to the other side of the street, just to get away from the egg covered, laughing weirdos.

Finally, when they have laughed all the tension off, they grow quiet just as quickly as they began.

"The chicken gang." Goliath shakes his head.

"Yeah."

Tiny begins picking egg shells from his hair, and he looks a bit sad, as if Goliath's words just reminded him of something he didn't want to be reminded of.

"You know them or what?" Goliath asks.

Tiny nods, while not very pleasant memories flash through his head.

"They've always picked on me."

"Sorry," Goliath offers, and picks some shells off of his cape, because he knows that's the one thing you can say when you don't know what to say. They sure are a strange looking pair, Goliath thinks. Dracula in his wheelchair, next to Frankenstein, picking eggshells from their clothes.

Goliath's eyes suddenly brighten.

"You said they've always picked on you?"

"Ever since I was little."

Tiny reflects on this for a second.

"I mean, younger."

"Does that mean you know where they live? "

A determined look spreads across Goliath's face.

"Well...yes," Tiny says carefully, not sure what Goliath is up to.

Goliath spins his chair around, ready to roll.

"Let's go!"

Tiny hesitates.

"What's wrong?" Goliath asks.

"I don't like... fighting."

"I promise there will be no fighting," Goliath says and plops his teeth back in. "Or my name isn't Dracula."

It's dark and only a single streetlight illuminates the corner. Across from the hedge that Tiny and Goliath are hiding behind, three mopeds are parked just outside the house. The light is on in the basement and they hear the steady vibrations of loud music. Goliath recaps the plan.

"Alright, so you do the rope, just like I told you. I'll do the bananas."

Tiny looks a bit nervous, but Goliath's confidence rubs off.

"OK."

They move from their cover and cross the street. Nobody else is out and they reach the mopeds without making hardly a sound. They immediately get to work. Goliath begins fiddling with the seats and Tiny goes to work on the wheels. It doesn't take long before they're done, and they sneak back across the street.

"There," Goliath says, "We've cast the net."

Tiny can't hide his excitement.

"Now what?" His eyes are eagerly watching the house, and the mopeds.

"Now we...," Goliath says and scoops up some gravel from the ground, "...Wait for our catch."

He throws the gravel in a big arch and hits the basement windows with perfect precision. POP, POP, POP! It sounds loud through the still night, and it only takes a few moments before the music stops. Not long after that the front door opens and there they are, Billy Buffoon and his gang. Goliath doesn't wait.

"Bwaaak! Bwaaak! Bwaaaaaaaak!"

Billy spies into the darkness and when he finally spots Goliath and Tiny he get furious.

"Get 'em!" Billy screams, and they run towards their mopeds.

Seeing as they are about to be charged again, Tiny has lost some of his bravery.

"Let's go," he says and grabs the wheelchair.

But Goliath couldn't be any cooler in the face of danger.

"Just wait and see," he says, and even though he wants to run, Tiny stays.

Billy and his gang jump onto their mopeds and start them up with three swift kicks. They are gunslingers again. They rev their engines and, as if on a signal, they all let go of the clutch at the same time. Tires screech against the asphalt, and they aim straight for the hedge.

With a battle cry Billy shoots across the street. But he only makes it halfway across. Suddenly the rope that is connecting all three mopeds is stretched tight and there is a sudden jerk. The three of them fly off their seats, landing in a disorderly pile of bullies and mopeds. They are not sure what just hit them. A second ago they were burning rubber, and now they are lying on the ground. Then Billy spots the rope.

"They ruined our bikes," he says, gritting his teeth.

One of his accomplices notices the banana before he does. It's all over Billy's pants.

"Ehm...you have something there, on your butt."

Billy reaches back to examine his pants and feels a sticky mess. He smells smells his hand with a disgusted look on his face.

"Banana?"

He looks across the street, defeat and anger burning in his eyes.

"You put banana on my seat?!"

He can't believe that somebody actually played a trick on him, for a change.

"You can call yourselves the monkey gang!" Goliath says, and nudges Tiny. "Now is probably a good time to leave," he whispers.

Billy rises from the pile of mopeds, mashed banana all over his backside.

"Get the freaks!"

That's all Tiny needs. He sets off, running down the street, pushing Goliath in front of him. His strong legs club the pavement, and it's not long until they have left Billy and his gang far behind. After a while they can't even hear Billy Buffoon's swearing.

They pause to catch their breaths, giggling like little boys. Goliath high fives Tiny.

"Good job, Frankenstein!"

Their hands connect, one large as a barrel lid, the other small as a sparrow.

"Let's go home," Goliath says. "It's freezing."

Goliath starts rolling, but Tiny stops him.

"Thank you," He says earnestly. "Nobody's ever defended me before."

"That's what friends are for," Goliath says with a shrug, and the two of them continue down the street, past houses where only ghosts, goblins and pumpkin heads are awake.

_____

The next morning Goliath is wearing his Dracula cape over his pj's. He looks tired and pale at the breakfast table.

Susy is buttering a toast on the counter, her back to him.

"You were up late last night. You and Tiny have a good time?"

She dips a tea bag into a cup of hot water, once, twice, thrice, and slices the cheese.

"What did you two goblins do?"

When Goliath still doesn't answer she turns around to find him wheezing and grabbing his throat. His face has gone from pale to purple.

"Goliath!"

_____

Doctor Gupta sits behind his desk, Susy and Goliath across from him. They've been here many times before. In fact, Goliath has been in that very spot, with the bandage on his arm from where the nurse drew his blood, the tiny hole in his arm itching like crazy, more times than he cares to remember. Today he's too tired to even scratch it.

"How are you feeling? Breathing any easier?" Dr. Gupta asks.

Goliath doesn't think anything feels particularly easy, but at least he can breathe.

"I'm OK, I guess."

"You need to get plenty of rest, you hear me?"

Dr. Gupta makes a futile attempt at a sharp look. But he still looks like a golden retriever. Some people just can't look angry, Goliath thinks.

"There will be no more running around late at night in the cold, young man."

Goliath is too weak to speak, so he nods instead.

"For how long?" Susy knows that she can't keep Goliath locked in for long. She might as well try to lock a rhinoceros in the kitchen cupboard.

Dr. Gupta's reply is quick, as if he was waiting for that question.

"At least a month." Then he adds, as if a whole month wasn't long enough, "Maybe more."

Images of pirates being thrown into a dungeon flash through Goliath's mind. Suddenly he isn't too tired to speak.

"A whole month?" Goliath looks at his mom.

"Is that really necessary?" Susy asks.

Dr. Gupta actually manages to look, if not angry, at least concerned. "Can I talk to you in private?" he says to her.

Just the look on Susy's face tells Dr. Gupta that he has stepped over an invisible line. There's not yet a fire in her eyes, but there are glowing coals. Susy keeps no secrets from Goliath. Especially when it's about *his* health.

Susy swallows once and counts to five.

"You can tell us right here. Goliath needs to know."

Dr. Gupta looks uncomfortable. He's not used to being the one who breaks the bad news. You'd think he would be. Doctors usually have half good and half bad news.

Dr. Gupta looks at them nervously, and begins.

"Goliath is deteriorating. He's not going to get any better. Only worse."

He glances at Goliath when he utters that last part. His eyes seem to be apologizing for the bad news. But Goliath doesn't really blame him.

Susy can't let it go. She's always known, deep in her heart, that there would come a day when Goliath stopped developing, stopped progressing. He would start going backwards, shrinking. But it's a hard pill to swallow. Your own child, shrinking in front of you. She just can't accept it.

"We've been in such a steady period lately. Everything has been going so well–with the exercise, with school. I mean, Dr. Gupta, there must be something we can do?"

She fights back tears. The glowing coals in her eyes are quickly put out.

Dr. Gupta tries his best to speak with a gentle and comforting voice.

"There isn't much we can do but prolong it as much as possible. Resting is vital."

If there's one thing that Goliath doesn't like, even more than talking about his own condition, it's seeing his mom cry.

He knows it's not Dr. Gupta's fault but he can't help that the words come out sharp like hand claps.

"What does "it" mean?" Even though Goliath knows exactly what it means.

Dr. Gupta now looks both confused and embarrassed. He finds Susy's eyes and without words he makes it clear that this is exactly where he didn't want to end up.

*I told you we should have done this in private,* they say.

Susy gets up, and dabs quickly at the corners of her eyes.

"Let's go home," She says and pushes Goliath out of the office.

Susy makes sure Goliath is strapped in before she closes the door. She folds the wheelchair without hesitating, putting it in the backseat. She's done it a million times before; she could probably do it with her eyes closed. Then she hurries around to the driver's side and as soon as she gets in Goliath blurts it out.

"Am I going to die?"

This is the question Susy has feared ever since Goliath was a toddler. She's known it was coming, but t

here is no good way of saying it. No way of making it all right. This is just how things are. This is their life and they have to accept it. Just like summer has to accept winter. So she begins.

"You know..."

She bites her tongue. The pain is sudden, then dull, but nothing compared to the fear she's feeling. Some words are impossible to speak and sometimes your mouth, or your tongue, won't allow them. Your mouth and tongue are trying to protect you. Saying them anyway, forcing them through her tightly bound lips would be...giving up, she thinks. And giving up is not OK.

There's a moment where nothing else exists. Life balances, like a tennis ball on top of the net. Then the fog lifts, and she sees clearly.

"No, you are not going to die. And anyone who says so will have to deal with me," She starts the car, her lips and mouth happy with her decision, and her face determined. She lets out a sigh of relief, as if she just dogged a bullet.

---

Susy carries a tray of cookies and milk into Goliath's room. He's in bed reading, and all around him are more books, spread out across his bed.

She puts the tray on the bedside table and brushes some crumbs from her waitress uniform.

"Are you sure you'll be OK by yourself?"

"Mmmm," is all Goliath says, his gaze not lifting from the book even for a moment.

"I'll call at lunch to check in on you."

She just gets another "Mmmm" in response. Whatever Goliath is reading is *that* good.

"And remember what the doctor said. Stay in bed and rest."

She kisses his forehead. "OK, honey, I have to go."

But it's like she's talking to herself, because Goliath is totally mesmerized by his book. He doesn't even look up when he reaches out to grab a cookie. His hand, living a life of his own, searches for it in midair, before it finally finds the tray.

"Snapping turtle," Goliath says, and it must be to himself because nobody else is there. He munches on the cookie and imagines he is a snapping turtle with a mom that bakes him cookies, and turns the page.

"Roadrunner," he says and takes another bite, this time thinking he is a roadrunner with long legs and a pointy beak.

He turns page after page. Every now and then Goliath says the name of an animal, and chews a cookie in a manner that mimics that animal eating a cookie.

"The orchard snapper," Munch, munch. "The white rhino," chomp, chomp. "The tongue lemur," snack, snack.

He's so engrossed in his book that at first he doesn't hear it. Some part of his mind picks up on a train whistle bouncing along the ridges in the distance, but it's the kind of sound that you stop noticing when you've lived in the same place all your life. This sound is definitely not the train whistle. Goliath hears it again. This sound seems to be coming from somewhere close by. It sounds as if something is scraping against a jagged surface, and at the end of the scraping there's a hoot. A hoot? Maybe an owl!

Goliath sits up in bed so fast the books fall to the floor. He pulls his wheelchair close and eases into it as quickly as he can. He rolls over to the balcony door. As he opens it he hears it again: it's definitely a hoot!

He forgets all about not getting cold, and rolls outside wearing just his pj's. It must be in the chimney at the top of the roof. He cranes his neck, his back to the garden. The chimney just looks like it always has, rectangular and black. From where Goliath sits there's no way of seeing down into it. That's where owls like to hide. It's common knowledge, at least for anyone that knows anything about owls. Is that a   feather stuck there or is something building a nest? They can't use the fireplace or it will smoke the poor bird out. People think that there are owls around every corner but that's not true. They are in fact pretty rare, and when you get one in your chimney the last thing you'd want to do is smoke it out. That scraping sound must be claws against the inside of the chimney, perhaps a beak sharp as a tiger's claw! But wait a second.... it sounds like it's coming from down below? It's coming from the garden!

Goliath turns around to look over the garden. A gust of wind blows, filling his pajamas with cool air. He shivers. But not from the wind. He shivers from what he sees standing in front of him. Just below the balcony.

The giant moose is rubbing up against an apple tree, scratching an itch. Moose don't have arms with hands and fingers to scratch an itch, so they have to find an apple tree to rub against.

Goliath just stares at it. The tree sways from side to side, the moose wielding its head, knocking down leaves with its huge antlers, and a couple of apples, which Susy would not have approved of had she been there to see it. She also wouldn't approve of the moose stepping through her flower bed and, God forbid, turning her pansies into moose hoof pancakes. But none of that crosses Goliath's mind. All he can think is: THERE IS A MOOSE IN MY BACK YARD!

Suddenly the moose lets out a brawl. BAROOOOOUUU-GA! It doesn't sound like any other moose Goliath has ever heard, and it doesn't look like any other moose Goliath has ever seen. Then again, he's never seen a moose before. Except in books. That's why he knows that moose don't, at least not usually, have two legs.

Tiny swings the moose head around, getting the antlers caught in the apple tree again. It's completely dark inside and impossible to see anything. As Tiny lifts the head, just for a moment, to catch his breath, he sees Goliath peering down at him from the balcony. His whole face is lit up.

Tiny puts the moose head down on the bed. It takes up half the mattress.

"Ohboy, ohboy, ohboy," Is all Goliath says, as he studies it. He couldn't hide his excitement even if he tried. He claps his hands he's so happy. He looks like a little scientist that has just succeeded with a difficult experiment.

"Yup, it's definitely a Grey Moose," he says with great confidence.

Just to make sure, he leans in and examines the ears closely.

"Native of Alberta, Canada," he continues, speaking into the ear.

His voice comes out through the moose's mouth.

"Where did you get it?"

Tiny seems wholly engrossed by the whale poster on the wall.

Goliath pulls his mouth from the moose's ear.

"That's a blue whale. Largest mammal in the world."

Tiny touches the poster, tracing the outline of the big whale with his finger, as if it's the most incredible thing he's ever seen.

"Cool, huh?" Goliath says.

Tiny nods softly.

"Beautiful..."

Goliath turns his attention back to the moose head . He looks at its mouth.

"Did you know that moose don't have upper front teeth?'

He runs his finger around the moose mouth, as if to demonstrate.

"I've seen it," Tiny says softly.

"Moose upper front teeth?"

Goliath looks at him with wide-open eyes.

But Tiny is still staring at the whale.

"Wait, you mean a blue whale?"

"I think it was a blue whale. I'm sure it was at least a whale," Tiny says.

"Where?!"

Besides the moose, the whale is Goliath's favorite animal. He just can't believe the luck he's having!

"From the hill," Tiny says, and nods towards somewhere inexact, across the city.

"I can show you, if you want?"

Goliath doesn't waste a second. This is really happening. He's officially an explorer.

"Let's go before my mom gets home." He spins his chair around and pulls open a drawer. Goliath knows she won't much like him going on a whale safari, so he decides he just won't tell her.

He will do his best to dress warm, however, and puts a sweater on over his pj's before threading his feet and legs in long, yellow socks that look like something a soccer player would wear. They reach well above his knees. An explorer can't be too picky about how he looks. It's about being utilitarian. His wheelchair isn't exactly a fashion statement anyway.

"Let's go whale exploring!" He says, grabbing his wool hat, and leads the way out of the room.

———————————

Moments later, as Goliath rolls out through the front door and stops on the stoop, it's clear that something has changed. His energy has disappeared, and all the excitement has gone from his face. He suddenly looks very tired again.

He turns his head towards the clouds, then at the wind that rustles the leaves in the trees, and pulls his sweater tighter.

"Is it OK if we do it another day? I feel a bit dizzy."

"OK," Tiny says.

As quickly as he rolled out onto the stoop, Goliath rolls back inside and lets the door close behind him.

Tiny stands there for a moment, not sure what to do now. Could it all be a joke? He looks at the closed door, hoping it will open again and Goliath will burst out, all smiles, ready to go whale exploring. The two of them will have an adventure, just like two regular friends. But Tiny's never been regular, and he's never had a friend. Well, Kurt of course. But never someone his own age. He stares at the door and tries to will it to open again. Any moment now Goliath will pop his head out yell "Gotcha!" and they'll hurry towards the hill where Tiny will push the chair up the grassy incline, all the way to the top where they see the city on one side, and the open ocean on the other. There they'll try to spot whales swimming by like blue-grey, leathery oil tankers.

But the door remains closed and after ten minutes Tiny turns around and walks home.

---

Kurt can tell that something is wrong by the way Tiny sits at the dinner table. He is staring at his plate, his hulking body leaning forward. Like a withering plant.

It doesn't take much to understand the reason, even though Tiny mostly answers with yes or no. Kurt does his best to explain.

"It's a disease. There's really nothing they can do about it. That's why Goliath is in a wheelchair. Because of this muscular disease. That's also why he gets tired and needs to stay home to rest."

Tiny doesn't feel like eating. He leaves the hotdogs and potatoes untouched. Kurt knows that if Tiny turns down food he really must be feeling blue, and he scrambles for a better explanation.

"It's like...it's like this old ship," he says and knocks on the railing. "Sure, Bertha's got a few things wrong with her. That's why we keep her here, on land. But she's still here, right? And we really like her company. So what does it matter that she doesn't sail anymore?"

Tiny looks up from his plate.

"But you can fix boats, right? I've seen it in the harbor."

"Sure, you can fix boats but..."

"Then why can't they fix Goliath?"

It's a fair question to ask. Although, sometimes just because a question is good doesn't mean there is a good answer.

"Well...I think they've tried but it just didn't work," Kurt says.

"But you always say there's nothing you can't fix."

Tiny isn't trying to be difficult. He just wants to understand. A lot of things in the world confuse him, and some things, like this, just don't make any sense.

"I do?"

Kurt is caught off guard. As a matter of fact, he does say that, and it is true. There are not many things he can't figure out how to fix.

"So how come nobody can fix Goliath?"

"Well, it's also a matter of other things. Like money. Susy mentioned that there is an experimental treatment in Boston that might help, but it's very expensive and not available for everyone. The doctors here do the best they can."

Tiny doesn't know what to think. Part of him knows that

Kurt is doing his best to explain it, and he's not to blame for Goliath's sickness. Nobody is. It's just not the answer he wants to hear. It's not an answer at all.

"Don't worry. Everything is going to be alright. OK?"

"He's *my* friend," Tiny says defiantly, as if Kurt, Susy and everybody else are in a separate group. He and Goliath share something special. It's them against everybody else, like with Billy the Buffoon and his gang.

Except he knows that's not true, so he softens his voice.

"He's my only friend."

Kurt pats Tiny's hand. His hand is weathered and calloused from a lifetime of hard work, but Tiny can still feel the warmth through his skin.

"Things are going to be fine, you'll see. Now let's lighten up and watch some TV while we eat."

Kurt turns on an old TV in the corner. As if the TV was somehow only capable of playing programs as old as itself, a black and white documentary comes on. It features a man named Jack Lalanne, and shows a segment featuring him swimming from an old prison, in the bay outside of San Francisco. The prison is called Alcatraz. The water around it is cold and the current very strong. Some say it's even filled with sharks. As if that wasn't hard enough, what makes it really incredible is that Jack Lalanne swims with his hands and feet tied together. It doesn't even look like he's swimming, because he can't move his arms and legs like a swimmer normally would. He squirms his way forward through the water, like a worm that coils and recoils.

A big crowd is standing on the beach, watching and cheering him on.

"Oh, I remember this," Kurt says fondly. "It was big news, even over here. What a guy, that Jack Lalanne. A real, live superhero."

Tiny looks at Jack Lalanne moving through the water, moving closer to the beach with every squirm. Camera flashes make the entire scene look like it's jumping up and down, or maybe that's just the old TV. News reporters push their pads towards the sea, as if the closer the pads are to Jack Lalanne, the more information they will get for their stories.

Suddenly, he emerges. The mighty Jack, who just swam through the cold, shark-infested waters surrounding Alcatraz, and everybody in the crowd cheers. Even the seagulls join in.

Tiny's hotdog is now cold. He doesn't care about food. He doesn't even notice the crowds cheering. What he does notice is how Jack moved through the water, even with his hands and feet tied, as if the water was his friend. As if he was part of the water himself.

Everything is clear. He doesn't know how, or even exactly what, but he knows that the answer lies in the water. To save his friend he must do what he's always done when the world presented him nothing but problems. When everything threatens to overtake him, the one place he can find peace is below the surface, in that silver blue liquid that feels like home. A place where nothing can harm him. How could he forget? The ocean will tell him what to do. It always does.

Tiny swims straight out from the harbor, following the coastline to a special place where the rocky bottom gives way to what looks like a huge, underwater swimming pool. Tiny loves this place. It's shallow enough to keep boats away, but the beach is inaccessible enough that other people don't come here.

He dives into the underwater pool and swims within the rectangle, the sea there covered in a roof of kelp above him, and the bottom scattered with starfish amongst the smooth, round boulders. This is where Tiny feels safe. He can hold his breath for a long time and somehow the salty water never bothers his eyes.

He takes his time, feeling the rocks covered in slippery moss, watching crabs scurry sideways from hideout to hideout. Every now and then schools of fish will swoop into the pool, moving as one even though there are hundreds of them, sometimes even thousands.

Tiny swims further across the pool, gazing at the bottom that never ceases to amaze him. It is a grey day, and light doesn't illuminate the rocks the same way it does when the sun is out. Each type of weather and each season has it's own color. Right now, everything is a shade of green, from the dark, wet moss to the lighter, shiny apple green of the towering seaweed. Tiny feels as if he is not swimming but flying through a thick forest. He feels small waves lap over his back, and he moves one arm up in front before pulling it back through the water, shoveling a mass of the salty liquid with his big hands. Back and forth he goes, pulling himself through the water, one arm at the time, tumbling from side to side and kicking his legs.

The bottom moves quickly beneath him as he picks up speed.

Tiny is really flying now, his mind emptying into the vastness of the sea. This is the moment he's been waiting for, the moment he lets go of who he is, when all his thoughts become one with the ocean. It is in this moment, when Tiny is completely free, that an answer bubbles to the surface within him. He will swim. Just like Jack Lalanne had his feet and hands shackled, so is Goliath shackled to his wheelchair. And just like Jack Lalanne, there's only one way to set him free. Tiny will swim.

---

It's dark when Goliath hears the tapping. He's reading a book about the Antarctic in the light of a flashlight when a marble hits his window, pulling him out of the walrus' life underwater. He slides out of bed and into his chair, and rolls quietly towards the balcony, careful not to wake his mom. He opens the door and looks into the dark garden, expecting to see the moose again even though the head is still resting on the floor in his bedroom.

He spots Tiny right away. His hair is wet and shimmering in the moonlight, as if Tiny was made out of metal.

"Hey there," Goliath whispers.

Tiny whispers back in his best soft voice. It's strange to hear such a soft voice come out of such a big body.

"I figured it out," He says.

"What?" Tiny is doing such a great job at whispering that Goliath can't really hear him.

"Figured out how to fix things. You, how to fix you," Tiny adds.

He continues without waiting for Goliath to speak. He fears that if he doesn't get it all out at once he'll forget what he needs to say, now that he's no longer in the embrace of the ocean.

"We will swim. I mean, *I* will swim, very far, and when I get there reporters and cameras will be there and TV, and they will give you the treatment. All right?"

Goliath can tell Tiny is excited because he's never spoken so many words at once before.

"You mean… like breaking a record?"

Tiny nods, happy that Goliath understands.

"Yes, yes, breaking a record."

"And we'll be on TV?"

Tiny nods again.

"And you'll swim?" Goliath goes through all the points again.

"I will swim."

"Sounds good to me. I would have to check with my mom first though."

"OK," Tiny says. This conversation went better than he thought it would.

"I've got to get back to bed now but we can talk more about this tomorrow."

"OK," Tiny says again because he doesn't really know what else to say. Although it feels as if he's forgetting something. Something important.

Goliath turns his wheelchair around to go back inside when he thinks of something. Tiny has started to walk back through the dark garden when he hears Goliath whisper.

"Tiny?"

Tiny hurries back to his spot below the balcony. "Yeah?"

"Where would we go?"

"Where?" Tiny doesn't understand the question. He wants to go home to sleep.

"Yes, where would we swim?"

"Oh." Tiny realizes what he forgot to mention.

"Across the ocean," he says, matter of factly.

"To England?" Goliath asks, raising his eyebrows. Swimming to England is impossibly far, through open water with waves and storms. It would take days.

"The *other* ocean," Tiny says.

"The other ocean?"

Goliath has to do a quick visualization of a world map before he realizes what Tiny is really talking about.

"You mean the Atlantic?!"

"Yes, that ocean! The Atlantic." Tiny is elated that Goliath understands the plan, and he waves his hand goodbye, like it was the most natural thing in the world to talk about. Like they were just planning to go to the movies or something.

Goliath watches him disappear behind the trees.

"Oh, boy," Goliath says to himself. What else can you say when someone, in all seriousness, has just told you that he'll swim across the Atlantic Ocean?

Oh, boy.

---

Goliath pours over the large map spread open on the table, his nose right up against it.

"The Atlantic," he says, tracing his finger from Ireland, which is just a small circle on the large map, and glides it west across the shiny paper, across the ocean. As far as they can see, it's all blue. Goliath looks up.

"We're going to need a boat," he states, as if suddenly realizing how large the Atlantic really is.

"We live on a boat..." Tiny offers.

Goliath seems to have regained some energy from his last spell, with just the thought of him and Tiny on such an adventure. Like real explorers!

"We just need to convince Kurt and then - the tricky part - my mom. How long do you think it will take to swim?"

"I don't know."

Goliath puts the tip of his finger on the map again.

"Let's say you swim one fingertip per day."

He walks forward, one fingertip after another, across the map. His lips are moving to an inner count. He stops halfway across, his fingers surrounded by blue.

"We're going to need a boat," he says again.

---

Kurt is working on the pool pump as Tiny and Goliath approach from behind. They look like two people who have things to say but don't know how to say them. Goliath pushes Tiny up front. Tiny looks unsure, and pushes Goliath up front. Goliath clears his throat.

"Uhmmm..."

Kurt looks up, sees them, and continues working his wrench.

"Hi lads. What are you up to?"

"We had a question and thought... maybe you could help us?"

"Sure thing," Kurt says, thinking that the question is about how to fix something at the pool, or maybe fishing, or even old cars.

But Goliath and Tiny don't want to know about old cars.

"If you had a really great idea that you knew would help someone that really needed it, and also make a lot of other people happy, but you were afraid that if you talked about it with anyone before you actually did it some people would try to stop you, even though your idea was really, really good, because that's just how people are, what would you do?"

Kurt puts down the wrench and scratches his head. A simple yes or no won't do in this case. This is a real question.

"Well, I suppose that if I knew in my heart that it was the right thing to do, I would trust that, regardless of what other people thought about it, I would do everything I could to make it happen."

Yes, Kurt thinks, that is sound advice to any growing young person. Follow your heart. What could go wrong with that answer?

Goliath and Tiny look at each other, as if that conversation went better than expected.

"OK thanks!" Goliath says,      and he and Tiny turn to leave.

After a few feet he stops his wheelchair and turns back.

"Oh, one more thing."

"Sure." Kurt says, already back on the pump.

"We're going to need your boat."

Kurt drops the wrench. It hits the ground with a clank.

"What?" He says, peering out from under the pipes. But by then Goliath and Tiny are gone.

Susy stands by the kitchen window, waiting for orders. Antoine slides two plates of pancakes through the slot, glancing into the diner.

"You've got visitors," He says.

Goliath and Tiny sit at a table in the corner, trying to hide behind their open menus. Susy serves the pancakes to an older couple on her way over and pulls out her pad, pretending they are ordinary customers.

"Gentlemen. What can I get you this fine morning?"

Tiny and Goliath lower their menus. Susy feigns surprise.

"Oh my gosh, I thought you two were truck drivers."

"Funny, mom." Goliath taps Tiny's knee under the table.

Tiny nervously stares at his menu, pushing Goliath's hand away.

Susy is the only waitress at the diner, and is in a bit of a hurry.

"What can I do for you, boys?"

"Ehm...," Goliath starts, before tapping Tiny's knee again, only this time harder.

More customers are coming in.

"I don't have all day, boys."

"Ehm...," Goliath says again, fighting with Tiny's hand

under the table.

"How about pancakes?" Susy suggests.

"OK," the boys say in unison, relieved not to have to decide.

Susy hurries back to the window.

"Why didn't you tell her?"

"You tell her," Tiny says.

"I could. I just think it would be better if you did."

Susy returns with two plates of pancakes.

"These were for another table but Antoine said you could have them. Wasn't that nice of him?"

She puts the plates in front of them.

"Tiny has a great idea," Goliath says, slapping his friend's knee.

"Oh, what is it?" Susy gives a wave to a table ready to order to give her just one more second.

"Can I please have syrup?"

"Sure thing, honey." Susy says, grabbing a bottle from the next table over.

"Anything else?"

The boys look at each other. Goliath wiggles his eyebrows, trying to convince Tiny to speak. Tiny just looks down at his pancakes.

"Alright, then. I'll get back to work."

She's about to turn around when Goliath speaks.

"If Tiny swims across the Atlantic we can get that treatment in the US."

A family of four is sitting two tables away. The man looks unhappy, as if the world is against him, and he doesn't wait for Susy to come over before calling across the tables.

"Ma'am? Where are our pancakes?"

"What?" Susy says.

"I said, where are the pancakes we ordered 20 minutes ago?"

"Hang on." Susy says to the father, before returning to Goliath and Tiny.

"Sorry, what are you talking about?" She is rightly confused. What on earth do pancakes have to do with swimming across the Atlantic?

"Swimming," Goliath says. "Tiny is a really good swimmer."

Tiny finally looks up from his pancakes, and nods.

"Ma'am, our pancakes?"

---

After a long day at the diner Susy and Goliath are on their way home. Tiny had to leave to go work at the pool but Goliath stayed behind. He listened to Antoine tell stories about cooking frog legs in France, until Susy's shift was over.

"That is the craziest idea I've ever heard, sweetheart," Susy says to him when he brings the plan up again.

Susy is driving their beat-up Volkswagen beetle. It's a quirky car—it's got a stick shift—and the second gear is no longer working. But it has character, Susy always says, and character makes up for a whole lot. Goliath thinks that if the car were a fishing boat it would have been on pallets behind some pool a long time ago.

"It's very sweet of Tiny to offer," she adds with a smile.

Goliath feels like she doesn't get it.

"Why can't we do it? Jack Lalanne did it from Alcatraz, and he had his feet and his hands tied together!"

"Who?" Susy says, looking both ways at an intersection.

"This man," Goliath begins but then thinks better of explaining the whole story.

" Anyway, it was a long time ago. The point is, he did it and so can we."

The car comes to a stop in front of a red light. Susy turns to Goliath.

"Honey, I know how much you want to get better. I want it, too. More than anything."

She looks sad now. She *feels* sad that she has to talk about things she can't control. Sad because she hates making Goliath disappointed.

"We just have to accept what Dr. Gupta tells us."

Goliath isn't giving up that easy.

"But you said that the doctors in the US might be able to help."

The light turns green but Susy doesn't move. She's deep in thought. A car behind them honks and Susy snaps out of it. She still doesn't go. Instead she turns to Goliath.

"OK, you want to know why it's a crazy idea?"

Goliath nods as another car honks.

"First of all—and this should be reason enough—it's not humanly possible to swim across the Atlantic. It's too far, too cold and too dangerous. Number two..."

Susy puts two fingers up.

"Even if Tiny *could* swim that far—and he can't—what good would it do for your treatment? We still can't afford it. We're not covered by insurance in the US."

Several cars are now behind them, honking. Susy glances at the light and gets ready to go.

She puts the gear in place but just as she's about to drive it turns to red. One car gives one last, angry honk.

"That's only two," Goliath says.

"What?"

"You said three reasons."

Susy again turns to Goliath.

"And number three. Even if it was possible to swim across the Atlantic, which it isn't, and even if that somehow paid for your treatment, which it wouldn't, it would take weeks, maybe even months on a boat for such a long journey. Your health won't allow that. And that's not even counting seasickness.

Goliath is silent.

"Do you want more than three reasons? Because I can probably think of plenty more."

"Green," Goliath says.

"What?"

Cars behind them begin honking again.

"The light. It's green."

Oh, right." Susy finally puts the gear in place and drives.

------

Goliath sits quiet in his seat the rest of the way home. Susy thinks she's upset him. But it's better to give him the truth. The truth is always better, no matter how much it hurts at the time.

She's wrong. Not about the truth – it *is* better to get the truth. She's wrong about Goliath being upset. That's not why he's quiet. He's quiet because he's thinking. When life hands you lemons, you either cry about hating lemons, or you figure out a way of making lemonade, selling it by the street corner and buying something cool with the money. Goliath is thinking about how to turn this into lemonade. He's thinking of a plan to convince his mom to agree to the transatlantic swim. He's thinking so hard that he can hear the cogs in his head turning. Ka-chunk, ka-gronk, ka-plonk.

---

Tiny and Goliath are sitting at the back of the boat, with the map between them, when Kurt walks by with a rope over his shoulder.

"What're you lads up to?"

He spots the map.

"Still working on your secret plan?"

He crosses to the other side of the boat.

"Well. Don't give up lads, dreams are important."

Goliath looks at Tiny.

"OK, this is what we have to do. Number 1...," Goliath scribbles something on the blue of the map before he continues.

---

At the next doctor's visit, Dr. Gupta gives Susy and Goliath his recommendations.

"One hour every day?"

Susy wonders where she's going to get an hour every day out of her busy schedule to sit by the sea with her son.

"Preferably. The more the better," Dr. Gupta says.

"And just being there, breathing the air will help?" Susy asks.

"Exactly. The sea air is filled with minerals that are both soothing and strengthening for the lungs and heart. The best thing would be to actually be on the ocean. But sitting next to it is the second best thing."

Susy seems to accept the doctor's recommendations, and nods.

"Alright, well I'll try to rearrange my schedule."

She turns to Goliath.

"We'll find time, don't worry, honey."

"Thanks, Mom. I know it will be hard on your schedule."

Susy gets up.

"Thanks, Doctor."

She seems to be in a hurry, so much she tries to push Goliath's wheelchair for him.

"I've got it, Mom."

"I'm double parked. I don't want to get a ticket."

"I'll meet you outside. I have to go to the bathroom anyway."

Susy hurries into corridor, and Goliath slowly rolls towards the door.

"Was that OK?" Dr. Gupta whispers from behind his desk.

Goliath peeks into the corridor.

"It was perfect," Goliath whispers back.

---

Back at home Susy opens the mail pile on the kitchen counter. One letter is addressed to Goliath.

"Goliath! You've got mail!" She calls and looks closer at an electric bill, before shaking her head. "What do these people think we do with our electricity, run an amusement park in our backyard?"

Goliath rolls into the kitchen and grabs the envelope. It is addressed "Goliath O'Callaghan, 3241 Hazy Lane Drive, 4321 Galway".

He quickly rolls into the living room, out of Susy's view.

He rips the envelope open, pulls the letter out and begins reading it out loud, with great excitement.

"Dear Mr. O'Callaghan, We are pleased to inform you that the first official world record for swimming the Atlantic is still open, and that, providing proper ratification, such a swim would indeed qualify for an official Guinness Book World Record."

"Did you say something?" Susy asks from the kitchen, chewing on a carrot as she goes through the water bill, while muttering. "What do these people think we do with our water, have our own lake in the backyard?"

But she gets no answer. Goliath is already gone.

---

He rolls down the street, towards the bus stop, and reaches it just as the bus pulls away. He gazes after it for a moment, but only for a second before he returns his hands to the rubber wheels. His arms really are the only things on his body that are somewhat strong. He gives himself a hard push forward.

He rolls through his neighborhood, then into the next, then past the school and past the church and eventually past the cracker factory where the smell of saltines hangs heavy in the air. He rolls all the way over to the north part of town, and the pool.

Tiny is on his knees, his muscular arm deep into a drainage hole when Goliath rolls in. Goliath is sweaty and out of breath after the long ride, his heart beating hard inside his chest, but his eyes are lively and full of energy. He takes a moment to catch his breath, before he holds out the letter.

"Read this."

Tiny takes the letter and goes through it slowly, letter by letter, word by word. It's a bit too slow for Goliath. Not because he doesn't want Tiny to learn how to read, but because he is too excited to wait.

"It says that we'll set the record if you swim."

Tiny stares at the letter. The words float into each other, as if he was reading under water.

"Now all we have to do is convince my mom."

Tiny's had enough reading for now, and hands the letter back.

"OK," He says, and takes off his shirt.

---

Goliath is sitting by the pool as Tiny swims when Kurt walks by carrying a tool kit.

"Tiny's swimming?"

"Yup," Goliath says.

"Keep an eye on him. He might need *you* to save *him* one of these days," He says and winks.

Kurt continues to cross the yard, and starts working on a bench that needs a touch up.

---

Later in the afternoon when Kurt walks by again, this time with a big hose over his shoulder, he notices the boys are still there.

"Still at it?"

This time Goliath doesn't say anything. It's obvious that Tiny is still swimming. Back and forth he glides, length after length.

"That lad sure can swim," Kurt says, a hint of pride in his voice.

The third time he walks by it's getting dark.

"You lads trying to break a record or something?"

Goliath yawns.

"I dunno."

"Your mom called. She's coming to pick you up in a bit."

"Alright," Goliath says, but doesn't take his eyes off of Tiny.

This is how to make lemonade. By not giving up.

When Susy arrives Tiny is still swimming.

"I've got supper ready at home, honey. Does Tiny want to join us?"

"Nah, he's swimming," Goliath says, pointing to the pool.

"Oh. Well, we can wait. How long has he been in?"

Goliath looks at his watch.

"About 5," He says after some figuring.

"Since 5 o'clock? Then he'll be done soon."

"No," Goliath says and makes sure to pause long enough for effect. "Five hours."

Susy looks taken aback.

"My goodness. Is that normal?"

Goliath shrugs, trying to act as if it is a perfectly normal day of swimming.

"He just likes to swim."

The next day Susy and Goliath are sitting at the breakfast table. Susy is scanning the morning paper. Goliath is concentrating on enjoying a peanut butter and jelly sandwich. Or is he...? Well, *he* is, because who wouldn't enjoy a peanut butter and jelly sandwich. At the same time, though, in the back of his mind, he is waiting. He expects it any second now. He can't say for sure, of course. It's just the only logical conclusion. Scientists and explorers are big on logical conclusions. Jelly pools perfectly in the crater formed by the peanut butter. That's only logical. Goliath imagines a planet made entirely from peanut butter, where all land is the hardened crust with creamy peanut butter underneath, and oceans and lakes are all jelly. KNOCK, KNOCK! And there it is, Goliath thinks, as Susy gets up to see who's at the door. The logical conclusion.

He still acts surprised when Kurt walks into the kitchen. Maybe a little *too* surprised.

"He's doing whaaaatt!?" Goliath nearly drops the sandwich but manages to catch it just before it lands on his foot. He tries again, this time with less enthusiasm.

"I mean, Tiny is doing what?"

"The lad is still swimming," Kurt says, and looks at Susy as if she held the answer to the question everyone wants to know: why is Tiny swimming?

Then they both look at Goliath, who shrugs once, then twice, just for emphasis.

"That sounds strange...,"he says.

Susy's seen them all before. The things Goliath does when he's got a secret. She's got a nose better at detecting lies than a truffle dog has for detecting truffles. It twitches as she sniffs the air. She gives Goliath The Look.

"Do you know anything about this?"

It's not that Goliath can't lie, it's just that Susy can see right through him. It's really irritating, a real invasion of privacy.

"I think we'd better go to the pool," he says.

When they arrive at the pool, Susy is still in her bathrobe, the newspaper clutched under her arm as if she just got up from the breakfast table to answer the phone. Tiny is still swimming.

Goliath rolls up to the edge. Tiny comes gliding in after another length, the water around him frothy from his constant movement.

Goliath leans forward and yells into the pool.

"Hey, you can stop now!"

Just like that, Tiny stops swimming. He stands up, the water only waist high on his big frame. Even though Kurt and Susy are standing only a few feet away, he looks at Goliath and speaks as if there was nobody else there.

"What did they say?"

His breathing is calm and steady. His body doesn't even remember that it has just swam for nearly 18 hours straight.

"Say about what?" Susy asks, and only when Tiny looks up does he seem to realize she and Kurt are there.

What follows could be something straight out of a Western movie, with Goliath and Tiny as gunslingers, and Susy and Kurt the sheriffs. The four of them look at each other: Goliath at Susy, Tiny at Kurt, Susy at Tiny, and Kurt at Goliath, as if at any moment any one of them is going to draw a gun.

"Well...," Goliath begins, and draws a deep breath. This is it.

"You know how Dr. Gupta said ocean air would be good for me?"

"Yes...," Susy says.

"And you know how you said that nobody could ever swim across the Atlantic because it was too far?"

"Yes..." Suzy suspects she knows where this is going, but can't stop it.

"And you know how you said that even if someone could swim that far, how would that pay for my treatment?"

"Yes, but..."

Goliath doesn't let her get another word in because he is afraid that if he doesn't get everything out now she will put a stop to their plans. He empties all his words at one time.

"Tiny just swam for 18 hours and he's not even tired. Right?"

He turns to Tiny. "Tell her."

"I'm not even tired," Tiny says and Goliath continues.

"And we also got a letter from uhm…"

He pulls a letter from his pocket.

"Guinness World Records. They say we will set a record for the longest swim in the world, and that a world record is worth something. Money, I mean."

"Alright, I see now what…"

"And you heard what Dr. Gupta said. I need ocean air."

Goliath doesn't mean to cough but it works out perfectly that he has to, so he puts some extra effort behind it.

"In fact, I could use some ocean air right now."

Susy puts her hands on her hips. Goliath feels his heart sink. That is a surefire sign that something bad is going to happen. Once, when he painted the apple tree blue, he saw the hands on the hips before he was sent to his room. Another time he entered the cart race with his wheelchair and almost got hit by a truck, and then there was the time he put the baby bird he found under a bus stop in her underwear drawer because it was the only soft place he could think of.

Hands on the hips, every time.

"Are you done? Susy asks.

Goliath and Tiny look at each other. This is where, if this were a Western, they would jump on their horses and gallop out of there as fast as they could.

She turns to Kurt. "Did you know about this?"

"About what?" It's clear that he doesn't know what they are talking about.

She turns back to Goliath and Tiny. Here it comes, Goliath thinks. The laser beams. Every mother uses the laser beams to annihilate their children. One look is all it takes. BOOM! You're gone.

"Let me get this straight. You dragged me here on my day off, before I've had my morning coffee or had the time to read the newspaper, for...this?"

Without a word she turns around and starts for the exit.

Goliath sighs and pats Tiny on the shoulder.

"At least we tried."

That's all you can do sometimes, try and fail. He's read about explorers who've gone out for months, even years, without finding what they were looking for. There's lots of failure in exploring. And it's not like he and Tiny have spent years preparing or anything.

But somehow it's easier to read about trying and failing, than actually doing it. Failing stings.

"Is she still sea worthy?"

At first nobody seems to know what the question refers to, or even who it's for.

"Huh?" Kurt says, because this entire morning is still a big mystery to him.

"Your boat. Is she still sea worthy?" Susy asks again.

"Oh...," Kurt says, still not sure what anything is about, but concluding it doesn't matter. He can talk about Old Bertha for hours.

"Yes ma'am. I'd trust her with my life."

Susy gives the three of them a look. She seems to contemplate something for a moment. She looks like she could be sucking on a mint, but Goliath can't remember any mints at the breakfast table.

"She needs new drapes. A woman's touch," she says, before turning around and walks towards the exit.

Kurt *still* doesn't know what this is all about.

"Yes ma'am," he says to her retreating back, just to be on the safe side. While in his head he is thinking, "why does Old Bertha need new drapes when the drapes she has have been fine for twenty years?"

He just doesn't get it.

Tiny is confused too. "What just happened?"

Goliath thinks maybe he gets it.

"I'm not sure but I think..." Did his mom just say they could do it? "...I think, we are going on an adventure!"

"Really? You mean...?" Tiny asks, beginning to understand.

"Yes, we are swimming across the Atlantic!"

It's been a couple of days and Goliath hasn't stopped talking about the swim. It's the weekend, and Susy and Goliath are on their way to the pool to work on old Bertha. The back of the car is packed with drapes, cushions…even a knitted wall hanging that will help make the old fishing boat a comfortable place to spend eight weeks in. That's how long it will take for Tiny to swim across the Atlantic. At least, that's what they think. They really don't have anything to compare it to. Kurt thinks they could do it in six weeks if they would just ride the currents going south and then west. It would be like stepping onto one of those moving walkways they have at airports and not getting off for six weeks, until you reach land. It's a nice thought, except the currents going that way would only get them to the West Indies, and Goliath's hospital is in Boston, which is another 800 miles north. And the weather in the South can be tricky, with plenty of storms. What they have to do, they conclude after they lay out rulers on a large map about a hundred times to calculate the best way, is go straight out from Ireland and stick to the Northern route. It's going to be a lot tougher than stepping onto a moving walkway, but Tiny swears he doesn't need currents to swim.

Susy pulls into the gas station.

"Wait right here," she says, and runs inside.

When she comes back she's carrying a 12-pack of the little scented pine trees you can hang from the rear view mirror.

"To get the fish smell out," she explains before starting the car.

When they get to the boat Kurt and Tiny are busy patching

the hull with tarpaper.

"How's it going?" Susy asks as she and Goliath balance a pile of cushions and drapes.

"Just plugging all the holes," Kurt says.

Susy stops short.

"Holes?"

"Yup. We don't want any leaks where we're going," Kurt says matter of factly.

Susy drops her load of pillows on the ground. She looks flustered.

"Leaks?! Now wait a minute. Nobody said anything about..."

"Mom," Goliath says behind his pile of fabric, his face completely hidden.

"He's kidding."

Kurt is laughing so hard his face is bright red. His laughter sounds like an old engine puttering, and coughing.

"Oh you..." she says, throwing a pillow Kurt's way. "You almost gave me a heart attack!"

Kurt grabs his chest and calms down his breathing.

"I'm sorry. I couldn't help it."

"Speaking of help," Susy says, looking at Tiny. "I could use some help getting all this stuff on board."

"OK," Tiny says, putting down the tar-covered brush.

Tiny likes helping Susy. It makes him feel good when she smiles and thanks him. He quickly gathers all the pillows from the ground, and the fabric from Goliath, and hoists them on board without having to use a ladder. Susy, on the other hand, has to climb up. As soon as she is out of sight Kurt whispers Goliath's way.

"Psst..."

"Yeah?"

"Can you help?" He hands Goliath a brush. "We have to fix these holes before your mom gets back."

Goliath looks at him to see if he's joking again. But Kurt isn't laughing. He looks dead serious, so Goliath grabs the brush and begins patching the holes with the thick, black tar.

Several hours later they are finally done sealing the hull. By then Susy has left for her shift at the diner, and Kurt openly vents his concerns about leaks.

"I mean, she should be fine, especially with this last coat, but..."

"You never know?" Goliath offers.

"Right, you never know. You never know until you put her in the water."

Goliath sees it clear as day; how they get to the harbor with all the bags and equipment, ready to go. His mom has got about a hundred Tupperware containers filled with sponge cake - she's got to have a piece of sponge cake with her coffee or she might as well not drink coffee at all, and that's never going to happen. There's a crowd seeing them off, just like the crowd that greeted Jack LaLanne in the clip he and Tiny have now watched about a hundred times in a little video booth at the library. There are news reporters and maybe even TV cameras, and they all get on the boat (except Tiny because he is in the water), and the big crane lowers them into the water and then it begins. A world record attempt, with everybody cheering and cameras flashing and Tiny starts swimming the first of millions of strokes, and then...old Bertha begins taking in water. It's a total fiasco. They never even make it out of the harbor.

Goliath opens his eyes.

"Isn't there a way we can test it outside of the harbor?"

Kurt scratches his head, pondering this idea.

"I guess," He says and glances towards the entrance. The last part he only mumbles to himself. "But it won't be popular."

---

General Shito - who isn't a real general at all, he just enjoys the respect his title gives him in the locker room, where there is already a butcher, a mechanic, a baker and an engineer, but no general until the day Shito announced his presence amidst curt nods and even a salute - walks to the pool in his usual brooding fashion. He stares at the ground. He leaves his slippers by the edge, before he turns around, descending the ladder backwards into the water. When it reaches his armpits, he lets go with a sigh, floating into the pool.

This is how General Shito always enters the pool, because

General Shito is a man of habit. He doesn't like change. If it were up to him the seasons would never change and the weather would always be the same. That's why General Shito is so surprised when his head collides with something hard in the middle of the pool, where there has never been anything hard before. Just moments after the dull thud echoes across the lawn, a loud voice booms from over by the entrance.

"What in the mighty Zeus is that!?"

General Shito and Mr. Buskly can't believe their eyes because in the middle of the pool, as if a hurricane had picked her up from a harbor in Dublin and plunked her down in their pool, sits old Bertha. Kurt looks over the railing.

"Good morning, General, Mr. Buskly," he says, giving them a salute.

General Shito doesn't know what to say. This is not part of his daily routine.

Tiny comes up on deck.

"I've checked it. She's all dry," He says.

"Excellent."

"Get that boat out of the pool and off my property!" Mr. Buskly yells.

Kurt waves at him, because you can't really be angry with people that wave at you.

"And you're fired!" Buskly says. "Both of you!" he adds, in case they didn't understand.

Kurt pats Tiny on the shoulder.

"I was getting tired of this place anyway. It's time we had an adventure."

———————

Goliath's bedroom is overflowing with things. If it really was a hurricane that picked old Bertha up and put her in the pool, that same hurricane must have opened all Goliath's closets and drawers, and emptied the content on his floor.

He sits in the middle, packing his bag for the big trip.

"Binoculars."

He puts a pair of binoculars in his bag.

"Check."

He continues with a pair of rubber boots.

"Rubber boots, check."

Next is a fishing pole.

"Fishing gear."

He puts it on the rubber boots.

"Check."

He rolls to his desk and grabs a camera.

"Camera."

He puts it on the fishing gear.

"Check."

He rolls to his bookshelf.

"Books."

He puts five books on his camera.

"Check, check, check, check and check."

He tries to move his bag but it won't budge. It's too heavy. He removes one book, puts it in his lap and rolls out of the room.

Susy has all her photo albums spread out on the floor as Goliath enters.

"Mom, do you have room for this in your bag?"

"Sure honey," She says without looking up. She holds up a photo.

"Look at how cute we were here."

The photo is of Goliath as a baby, lying flat on his stomach on the floor. Susy is wearing a flower-patterned dress that looks older than the twelve years since the photo was taken, and she is smiling widely at the camera. She's lying next to Goliath on the floor. He spots it right away, as if it wasn't he that noticed, but his subconscious.

"Look at my legs," he says, and points them out. "They're as thick as my arms."

As if reading his mind Susy comes to her son's rescue, like she has done so many times before.

"You look so much better now." She adds, "In fact, you were a pretty ugly baby, if I'm being honest. I couldn't even get you into day care. I tried but they just said, "No, Mrs. O'Callaghan, your baby is too ugly. He'll scare the other kids with those thick legs of his.""

Over the years Susy has developed a patented approach to any situation when Goliath is feeling sorry for himself. She won't allow it, and uses humor to disarm him.

"Ha, ha. Very funny, Mom."

It usually works. But this time, perhaps because of the excitement of the trip, Goliath notices something else about the photo. Something that he hadn't thought about before.

"Who took that photo? Was it Dad?"

The question takes Susy by surprise. They don't talk about Goliath's dad very often. When they do it usually leaves Goliath in a bad mood.

"I don't really remember. You know, it might actually have been Deirdra. You remember Deirdra, right?"

Goliath does remember Deirdra. She was his mom's friend from up north. Goliath always thought she smelled like cooked spaghetti. As if she rubbed her clothes in macaroni before every visit. Without a word he rolls out of the room. Moments later he returns holding a magnifying glass. He takes the photo and studies it closely.

"Yep, it's him."

Susy looks at the photo again, skeptically.

"How do you know?"

"The reflection in the TV. I see his glasses."

Susy looks again and while she'd rather not talk about Goliath's father, there's admiration in her voice.

"Well aren't you a little Sherlock Holmes."

"Where do you think he is now?"

"I don't know."

Part of Susy wants to say exactly how she feels about being abandoned by the man she loved and she thought loved her. She's angry, even after all these years, but not for her. For Goliath. For the fact that he left her with talks like this, where she has to scramble to come up with an explanation where there really isn't one, and Goliath has to scramble to make sense of her answers, when there really isn't any.

"He moved to New Zealand a year after he left. There were a couple of postcards and then we never heard from him again," This is always what she says when he asks.

Facts are what they are, and she'll never lie to him about anything, no matter how painful. He deserves the truth. That's how much she loves her son.

Goliath thinks about her answer. He approaches it as if he really is Sherlock Holmes and this is the first time he's heard the story. Neither of which is true. There's something about the moment, about packing for the actual moment of their lives where they'll be heading off into an unknown future, that makes him want to know about his past.

Susy puts Goliath's books in her bag.

"Did he leave because of me?"

Susy freezes. It's as if what she just heard was the most ridiculous thing she's ever heard in her life, so ridiculous her body couldn't comprehend and stopped moving.

"That is the most ridiculous thing I've ever heard in my life."

With the words her body breaks free, and she puts the albums down and kneels in front of Goliath. She looks at him with the most serious face she's ever made.

"Now, you listen to me, young man, and you listen good."

Her eyes shine like flashlights, right into Goliath's heart.

"You are the best thing that has ever happened to me. To your father, too, if he was ever so lucky to realize it. One day he will and then he'll be sorry. You are a handsome young man with values and goals and aspirations and a great, big heart. You are a blessing. I am without a doubt the luckiest mom in the whole world."

It's hard for Goliath to look at her because her eyes are so bright.

"So...what you're saying is that...he left because I'm in a wheelchair?"

Time stands still. How can she explain it to him so that he understands? He is the most precious....oh...she gets it now. Sucker. Goliath winks and cracks a smile. Susy grabs the nearest pillow and whacks Goliath right in the head with it.

Not too hard but hard enough for him to wake up.

"You little trickster!"

Goliath laughs hard.

"You should have seen your face!" He catches his breath and becomes serious again.

"I do miss him, though."

"I know, honey. In a way I do too."

She searches among the pile and pulls a picture from one of the photo books.

"Here", she says and gives it to Goliath.

"Bring him with you on the trip."

Goliath looks at the photo. His dad looks young. Older than he is, obviously, but young for an adult. He has a moustache that looks like a bicycle handle across his face, and his shirt is only buttoned half way. A rug of fuzzy hair sticks out from his chest.

"What's all that?"

"Your father was very hairy."

Susy moves around the feathers, and continues packing.

"He just woke up one morning with that jungle on his chest."

Goliath looks surprised.

"Really?"

He doesn't want to have a hairy animal growing on his chest, ever.

His mother shrugs. "Nothing you can do about it, I'm afraid. It's in your genes."

There's something in her tone of voice that makes Goliath suspicious.

"Wait a second...," he says as he grabs the nearest pillow.

He whacks his mom in the back with the pillow, perhaps a little too hard, because it splits open, and the room fills with a cloud of feathers.

"You trickster!"

Feathers slowly float down around them, turning the room into a winter wonderland.

---

Susy is reading mental lists out loud over every detail they have had to remember, and she's starting to repeat herself.

"Give old Mrs. Robinson the key to the garden shed so she can pick the apples and not let them go to waste."

"Let Ben know we're gone so he doesn't stuff our mailbox full."

She turns to Goliath.

"Did we let Ben know?"

She looks confused.

"There are so many things to keep track of that I don't remember."

Goliath scans the harbor, expecting to see Old Bertha suspended from a crane, ready to be lowered into the water, surrounded by a large crowd of journalists. But he can see neither.

"Wait, I think I did tell Ben. OK, moving on," Susy mumbles.

"Where's the boat?" Goliath says.

"It's right there." Susy responds, pointing to the right.

Old Bertha is already in the water.

"It's already in the water?" Goliath can't hide his disappointment.

"But where's the crowd?" Goliath says this mostly to himself as Susy is back to going through her mental list of things to remember.

"Water all the plants and take out the trash..."

Tiny steps ashore to help them carry their things.

"Where are all the journalists?" Goliath asks.

All explorers needs someone to write about them, otherwise it's like they don't exist.

Tiny shrugs, and grabs all their bags at once.

"Dunno."

He glances over the empty car.

"No pillows?"

Goliath doesn't hear the question and he doesn't have time

to explain the pillow fight. He's spotted something across the harbor.

"What about that guy over there?"

On the other side of the dock there is a middle-aged man eating fish and chips. Goliath waves at him.

"Over here!"

"Hi Tiny," Susy says, and gives him a hug with one arm. She is clutching the phone to her ear with her other hand.

"Thanks, Debra", she says into the phone. "So the car is parked by the fishing dock. Yes, the key is under the mat. No, I didn't lock the door. How could I lock it and still have the key under the mat? Now listen..."

"Hello, you over there!" Goliath says, continuing to wave at the man with the fish and chips.

The middle-aged man holding the fish and chips finally notices Goliath, and waddles over.

"Are you with the press?" Goliath asks when he's close enough.

The man looks confused.

"A what?"

"The press, like a journalist. Are you one?"

"Me? No, I'm just..."

Goliath doesn't wait for an answer.

"Here, take this notebook and this pen and ask us some questions."

The man doesn't know what's going on but takes the notebook and pen because Goliath is pushing them into his hand.

"Ehm..., what questions?"

"About our trip."

The man thinks for a second, then decides to play news reporter.

"Alright, where ya going?"

"Boston," Goliath answers. When the man hesitates, he adds, "Go on, write down the answer."

"Okey doke. Boston," The man says, scribbling in the notebook.

Goliath and Tiny patiently wait for him to finish. After a long pause, he's ready for the next question.

"Ehm..., why ya going to Boston?"

"There's a hospital there that specializes in treating Duchenne muscular dystrophy."

The man writes the answer down, word by word.

"How ya spell that? D-u..."

"C-h-e-n-n-e," Goliath says.

"Gotcha. And uhm...how are you getting to Boston?"

"Well, *we're* going on that boat over there," Goliath says and points at Bertha, "But Tiny here is going to swim. Isn't that right, Tiny?"

"Yup, I'm going to swim."

The man starts writing down the answer before it hits him. Did he say swim to Boston?

Then Susy calls them from the boat.

"Tiny, Goliath, let's go!"

"See ya," Goliath says and rolls towards the boat with Tiny alongside him.

"Wait, did ya say swim?"

The man is even more confused than when he began. All he can do is watch the big boy lift the little boy's wheelchair onto deck, and then swing himself after as if it was nothing.

---

Kurt is zipping around the boat checking a million things. There's the gas tank that needs to be filled - enough for 3000 nautical miles - because there are no gas stations where they're going. That's one of Kurt's favorite sayings. There are no gas stations in the middle of the ocean.

Then there's the water tank that needs to hold almost as much as the gas tank. It's weird that one of the most important things to bring on a trip on the ocean is water. But it is.

Goliath and Susy wait in the middle of the deck, not sure what to do. There's a lot of commotion going on around them. Tiny does seem to know what to do, though, as he follows Kurt around. Kurt barks orders left and right. Check this, tighten that, double check this, double tighten that. It's a whirlwind of tasks for Tiny who's never been on a boat at sea. But he's so used to old Bertha from years of living on her that he knows exactly what Kurt means when he says things like "batten down the hatches," and "on your beam ends". Tiny is so busy that he even forgets for a little while that he isn't actually going to be *on* the boat, except for when he's having dinner and sleeping at night.

A truck arrives with food, and so Susy and Goliath take charge of stocking the pantry. For hours, or at least it seems like hours, Goliath rolls back and forth across deck with boxes, bags and cans. After a while the sun is high in the sky and when it's starting to feel like he is trapped in a dream where everything just repeats itself, box after bag after can, and then more boxes and cans and bags, they finally finish. The deck is clean, the pantry is full and all the tanks are filled. Everything is tied down and tucked away. They are finally ready to go. There's finally a small crowd on the dock, gathered around the man pretending to be a journalist. He points at the boat, then at the notebook, then back at the boat.

"I think that's everything," Kurt says, and looks out from the captain's window.

"Food's squared away, we have our bags, and of course, Goliath and Tiny," Susy adds.

Everything finally seems ready for departure. As if on cue, Tiny pulls off his t-shirt, swings his legs over the railing, and sits down. His legs dangle over the edge, big toes dipping into the water. This is how it begins, Goliath thinks. When Tiny jumps into that water and they steer old Bertha out through the harbor, past the breakwater built to keep the storm waves from reaching land, their lives will change. There's only one thing beyond that stony ridge - open water. A big, unbroken ocean that stretches for weeks on end.

Goliath turns his gaze to the horizon. There's no saying what they will find along the way. It's a fact of life for any explorer. Goliath thinks about that for a second, and then changes his thought. It's the simple fact of life, period. The hairs on the back of his neck stand up. He feels cold even though he's standing in the sun. He can see it glimmer out there, the ocean. She's like - she's always a she, Kurt says, just like every boat is always a she - a mysterious animal. Silent, waiting, breathing calmly, chest heaving up and down. It's a big, big place where they are going, and Goliath can't help but feel a little bit afraid.

"All right, ready to go?" Kurt asks through the window above them.

Tiny jumps in the water. Something doesn't feel right to Goliath, though. They are forgetting something. He can feel it in his bones. Something very important. He goes through his mental checklist again, then his mom's mental list, while Kurt unties Bertha and collects the ropes in neat, round piles. He can't put his finger on it so he starts again, from the beginning. We are swimming across the Atlantic. We have a boat, we have gas, water, food and all our stuff. Everything seems in order, so Goliath tries to push the feeling away. Old Bertha shudders when Kurt presses the button and the engine ignites. The propeller churns up the water, and, slowly, Bertha begins inching away from the dock.

Suddenly there's movement in the corner of Goliath's eyes. By the parking lot above the harbor a man jumps out of a taxi and begins running down the path towards the dock. His jacket is half on, half off, and he drags a suitcase behind him in a way that makes it look very uncomfortable. He stops briefly by the crowd, the one around the man who pretends to be a journalist who is now pointing towards the boat. The man with the suitcase starts running again, this time waiving his one free arm and shouting something that sounds more like the bark of a sea lion than a human.

"Arf! Arf! Arf!"

Bertha is slowly widening the gap between her and the dock, and suddenly the penny that was stuck in Goliath's head shakes lose. He remembers what they've forgotten.

"Stop the boat!" he yells up at the captain's cabin.

Kurt quickly pulls the throttle to neutral. Bertha shudders once before coming to a stop. There's a gap of water the width of a car between the boat and the dock.

"It's the controller," Goliath says to his mom, as they all look at the strange man running towards them.

"Arf! Arf! Arf!"

"The what?"

The man gets closer and closer. He doesn't seem to want to slow down.

"Is he going to...." Susy says, but the last part is lost when the man reaches the dock. He continues towards the edge, where he pushes off and takes one giant leap, aiming for old Bertha.

Goliath sees him coming like it's in slow motion, one jacket arm dragging behind as the suitcase pops open and clothes spill out. The man's face is saying "Get out of the way, I'm going to land on deck!" and Goliath, who is about to answer his mom's question, has to throw himself to the side, his wheelchair falling on end. The man suddenly stops moving through the air and falls straight down into the water. He hits the surface with a giant splash.

"The controller from the Guinness Book of World Records," Goliath finally says, as he crawls back in his wheelchair.

———————————

His name is Harry Belafonte, like the famous West Indian singer. Although this Harry couldn't be less West Indian, or more Irish, if he tried. He sits in a rather sad pile on deck, a towel around his shoulders with a pool of water forming around him. Tiny, who quickly hoisted Harry on board, also picked up all the items that spilled from Harry's suitcase. Susy has hung them from the railing to dry. Harry offers an explanation.

"My alarm died, then the train was late, and then the taxi was late and then..."

"You were late?" Kurt offers.

Harry gives him a glance through his fogged up glasses.

"Exactly."

Goliath tried his best to explain it while everyone was running around deck in the general commotion after Harry hit the water. Harry was the official controller sent by Guinness to verify the record. No Harry, no official record. Something Harry, who seems to be a man who likes rules and protocol, seems happy to remind them of now. He pulls from his bag a plastic sleeve filled with an official rulebook, and begins reading from it out loud, in a very official sounding voice.

"One: witness statement template. Every record attempt requires TWO witness statements. Witness statements are statements of authentication that must be filled out by independent individuals who verify all relevant details of a record attempt. Refer to guide and...."

Goliath, Tiny, Susy and Kurt have trouble paying attention. The subject is awfully boring, and so is Harry's monotonous voice that just keeps going and going and going, and going...It's not long before everyone is daydreaming.

---

Everyone wakes up with a jerk as Harry, finally, reads the last sentence on the last paper.

"These Terms of Use, and any rights and licenses granted hereunder, may not be transferred or assigned by you, but may be assigned by us without restriction.

These terms shall be governed by and interpreted in accordance with the laws of Ireland which shall have exclusive jurisdiction over any disputes."

Everyone is silent. It takes a while for them to notice that Harry has stopped rambling. It's Kurt who breaks the silence. He's getting impatient. The whole ocean is in front of them, every inch of it yet unswimmed and uncrossed. The longer they sit here the longer it's going to take them to get to Boston.

"I'd say that about covers it," he says, and trudges up to the control deck.

He slides open the window and sticks his head out. He's wearing his old captain's hat and Goliath realizes that this is it. He knows that this is the beginning, even before Kurt fires up the engine and old Bertha shudders and starts creeping away from the dock. The man who isn't really a journalist understands the gravity of the  situation too, and starts waving. The people around him start to wave too, and Tiny jumps in the water for a second time and starts churning his arms like a windmill, round and round in a steady beat, gliding through the harbor. Goliath knows that the adventure of his life has just begun.

## 53.2707° N, 9.0568° W, Galway, Ireland
## 12:37 PM, Sunday, May 15, 1988

The buzzing from the propeller fills the water, and the moment Tiny hears it he lifts his feet back and puts his arms out. He stays like this for a minute, horizontal, face down, just floating, while Kurt gets Bertha ready for their voyage. Again.

It's true that Tiny is a bit slow, and that he doesn't really have a concept of how far he has to swim. Halfway around the world - they are just words to him. Tiny, who has never even been out of Galway. But despite that, or perhaps because he doesn't understand, he isn't afraid. The water always soothes him. Being in it, floating on the surface like now, or diving deep down, always feels like coming home. Like the water reaches out and hugs him with a thousand little arms.

Tiny can see the bottom here. Not many plants, mostly sand and some empty bottles. A typical harbor floor. Part of Tiny wishes there were no harbors, no boats, no garbage and sometimes even no people. Just the pure, clean ocean. But then he thinks about Kurt and Goliath and Susy and he adjusts his day dream to no harbor, no boats, no garbage and just a few, very special people. He's about to dive down to get the bottles when the buzzing increases in strength and Bertha starts moving beside him. He lifts his head up, just for a moment, and takes one quick look back at the land he's leaving for the first time. The last land he'll set foot on before the US coast a million miles away. He takes a deep breath, so deep he feels it would be enough to carry him all the way to Boston, puts his face back in the water where it belongs, and starts swimming.

Tiny swims alongside Bertha at a distance of twenty-five feet from her hull. This is the distance Kurt has decided, in order to avoid any accidents. As if that would ever happen, Tiny thinks. There's not a move in the water he isn't aware of. Still, he knows it's important to Kurt, so he agrees.

So many memories are coming now that he's in the water, and they play like a movie in his mind. Although there's not much time to sit back and watch clips of his own life because it only takes moments for them to clear the breakers at the outer harbor lip, and before them the open ocean spreads out.

It has started. Their crossing. Oddly, Tiny doesn't feel like he is leaving. It feels like he is going home.

There are two things that Goliath notices as Bertha breaches the stone jetty, and the real ocean begins. Number one: the wind that suddenly hits his face. It's a real ocean wind, untamed. Number two: how pronounced the slow, steady vibrations from the engine are, traveling through the deck straight to his wheelchair.

Goliath sits next to the railing and watches Tiny swim beside him. Just as the engine settles into a rhythm, so, it seems, does Tiny. His strokes rise out of the water like the pistons on a machine, effortlessly, and in an unchanged rhythm. They tumble forward, one after another. To Goliath the two rhythms, Bertha's and Tiny's, match one another, as if they were part of the same engine.

Goliath watches Tiny for a while, not taking his eyes off of him, but anyone that has ever watched an engine run knows that it's not exactly the most interesting thing in the world. In fact, it's pretty boring. Parts go round and round...and that's it. Eventually, Goliath brings his binoculars up and scours the slowly shrinking coastline for birds. Just as he thinks he's spotted a Rare Jaygoose, he hears something fascinating from behind his back.

"Vablaah! Vablaah!"

That sounds like the Tufted Mousehawk! He quickly spins around but there is no Tufted Mousehawk to be found. Only Harry Belafonte, leaning over the railing, throwing up into the water.

"Vablaah! Vablaah!"

Harry's face is green like his mom's kitchen apron. "Are you OK?" Goliath asks.

The only reply he gets is, "vablaah!" as Harry throws up again.

A few moments later, in between breaths, he manages to speak. "Just seasick, that's all."

Goliath looks around at the water around them. There are no real waves to speak of. Just a few gentle chops in the water.

"Ehm...why did you go on a boat if you get seasick?"

It's a valid question, at least that's what Goliath thinks.

Harry wipes his mouth with a handkerchief. "Nobody else wanted to go." He pauses, as if more of his breakfast wants to go for a swim, but then he thinks better of it.

"But don't worry, I'll be fine. We won't be out here that long."

"What do you mean?" Goliath thinks Harry might be missing some vital info. "You know we're going across the ocean, right?"

Harry wipes his mouth again. "Listen, nobody—especially a kid—can swim across the Atlantic Ocean. No matter how great a swimmer he is. I'm an official Guinness Record controller, I should know." With that, Harry excuses himself and goes inside.

Goliath suddenly understands why there weren't any journalists to see them off. He feels so dumb for not getting it sooner. Nobody believes in them. Nobody thinks they can do it. He feels angry. Even the official Guinness Controller doesn't believe in them. Nobody gets anything. He might be small and Tiny may be slow with his words, but they don't know the superpowers the two of them have when they're together. He shapes his little hands around his mouth like a megaphone, and starts cheering Tiny on.

"You can do it! Come on! We can do this!"

It feels good to scream. In Goliath's mind he screams at all the doubters and he becomes the cheering crowd that wasn't there to see them off, and he becomes the journalists with their questions, and he becomes the radio host that broadcast their departure live, and he becomes the doctors and the hospital, and the wheelchair, and his dad and he puts it all behind his voice. His voice doesn't carry that far on the water, with the engine noise and wind, but still. He gives the strongest screams he can, hoping that his words will propel Tiny forward, across the ocean all the way to Boston.

"You look strong! You're a survivor! You never give up! You never ever give up!"

Even though he doesn't realize it right then and there, it's as if Goliath is cheering himself on.

---

Kurt stands on the bridge where he has a great view of the surrounding ocean. Below him Goliath is jumping up and down in his chair, shouting his lungs out at Tiny. But Kurt isn't looking at Goliath; he's not even looking out the window. He is bent over the table, studying a map. He charted the course weeks ago, planning each day and carefully marking the course on the map. He's thought long and hard about it. He's confident that it's the fastest, safest and best route. The Northern route. Similar to what Goliath and Tiny charted out, but for different reasons. He goes over it again. The distance from Galway to Boston is two thousand nine hundred and forty-six nautical miles. At a speed of two and a half knots, they will arrive in Boston in forty-nine days, just before hurricane season that begins in July and continues till November. His finger traces the route, inch after inch over the cool blue, until it reaches brown. Land. Everything checks out.

Then why is he feeling a lump in his stomach? Not a big one. Just large enough to feel like the coffee he just drank was not a good idea. Who's he kidding? After a lifetime at sea he knows why. He is an experienced sailor who's been through storms, high seas and emergencies far from any land. He is the oldest person on board, with the most life experience, he knows every part of old Bertha, and at least most of the ocean they are crossing, and, well, that's why. Kurt knows that the ocean is not a playground. No matter how smart and lucky they are, it will be a tough trip, even without the added sting of icebergs and fog. So many things can go wrong. If you are out on the water, far, far from land and something goes wrong... well that could mean thank you and goodbye.

The greatest dangers are mechanical problems, and Kurt has spent countless hours in Bertha's belly, checking tubes, greasing cranks, replacing washers and tightening bolts. If the engine stops and you can't get it going again, you are a sitting duck. That means you can't turn the boat into incoming waves, and if a big one comes along it will simply flip you over. And there are no gas stations out there, so Kurt has double, triple, quintuple checked the tanks to make sure they're filled to very tip of the brim. You run out of gas, it's thank you and goodbye.

Then there's the bad weather. If you're out to sea for a long time you are bound to encounter bad weather. There's just no way around it. Most of the time it looks worse than it is, with waves that seem to want to swallow you whole, and ocean spray covering the windshield making it impossible to see out. The boat rocks back and forth, slamming into wave after wave with a loud bang, falling and rising so quickly that the hair on your head lifts up. That's mostly the ocean trying to scare you. The boat can handle more than you think, and if you know what you are doing, a ride like that can be more fun than dangerous.

Then there are the times when nature, and the ocean, is in a bad mood. When they're both angry it's just best not to get in their way. There's no place to hide in the middle of the ocean. That's why a good sailor always, always, and always again, watches the weather. To know what is coming. If you know what to look for you can see the signs of anger long before nature throws a tantrum.

Kurt lights an old pipe and studies the map for the hundredth time, just to make sure his calculations are correct, and he listens to the weather report, and he checks the instruments again. There's no room for error when you are captain of a ship. Any mistakes and it's thank you and goodbye.

When Susy enters, carrying a tray of coffee, Kurt is still puffing on his pipe, mulling over the map. When he sees her, he starts frantically fanning the white cloud of smoke, and quickly opens a window.

"Sorry," he says. "Old sailor's habit."

Susy puts the coffee on his desk. "Oh, I don't mind. I've worked in my share of smoky diners."

"Well, in that case..." Kurt says, sticking the pipe back in his mouth. He takes a long drag and...starts coughing uncontrollably.

Susy smiles. "I think I'd rather have a cookie..." she says, and takes one from the plate.

"I'm not used to it," Kurt says, referring to the pipe, "after all my years on land. But it's for good luck. A safe crossing, you know."

Susy looks interested. "Oh, like the Native Americans smoking a peace pipe?"

"Sort of. It's an old seafarer tradition. Although I don't know if there's much truth to it."

"Better safe than sorry." Susy winks.

"That's right. God knows we need all the luck we can get." Kurt nods towards the window.

Susy looks at Tiny and Goliath below them. She watches Goliath scream and jump up and down in his wheelchair, as if he were at the horse races and bet all his money on the winning horse.

"Got valuable cargo," Kurt adds.

Susy feels something tug at her heart. Was this trip irresponsible? Was she a bad parent? If something happened to Goliath, or Tiny, she would never forgive herself. Her heart fills with warmth as she watches her baby boy. So full of life. She is so proud of him. He's on a fishing boat heading into the ocean. He may be limited by his wheelchair, but he's not limited to living life. Goliath is out there living it up.

In one quick movement she snatches the pipe out of Kurt's hand, and sticks it between her lips. She inhales, and seconds later, *she* starts coughing.

Kurt can't believe his eyes. "What on earth...?"

Susy's eyes are red. "In case we need a little more good luck," she says, handing the pipe back to him.

Kurt laughs, and then Susy laughs, but not before coughing again. When they finally catch their breath Susy looks serious again. She puts her hand on Kurt's.

"Thank you," she says earnestly. "Thank you for doing this for Goliath."

With the smoke tearing her eyes it looks like she's been crying, which isn't far from the truth. This man, who was a stranger not long ago, is willing to risk everything he has to help her and Goliath.

Kurt puts his hand on hers, just like her father used to do. It's coarse as sandpaper, but still warm and tender. "You want to know the truth?" he says. "I should be the one thanking you. If it weren't for you and Goliath, me and Tiny would be rotting away at that pool forever." He squeezes her hand. "An adventure is what this old man has needed for a long time now. Tiny too. So thank *you*."

Susy suddenly feels a great rush of love for this old man, with his weathered face, and kind, blue eyes. He's like the grandfather Goliath never had. Like the grandfather *she* never had. Her eyes keep watering, but this time it isn't the smoke.

She gives Kurt a big hug, wipes her face and looks at Goliath and Tiny again. "I'd better get down there before he gets so excited he jumps in the water."

As Susy leaves Kurt takes the pipe and taps it against the ledge of the open window, to clear the old tobacco. He watches the burnt leaves dissolve in the wind and sends a prayer to whatever sea god is out there. *All we want is safe passage*, he prays and hopes that his offering is enough.

As Bertha steams through Galway Bay, Goliath and Susy watch Tiny swim. It's an amazing sight. The green hills in the background glimmer like emeralds when the sun hits them. As awe-inspiring as nature is, they are just as in awe of Tiny. His arms are going round and round, like the wheels on an old riverboat. He has a good rhythm going: one, two, three, four. One, two, three, four. To Susy, who's not really seen Tiny swim before, except for in the pool, he's going awfully fast. She's worried he'll wear himself out. She's about to call out to him to take it easy, but there's something about the serenity of the motion that makes her change her mind.

"This is really something..." Goliath says, and then there's a pause, as if he's searching for the right word.

A pair of fishing boats is heading in the opposite direction, steaming towards the harbor, and Goliath wants to shout out "We're going across the Atlantic!", but there's no room in his head because he's already searching for the word he can't think of. When the fishing boats pass and eventually disappear behind them, the word finally comes to him.

"...special," he says. "This is really something special."

It doesn't quite sum up the whole weird experience, with Tiny swimming next to them, and this trip and everything, but that's all he can come up with. He and Susy settle back into silence.

One, two, three, four. Tiny's arms paddle on through the water. He's like a log with arms, or a seal with long hair.

"Yup. It's special alright," Susy says. Then they're both quiet again.

Bertha huffs and puffs below them, small waves splashing against her bow. One, two, three, four. It's a steady rhythm. Tiny's face is submerged under water, except after each fourth stroke when he turns his body like meat on a skewer, looking at his own armpit before drawing a breath. One, two, three, four…breathe.

"How many times do you think he breathes in an hour?" Susy asks.

She thinks it's a pretty good question, but Goliath's reply comes without much enthusiasm.

"Dunno."

Silence again.

Kurt comes out. Now all three of them are watching Tiny swim. One, two, three, four…breathe. They don't say anything. They just watch the same, endless rhythm. One, two, three, four…breathe.

Goliath pats the railing with his hand. "You know what this is called?" he asks his mom.

"A hand?" she says, because she's always been a smarty-pants.

"No, I mean the back of the boat!" Goliath says.

Susy thinks for a moment. It's a short name, she's certain. It's right at the tip of her tongue.

"St…" Goliath says, trying to help.

It's enough of a clue. Susy blurts it out "Stern!"

One, two, three, four…breathe.

Kurt points to the middle of the boat. "What about this part?"

"The middle…?" Goliath guesses.

"Pretty close. It's amidships," Kurt says.

One, two, three, four…breathe.

"I like this game," Susy says.

"What about the front of the boat?"

Goliath knows this one but waits to see if Susy does too. She just shakes her head.

"Bow, right?"

"That's right!" Kurt says. He points to where he steers Bertha. "What about that?"

Goliath and Susy work together to solve this one. "It sounds like some sort of game…" Susy says.

"Poker?" Goliath suggests, and tries to think of different games. "Monopoly? Trivial Pursuit? Risk?"

One, two, three, four…breathe.

"Oh wait! Bridge!" Susy shouts, jumping up and down with excitement.

Kurt points to the left side of the boat but neither Goliath nor Susy can figure it out. "Port," he says, then points to the right side. Still he gets only wrinkled foreheads and chewed lips as a reply. "Starboard," Kurt tells them.

"I know who else is bored," Susy mumbles.

One, two, three, four…breathe.

Kurt points at the small lifeboat suspended behind them. "And that is…" but he's interrupted by Harry, who comes running out of the door and races over to the railing, where he is sick again. Seagulls swarm down to start picking at the puke.

"… Disgusting," Kurt finishes.

They all feel a little sick suddenly, and turn to face Tiny.

One, two, three, four…breathe.

Anyone that's ever watched someone else swim knows it's worse than watching paint dry. Or grass grow. Nothing changes.

One, two, three, four…breathe.

One minute passes. Ten minutes. After twenty minutes the three of them are bored out of their minds.

"I don't think I can watch Tiny swim all the way to Boston," Susy declares.

"I have to get back up to the bridge," Kurt says before wandering off, relieved that at least he has a good excuse.

Goliath looks relieved as well. He thought he was the only one that was bored. He resorted to counting his heartbeats just to keep his mind occupied. He got all the way up to 387.

"I should really go look at how the…things are coming along…" Susy says before sneaking off as well.

Goliath feels OK leaving Tiny to do the swimming by himself for a while. He probably doesn't even know they were watching him anyway.

He rolls up to Harry, leaning over the edge, watching the seagulls feasting on the contents of his stomach.

"Mr. Belafonte? What is the world record for the biggest bird in the world?"

Despite feeling sick he answers without hesitation. "The largest known bird to ever live was an elephant bird from Madagascar. It grew to eleven feet tall and weighed over one thousand pounds."

Goliath looks at him with renewed interest. "What about the fastest mammal?"

After another cascade of vomit hits the water below, Harry says, "Cheetah. Sixty-four miles per hour."

It's like Harry is a computer with every record stored in his head. "The smallest insect?"

"The feather winged beetle of the family Ptiliidae."

"The longest animal?"

"The bootlace worm. One hundred eighty feet."

Goliath wants to find an animal record that stumps Harry's seemingly inexhaustible data, so he tries to think of a really hard record.

"Hmm...how about the longest dog tongue?"

Harry hesitates. Finally, Goliath's question has trumped his knowledge. Eventually Harry opens his mouth as if to speak but vomits again. Then he says, "Mochi the Saint Bernard had a tongue measuring seven point three inches."

Goliath is officially impressed. Maybe Harry isn't a dodo after all, he thinks.

"Captain?" Harry calls to Kurt through the open bridge window. Kurt pops his head out.

"How much further do you think we are going?"

Kurt looks confused. "What do you mean?"

"I mean, how far will the boy swim before we turn around?"

Kurt scratches his head as if he still doesn't understand the question. "Why, all the way."

"All the way?" Harry asks.

"Yeah, all the way," Kurt answers.

"I think we both know that there's no way this boy can swim across the Atlantic. I say we give him another day, two days max, and he'll be done. Good attempt and all."

Kurt pulls his head in without a reply. Goliath changes his mind. Harry's a dodo.

Harry calls to Susy. "Miss? Miss?"

Susy pops her head out from the door. "Yes?"

"Ah, there you are. I'll have my lunch out here, if you don't mind. Three eggs, toast and some bacon wouldn't hurt. And coffee." Harry rubs his belly and says to himself, "For some reason I feel empty inside."

Goliath looks down at the water, where the sea gulls are still picking up bits of Harry's dinner.

Susy isn't here to be anybody's waitress. She had quite enough of that on land and could tell Harry to get his own lunch. But she doesn't. If it helps make the trip easier for everyone she doesn't mind having to put up with some annoying things.

As far as Goliath is concerned, there's no changing his mind. Harry's definitely a dodo. Which is a shame since he was having such fun with the records and all. But the way he speaks about Tiny and the way he speaks to Goliath's mom unfortunately leaves no doubt. Harry is a dodo.

A couple of minutes later Susy comes out carrying a tray and puts it on the table in front of Harry. He takes one look at the three bouncy egg yolks staring up at him like yellow eyeballs, and vomits again, over the edge.

"Sorry," he says when he's done. "I can't eat anything." Susy takes the tray inside again.

It's confirmed. A definite dodo.

Tiny swims all day while Goliath reads a book called *Animals of the Atlantic*. Harry keeps feeding the seagulls and Goliath can't help but wonder where all that food is coming from. Eventually Kurt takes pity on him and brings Harry a box of saltines and a lime.

"I can't have you making the seagulls fat," he says, handing him the items, which are an old seaman's cure for seasickness.

At five o'clock Kurt honks the horn once. It's a deep, dark hoot that makes the air vibrate. For the first time since that morning Tiny stops swimming. One, two, three and...stop. Tiny looks up. There's a moment when his eyes are blank and his mind confused, like he doesn't know which world he is in. Then he sees the boat and he remembers. He reaches it in a couple of strokes, climbs up the hull and onto the deck, where Goliath is waiting for him.

Kurt parks Bertha for the night, making sure to mark the map at their exact location in case they drift during the night. That's how they'll have to do it to set the record, Harry has explained to them. Wherever they stop for the night has to be the exact same spot Tiny begins swimming from in the morning. So Kurt makes sure to mark the map.

He looks out the window and sees the Aran Islands. Once they pass the islands tomorrow there is nothing but ocean until they reach Boston. Not a beach, a mound, or a single rock big enough even for a seagull. Just water. If there was ever a last time and a place to turn around, this would be it. *And do what?* Kurt thinks. *Go back to the pool?* Once you make up your mind about something you follow through. They'll be fine. Just in case, though, he takes the pipe with him when he goes down to the galley.

At the dinner table everyone gathers around a big pot of stew Susy has made. Tiny's hair is still glistening wet but otherwise there is no sign he's been swimming all day. He doesn't look tired, and isn't even breathing hard.

Goliath is folding his napkin in the shape of something, and Harry seems to have finally overcome his seasickness.

"I'm hungry like a wolf," he declares, and Goliath shows Tiny his napkin. It looks like a seagull. They both giggle, because from the time Tiny came on board and quickly dried off and then lifted Goliath down the stairs in his wheelchair like he was no more than a jar of mayo, Goliath has been telling Tiny about his day. *The briefing*, as Goliath calls it.

"What's so funny, boys?" Susy says as she sees their sly smiles.

"Oh nothing..." Goliath answers, innocently, and Tiny hides the seagull in his big hand.

Harry seems to have forgotten all about his recent ills and loads a big bowl with stew. He also seems to have forgotten that the reason he is feeling better is Kurt's old sailor's trick.

"A little bit of sea never bothered anyone, eh, boys?" he says, slurping a big spoonful. "Us men of Abbeyknockmoy are known for our wills of steel. God nor man-made thing, weather nor nature, can stop us."

"What village is that?" Susy asks, mostly to be polite, but also because it's nice to have some conversation going during dinner.

"Seagullville," Goliath mumbles to Tiny, and they can't help but laugh some more.

"What's that?" Harry asks. "No, not whatever-you-said ville. Abbeyknockmoy. For generations the land there has raised a hardy crop, seemingly indestructible, and unaffected by trivial things such as weather, nature or...." Harry pauses. His face is frozen in a ridiculous grimace.

Goliath and Tiny pull back, fearing another bout of sea-sickness. Instead, Harry lets out a sneeze that nearly lifts the tablecloth.

"Achoo!"

"Cold?" Susy asks.

"No, I actually feel rather warm," Harry says.

"I mean, are you coming down with a cold?"

"Impossible. Us men from Abbeyknockmoy are not susceptible to..." His face freezes again. Then he sneezes. "Achoo!"

Susy smiles, her face comforting. "I think the Man of Steel from Abbeyknockmoy needs some more warm stew," and she pours another scoop into his bowl.

Everyone laughs. Everyone but Harry.

After dinner both Tiny and Goliath yawn. It's been a long day. They share a small room in the front of Bertha, where Goliath has the lowest berth, which is what a bed in a boat is called, and Tiny the top one. He looks much too big for it but seem comfortable nonetheless. He lies on his back, listening to Goliath.

Goliath uses a flashlight to illuminate the pages of his book *Animals of the Atlantic*.

"The Atlantic Wolffish. Did you see any of those down there?"

"Hmm, I don't know," Tiny says. "What do they look like?"

"They're purplish brown, five feet long and have a mouth like, well, a wolf."

"I don't think so," Tiny says.

Goliath turns the page. "What about the Spotted Eagle Ray?"

"What does it look like?"

"It's an eagle ray covered in white spots," Goliath reads from the book.

"I don't think so."

Goliath directs the flash light up into the ceiling, where it sits peacefully like a man made moon. "How can you not remember?"

"I don't know...I just...".

Goliath holds the book up. "Let's try this. *You* tell *me* what you saw, and I'll try to match it with something in the book, ok?"

"Well..." Tiny says and closes his eyes, because that's what you do when you want to see another world. And the ocean is a whole other world.

"I see...black."

"Black?" Goliath asks. He hopes there's more, because 'black' isn't really something he can look up in the book, nor is it very exciting.

There is more, so much more. A wonderful world, much more wonderful than what's above the surface. Magical, even, and Tiny wishes he was better with words so that he could explain to Goliath what it's like when the sun hits the water and breaks into a thousand little pieces, shimmering and twinkling like sinking diamonds. Or when a school of fish don't dart away out of fear because they believe Tiny is one of them, and they pack around him, allowing him to be part of the moving mass, staying close and mimicking his every move so they become like a body that constantly changes and evolves only to return to its original shape. If the fish are bigger they just cruise far below him, gently gliding through the water like slow moving torpedoes.

And there's the sound. The sound of the ocean beneath its surface is the most beautiful music nobody ever hears. There are pings and echoes, and weird burps and bubbles. They come from ocean creatures, or the bottom of the ocean itself, which is alive, and of course the water, always moving, slurping, swirling, packing up against itself, and pulling apart. It's a world of sound, and when all those sounds come together, it creates a beautiful symphony.

And then there are the plants, with their wonderful, extra-terrestrial designs. Each part has an exaggerated function and a purpose. The kelp forests, for example, that reach all the way from the bottom, with tiny buoys filled with air that allows the leaves to sit neatly under the surface, getting the sunlight they need to grow.

If Tiny could only be good with words he would talk about how seaweed makes sounds too, when a tube rubs up against another and causes water around it to vibrate.

How could Tiny describe all this without using words he doesn't know, and descriptions he doesn't understand? It would be like trying to describe a dream. And that's exactly what happens when Tiny jumps into the water. The moment his face sinks below the surface he starts dreaming. But they are impossible to remember because dreams are there one second, and gone the next.

"Well...black, green..." Tiny says, and then, for good measure, he adds "...and blue."

Goliath sighs before he puts the book down. He won't get better answers out of Tiny. There's a part of him that wishes he could see and feel what Tiny does when he's down there, part of him that feels a little bit left out. But he's learned a long time ago to not wish for things he can't have. This leads Goliath into a new set of questions.

"OK, what do you want most of all in the world?"

"You mean like a secret wish?" Tiny asks.

"Sure..., like a secret wish."

"Well...," Tiny closes his eyes again, and sinks back into his mind, when Goliath interrupts.

"Wait, let's guess each other's."

"Alright...."

"I can go first," Goliath says. "I'm guessing that you most of all in the whole world would not have your superpower webbed hands and feet, even though I think they're really cool. Your turn."

"Ahm, I guess the wheelchair," Tiny says.

They lie in silence for a while, listening to the ocean lapping at the side of Old Bertha, feeling her rock in the current. They stare at the full moon in the ceiling. They think about the cards life has dealt them. How, fair or unfair, they have become who they are.

It's Tiny who first breaks the silence. "I want to be smart."

Goliath doesn't have to think. He feels that with Tiny he can share anything. "I wish I had a dad."

They're quiet for another few moments before Goliath continues. "But I guess most of all I wish I was..."

Just like two parts connected as one, they say it at exactly the same time. "...normal."

They just want to be normal. Goliath turns the flashlight off and the room goes completely dark. They lie awake for a bit, quiet. What could they say that was as important and big as what they just did?

It's not long before they fall asleep. Two boys from Ireland that the world has never heard of about to enter into an adventure so great few dare even think it, fall asleep on an old fishing boat just outside the Aran Islands. And all they wish for is to be normal.

------

The next morning, the sun rises over the Arans and slings its sharp morning light across the ocean. The sea is completely flat and still, as if God himself had turned everything in the world off before going to bed.

Usually chatter boxes, especially Goliath, neither of them say a word as they stare at the giant mirror before them. They feel anything they would say would be trivial and cheap compared to this magnificent beauty. It's a sacred moment, like witnessing a dinosaurbaby hatch. It not only takes their breath away, it also takes away their words.

"It's called 'widow of the night' because it's the moment when all that is left of night meets all that has begun of day, and it's a moment of absolute stillness." Kurt has come up behind them, coffee cup in hand, his eyes taking in the serenity.

"It's beautiful," Susy whispers, as if she's afraid her voice might crack the surface.

They stand in silence, until a sound comes from deep within Bertha...

"Achoo! Oh my poor throat. I could use some tea..." It's Harry, sounding as if he's got a terrible cold. "Excuse me, a cup of tea please?"

Just like that, the moment has passed. Small waves have already begun breaking the surface apart. Little by little, the world starts turning.

"I suppose I'll bring the man of steel some tea," Susy says.

"Achoo!"

As Susy leaves, Kurt pats Tiny on the shoulder. "You ready for this, lad?" He nods towards the Aran Islands, then past them, towards the unknown.

"This is the last land we'll see for a very long time. Behind these piles of rock the real ocean begins."

"It's ok," is all Tiny says. Even if he was going to the moon, or the center of the earth on a moped, he'd probably say the same thing. 'It's ok.' Then, because he realizes that he should at least pretend to be a bit worried, he adds, "I'll be careful."

"That's a good lad," Kurt says as he starts towards the bridge.

---

Perhaps it's because of the moment that Goliath realizes the greatness of what Tiny is doing for him. It's Tiny that will jump into the cold water and won't come up until eight hours later, Tiny that will swim all day without food while they snack on whatever they can find in the pantry, and it's Tiny that will risk his life. So when Tiny pulls his t-shirt off and gets ready to climb over the railing, Goliath stops him.

"Wait."

Tiny waits.

"Raise your right hand."

Tiny raises his left hand. It doesn't really matter so Goliath doesn't correct him. He continues, and speaks with a clear, strong voice, just like he's seen and heard people speak in movies about knights.

"I hereby declare that you, Tiny, are my best friend for as long as I live."

Tiny can't believe his ears. Although he can definitely feel them, because they go bright red from all the blood rushing to them. He's never had a best friend before, and now it's official.

Tiny and Goliath are best friends! And he said for as long as they live!

"Ok, you can take your hand down now," Goliath says.

Tiny does and that's that. He climbs over the railing and as he jumps into the water it's like he can hear the steam rise from his glowing, hot ears. A best friend.

Tiny starts swimming next to Old Bertha, but it's not long before he forgets that she's even there. He forgets everything above the surface. Except one thing, which he repeats over and over again in his head just so he won't forget it: remember all the animals. Now that he is paying attention, oh boy, does he see things. Like a photographer looking through his lens for the first time there are suddenly thousands of things to notice, and not like before when Tiny was just one of those thousands of things.

It's not fair, Tiny thinks, that I get to see all this when Goliath is stuck in his wheelchair. He doesn't think it's unfair that he has to swim in the cold water for hours every day, while Goliath and the others are dry and warm, because that's not how Tiny's mind works. On the surface it appears he doesn't understand. But in the depths of it, just like in the depths of the sea, there are thousands of things going on. This time Tiny tries to notice them all. For example, the air bubbles.

Every time he moves his arms, a cascade of air bubbles forms in the water in front of him, encapsulating his whole body. He feels them tickle him, and it is as if they are alive. He even thinks he can hear them giggle, and can't help but giggle himself.

Outside the islands kelp grows from the bottom and rises all the way up to the surface, a distance of over a hundred feet. Its long, waxy leaves brush up against his legs as he zig zags through this aquatic forest. Every now and then groups of krill that hide behind the leaves look surprised when Tiny swims through, his air bubbles in tow.    If someone came swimming through your kitchen when you were having breakfast, Tiny thinks, you'd be surprised too. He giggles at the thought of it. And then at the air bubbles again.

Then there are the stretches of nothing, where there are no plants and no fish and hardly any bubbles, just a swirling, black-grey mass around him. Still, even the nothing is still something, because he can still hear the water rushing around him, and from the depths his ears and body pick up the occasional bleeps and beeps that are signals sent from creatures far away. They act like radio signals, and even though he doesn't understand what they mean he likes how they make him feel. As if he is part of a magic conversation.

Meanwhile, Goliath sits on deck and enjoys the day. The sun is out and the wind is but a gentle breeze. A family of Northern gannets are following the boat, having learned from other fishing boats that there's food to be found, if they are just patient enough. Goliath couldn't be happier. As they sail right behind Bertha he watches their every move through his binoculars. They glide and play so effortlessly on invisible bubbles of air, and Goliath comments his observations just like a documentarian.

"And now the gannet undulates its exterior wings, folks, ready to dive into the sea for scraps." He even has time to sketch them in his notebook.

"Good morning. Achoo!"

Goliath puts his binoculars down. Harry is wearing a big scarf wrapped around his neck. He speaks with a coarse voice.

"The Gannets can dive from a height of ninety-eight feet, achieving speeds of sixty-two miles per hour as they strike the water, enabling them to catch fish much deeper than most airborne birds."

Goliath nearly forgives Harry for being a dodo, but then he says something that forever condemns him to dodo land, with no possibility of pardon.

Harry looks over the railing, sees Tiny swimming, and immediately gets his rulebook out. He consults it for a moment.

"No, I can't allow it."

He turns and waves to Kurt up on the bridge, and motions to cut the engine. Bertha quickly comes to a standstill. Tiny, in tune with the old boat, pops his head out of the water. Susy comes out on deck and Kurt leans out through the window. Everybody wonders what is going on.

"We have to start over," Harry says.

"What?!" Goliath can't believe his ears.

"Is something wrong?" Susy asks.

"Yes," Harry says and waves his rulebook. "According

to rule seventeen, paragraph three, a controller—me in this case—has to be present at each commencement of a record attempt. And since the record attempter—Tiny in this case—started without my inspection, the attempt is not valid."

"But I've been out here all day! I've seen him swim," Goliath says.

"I'm afraid I can't verify that. Besides..." Harry waves the rule book, "...rules are rules and we have to follow them."

"Rules..." Kurt mumbles from the window.

"Yes, rules. Without them we might as well be monkeys, still living in trees."

"At least monkeys are fun...," Goliath whispers, and if Harry hears that, too, he pretends not to.

"We have to go back and start from where we stopped last night," Harry says.

"But..." Goliath says, because he's *seen* Tiny swim all day. If only Harry would listen to him.

"Or I will have no choice but declare this record attempt invalid."

They stand silent for a moment. It's Susy that finally breaks it.

"Tiny, come up and have some breakfast."

Tiny, who is the one who will have to swim the same distance all over again, seems to be the one who cares the least about starting over again. Either way he will be swimming, and that's all that matters to him.

Kurt mutters some curse under his beard, but he starts the engine and turns Bertha around. He leans on the throttle and steams forward, double speed now that he doesn't have Tiny in the water next to him, back towards the Aran Islands. Goliath vows to never speak to Harry, ever again.

Kurt makes it back in half the time, but by the time Tiny is in the water again, and Harry has waived his arm in a silly gesture as if starting a racecar, they have lost half a day. Again they pass the Aran Islands, and once again they face the open ocean. Again. Kurt feels how the more powerful sea tugs at Bertha, as they steam into the unknown, and leave the Aran Islands behind. Again.

The rest of the day is uneventful. It's just a repetition of the first half, after all. Tiny swims, now with Harry casting a glance at him every now and then, and Goliath is back looking at the gannets who also seem fine with repeating the first half of the day.

When the sun sets and the sky goes from pastel yellow to pink, then to red, Susy has to come out on deck to get them.

"Dinner is ready," she says and waves to Kurt, who gently eases the throttle until Bertha comes to a stand still. Just like before, Tiny somehow knows it's time, and climbs back on board. He wants to tell Goliath about all the things he's seen but dinner is waiting, and while they eat Goliath is in a bad mood because Harry made them go back and start over. He mutters something about "walking the plank." Susy is again the glue that keeps everyone together, though, and makes everyone focus on her lasagna and a story about her Uncle Steven who built an airplane in his living room. When her Uncle Steven was done he realized that it was too big to get out of the house. It's a good story and everyone laughs, even Goliath, but it makes Tiny forget all about what he was trying to remember for Goliath. When they finally go to bed, they both fall asleep as soon as their heads hit their pillows. It's not every day you have to live the same day twice.

---

Harry is sound asleep, his snoring like a misfiring engine, popping and gasping, dreaming about one of his absolute favorite memories: when he walked from France to Santiago de Compostela, in Spain, on a pilgrimage. In his mind he is on a beach after weeks of walking, soaking his aching feet in the cool water of the Atlantic Ocean. Everything is quiet and serene, with the calming sound of the water lapping the shore around him. He is at perfect peace with the world.

Suddenly there's an intrusion. A terrible sound is coming from right behind his head. "Pah-pa-rah!"

Goliath directs the trumpet towards Harry's face, and blows it as hard as he can. A loud, hacking hoot fills the small room, "Pah-pa-rah!". Harry wakes up with a jerk.

He jumps out of bed, and onto the floor, where he knocks over empty glass bottles that have been positioned to cover every square inch of the small bedroom. They fall against each other like bricks, clink clanking, and Harry's reflex is to waive his arms above his head. That only makes things worse as he hits the pans and pots strung to the ceiling, and one pan swings into the next, and it into the next, and together with the falling bottles it makes for an awful sound, and a rude awakening.

Tiny and Goliath laugh wildly outside the door. Mission accomplished. There's no chance Harry will miss Tiny's swim this morning.

However, there is another problem. When they get out on deck Kurt is there, toolbox in hand.

"Morning, lads," he says. "Just have to give Bertha some breakfast before we can go." He wiggles a jug of grease.

While Kurt disappears into the engine room Harry arrives on deck.

"I suppose you think that was funny? I'll remind you boys that I am an official controller of the very esteemed publication of..."

"Here you go," Susy says, handing him a cup of coffee, still making sure everyone gets along, and because you can't drink coffee and talk at the same time. Harry takes a sip, and the boys are off the hook.

"Where is Kurt?' Susy asks.

*Fixing something with the engine,* Goliath is about to say, but then Kurt returns from the engine room through the hatch, his face already covered in oil. "She needs a little more work."

"What's wrong?" Susy asks.

"Nothing major, I just have to change the gasket on one of the heads. You know, so the cooling fluid departs from the combustion fumes and..."

That's more information than Susy cares to know, so she turns to the boys. "OK, who wants eggs for breakfast?"

Kurt smiles and shakes his head. Sometimes he forgets that not everyone is as knowledgeable about engines as he is. Or, in this case, as knowledgeable about Bertha as he is. After fifty years he knows her inside and out. Not to say that she doesn't surprise him and break down every now and again. But Kurt can tell her mood just by putting his hand on the railing and feeling the way she hums. When he sleeps at night he hears the same sounds he's heard every night the last fifty years, give or take a few. The creaking, the bubbling....the two of them speak to each other without words. Just like an old married couple.

Susy leads the way into the galley. "Come on boys. I'll make pancakes too. Francois's secret recipe from France."

Unfortunately, Harry, who's been flipping through his rulebook, has some questions. "Wait a second," he says, and turns to Kurt. "How long do you think it will take?"

Kurt scratches his head, getting oil in his hair and on his left ear. "I'd say no more than a couple of hours. Four. Five, tops."

Harry checks his rulebook. "According to rule twenty-one, paragraph four, any long distance record attempt can't include a rest longer than twelve hours between stages. And..." Harry consults his watch. "...we're coming up on the twelve hour mark."

Kurt looks at the rulebook, then at Harry, and scratches the other side of his head, getting oil on that ear too. "I mean, does an hour or two really matter? We can make it up by starting early tomorrow," he says.

"It's a matter of up to five hours. You said so yourself. Yes, it does matter, or else we might as well..."

Goliath interrupts him. "...be monkeys living in trees, flinging our poop on each other."

"Goliath Pedigree O'Callaghan!!!" Susy looks at him like she can't believe her ears.

Goliath looks embarrassed, as if *he* can't believe what just came out of his mouth. "Did I say that out loud?"

They stand in awkward silence for a while. Finally Kurt can't take it, and says, "well, she's not going to fix herself so..."

"So what do we do?" Goliath asks, worried that their entire record is in danger.

"Let's just go have breakfast and let them figure it out," Susy says, putting her arm around his shoulders.

Tiny clears his throat. Everyone else thinks he's just clearing his throat, so they don't pay it much attention. So he does it again, only this time it comes out far too loud. "OOAH-HGHMPH!!!" It sounds more like an angry dinosaur than a throat clearing, but it works. Everyone turns his way. At least he got their attention.

"Sorry..." he mumbles and directs his eyes down at deck, his cheeks warm. "Maybe...I mean, what if I go...and then you catch up?"

Susy puts her hand on his arm, like she always does when she's speaking to Tiny. So he knows that she's speaking to *him*, and nobody else. "You mean with us here, and you..." She looks out over the ocean, "...out there? alone?"

"No, no, that's out of the question," Kurt says.

Susy, with her arm still on Tiny's, says, "Honey, that sounds very dangerous. Why don't you stay here until the engine is fixed, all right?"

It's Harry's turn to clear his throat. "Hrrmmmph," he says and pats his rulebook.

Everyone seems to be at loss of what to do, and they all just stand there. Goliath looks very disappointed. He reminds Kurt of a balloon left over from the fairground - deflated and sad looking.

He turns around and disappears below deck. They hear him rummage through his things and when he returns he has a coiled rope, and attached to the end of it, a red buoy.

"If you tie this to your waist we'll find you, or if you get tired, I know you won't, but just in case you do, you can hang onto this and rest until we come find you."

Kurt hands the buoy to Tiny and gives Harry a hard look. "Good enough for your rules?"

Harry, who isn't a very personable fellow to begin with, but is at least professional and true to the rules, because without rules, well....goes through his rulebook without letting any emotions shine through. "It says no flotation devices, but since he's not exactly floating on it I will allow it."

Tiny doesn't waste another second. He immediately takes his shirt off and begins tying the rope around his waist. When he's done Susy takes his hand in his and looks him in the eyes (though it's hard to look someone who is staring at his feet in the eyes).

"Now be careful out there, you hear me?"

"Yes ma'am," Tiny says, nodding his big head.

"Keep in mind everything I've taught you about the ocean, lad," Kurt chimes in, before adding, "I'll fix old Bertha as quickly as I can. Then I'll come get you." He disappears down into to the machine room.

Goliath follows Tiny to the railing. Goliath has gone from looking like a disappointed balloon, to a worried balloon. Tiny sees it, and does his best to calm his friend.

"It's OK," Tiny says.

"Don't do it if it's dangerous," Goliath says.

"What's 'dangerous'?" Tiny asks, as if Goliath was speaking about something completely different than swimming through the ocean all by himself.

"The ocean, out there, all alone," Goliath says.

Tiny turns and looks over the vast, flat landscape.

"It's not dangerous," he says, and Goliath sees that he really believes it.

Goliath looks out at the same view, at the same horizon, and although he doesn't see what Tiny sees he's starting to understand his big friend.

"Well, just be careful. I never had a best friend before and I don't want to lose this one already."

Goliath gives Tiny a friendly punch on the shoulder, just like guys do when they really want to hug but they don't know how to. Tiny is so excited about the fact that he has a best friend that when he punches Goliath he forgets all about how big he is, and that Goliath is in a wheelchair, and his giant fist sends Goliath rolling across the deck. If it isn't for Tiny's quick reflexes - he lunges forward and grabs hold of the wheelchair just before it's about to crash into the wall - Goliath might have flown right over the edge, and into the water.

"Sorry," Tiny says, and looks ashamed.

Goliath rubs his shoulder. It's probably going to be black tomorrow. "It's alright," he says, and they burst out laughing.

---

With Tiny swimming ahead of them, Goliath joins Kurt in the machine room. After he's had pancakes, of course.

Kurt is deep into the machine, one arm holding a wrench, the other trying to reach a bolt. "Now, you let go of that, you hear?" Kurt mutters to nobody else but the engine.

"What?" Goliath asks, because he's not touching anything.

"What?" Kurt says, wondering what Goliath is saying.

They realize what happened at the same time.

"Oh, OK."

"Oh, OK."

Kurt gets back to what he's doing, and Goliath watches him work. "Do you always talk to her?"

"Always," Kurt says, "and she talks to me," he adds.

"She does? But..." Goliath looks around, "...she's a boat."

Kurt pulls his arm out from the jungle of steel rods and oily valves, and leans against the wall, preparing for a story.

"I remember when we first met," Kurt says. "I had just come back from South America."

"South America?" Goliath interrupts. "What were you doing there?"

"I was on a banana boat," Kurt says.

"Wow," is all Goliath says, because what else is there to say when someone tells you they've been on a banana boat?

"Yes, wow," Kurt says, eager to continue his story. "So I come back and walk the docks in the port of Cork trying to find a new job. You may not believe it, but I was young and strong and there wasn't a job on any boat I couldn't do. The dock was lined with tankers and container ships, colossal vessels that were more like floating cities than ships. I walked among them trying to decide what my next adventure should be. Eventually I neared the end of the dock. The boats there were smaller, crabbier, and the further I walked, the more run down they looked.

At the very end of the dock a man was standing on a chipped and weathered old boat, chopping at her deck with an axe. Sure, it was old and had seen better days, but there was something about it, a sort of inner beauty underneath all that old paint and chipped planks. Seeing him taking an axe to her like that just made my gut wrench. So I called out to him. 'Ahoy, what are you doing?'. But the man continued sinking his axe into the deck. 'Firewood,' is all he said.

I watched for a few more moments until I couldn't stand it any longer. I called out to him again. 'Stop!' I said. The man stopped, axe lifted. He looked at me, about to swing again, when my mouth spoke words I didn't recognize as my own. 'I'll buy her from ya. Name your price and I'll buy her from ya.' The price he named all but cleared my bank account and before I knew how it happened I was without a job, and I had just bought an old fishing boat.

I didn't have an apartment at the time so I moved my few belongings to the boat and started living on it. There was so much to do – oh, boy was she run down - but I was determined to get her back to her original glory, whatever it took. And what it took was me working the night shift at a hospice, and then working on the boat during the day. I slaved away like this for six long months, working every hour of every day. I scoured the containers and empty warehouse lots for things I might be able to salvage and use on my boat, and then, one day, she was ready. I climbed down and took a few steps back to get a better view. You couldn't recognize her. The transformation was total. There was only one last thing to do. Give her a name.

At the hospice I had befriended an old lady that didn't have any family. She was a beautiful old lady, with snow-white hair and delicate features. We became fast friends because we were both alone in this world. We used to play cards on this thin metal tray that was about the only thing she owned. We talked about everything as we played. One day, I asked her if she had any regrets. 'Regrets about what?' she said. 'Well. About life'. She was quiet for a while and I thought I'd asked her the wrong question. I was about to apologize when she said something I'll always remember. 'Not having another life.' I asked her what she meant by that, even though I think knew the answer. She hadn't lived a life according to her dreams, she said. She had lived a life doing what other people expected of her. And now that she was old it was too late. I sat for a while and thought about that. 'What did you dream of?' She answered with no hesitation. 'To go on the Trans-Siberian railway, to dance the hula in Hawaii, to smell the hot lava in a volcano, to dive and see a coral reef, to.....'. It came out of her like a waterfall. Eventually I had to leave to do my rounds and I remembered that there was a video recording of a tango dancer in the library. So after my rounds I picked it up to bring it to her room. 'She will love it!' I said to myself.

But when I got there they were just lifting her body onto a stretcher. She had passed away during my rounds, and now two men were covering her with a sheet, rolling her out of the room, never to return. It was a hospice. People came there to die. But I was still so sad to see my friend leave me. I thought about her as I watched my boat that day. There was really only one name that I could choose. Bertha. Finally she could go places, see things and experience great adventures."

Goliath looks around the engine room. The engine is in the middle, like a heart of steel, the tubes and pipes like arteries, and the walls like bones. Suddenly he sees old Bertha differently.

Kurt continues. "Ever since, me and Bertha have been inseparable. We've weathered storms, healed broken bones, fixed leaks, endured heat and ice. We've had each other's backs and have taken care of each other the best we could." He pats the engine tenderly.

Suddenly Kurt seems to wake up from a daydream. "Right, we don't have time for this. Hand me that wrench, lad," he says, pointing to the toolbox.

---

Kurt and Goliath emerge from the hatch, unrecognizable. They are covered in black engine grease, and even though they've only been gone for three hours it looks as if they've been on an expedition to the center of earth.

"Let's see if that did the trick," Kurt says, and heads to the bridge.

The day looks different too, though it's only been three hours. The sun is gone and everything looks grey. The wind is picking up, and some clouds loom in the distance.

Back at the controls Kurt flips a switch that lights up a yellow button. When he presses it there's a distinct rumble. "That's my girl," Kurt says, and checks all the gauges.

"How does it look?" Susy says, coming behind him.

"*This* looks good," Kurt says and pats the instrument panel. "*That* doesn't," he says, nodding towards the darkening sky. A massive bunch of dark clouds has formed on the horizon. It's the shape of a massive donut, and it seems to grow larger every minute, as if it's sucking in all the clouds in the area.

"Looks like we're getting some weather," Susy says as she

takes a sip from her coffee cup.

"Sure does," Kurt says. His face is troubled.

"What does that mean for..." but she stops before finishing.

Kurt understands. "We'd better get going," he says, his look darkening.

Neither of them wants to say it out loud. They're second-guessing their decision to let Tiny go out alone. He is headed straight for the storm.

---

The waves have increased in size and Bertha rocks up and down as they steer right towards the darkness.

"Do you see him?" Susy asks.

Goliath spies through his binoculars at the swelling black mass that is an ocean far different from the one that morning. There is no stillness here.

"No," he says without taking his eyes from the sea for a moment.

A red buoy is what Goliath is looking for. Between the increasing wave sizes and the murky light, that's like looking for a needle in a haystack. Except this haystack is moving, and is millions of square miles.

The sky rips apart in a flash. It's as if the world stops, and when the sulfur smell reaches their noses on the bridge, and the clap of thunder smacks down over them so hard that the windows rattle, it is set in motion again.

"That's some storm," Kurt mutters, not taking his eyes

from the windshield.

Just moments after, nature displays her power again. A wall of water has risen from the sea, and is speeding towards them. It whips a white froth where it passes, and for a few fateful seconds it feels to Goliath as if Bertha is flying forward at warp speed. Before his mind can adjust, the wall is over them, and it runs right through them.

The windows shatter into a million pieces and a giant hand picks up the entire boat and shakes it. It happens so fast that Goliath doesn't have time to get scared. But he must have been scared, because he clamps his eyes shut. When he opens them the window is whole, the wall is gone and in its place he sees what it's become: rain.

A wall of rain with no mountains, trees or cities to stop it, ran right into them like an attacking army. In its wake a surge gripped Bertha and shook her like a bully on the schoolyard.

Heavy rain is pouring down and even though Kurt sets the windshield wipers at the highest speed it is still hard to see out of the window, let alone spot a red buoy. Goliath puts the binoculars down and rolls over to the chest. He begins rummaging through it.

"Feeling cold?" Susy asks, assuming he is looking for a sweater.

When she sees him pull out a rain jacket she gets scared.

"I can't see anything in here. I'm going out on deck," he says.

"Not alone, you're not," Susy says, and her foot literally

stomps the floor.

"But..." Goliath tries, but there's the foot again.

"No buts."

"I'll keep an eye on him," Harry unexpectedly offers. "I could use some air." He looks pale.

"Well..." Susy says.

"Come on, Mom. I'm with an adult."

Susy wants to stomp on the floor again, but this trip is also about letting go, letting Goliath grow up, and how will he do that if she constantly tells him what to do?

"Ok," she says, "but be careful. And come directly inside the moment I tell you."

"Sure," Goliath says, already halfway out the door.

---

Outside, the rain falls hard, and it hammers Goliath's raincoat. The deck is a wet mess but the coarse surface gives his tires enough traction to roll to the very front, where the anchor chain loops through a hole in the hull. Goliath positions himself right in front of it, flips the wheel lock in place, and lifts his binoculars. "A red buoy," he tells himself quietly, reminding himself to focus.

Beside him there's a loud "blaarhghmpf" as Harry throws up again over the railing, the saltines and limes no match for the storm. Moments after, there's sneezing. Wild, uncontrollable sneezing that seems to rock the boat just as much as the waves. Goliath shuts it all out and focuses on the circular view in his binoculars. "A red buoy," he says to himself again and again. "A red buoy."

---

The storm is getting stronger and the waves bigger. Standing on the bridge, Susy feels like she's on a roller coaster. A slow moving roller coaster, but still. Bertha dives into deep canyons of emptiness only to meet a wall of water at the bottom, crash into it and ride up a steep hill, before repeating the entire process again. The weather, or the waves, don't seem to worry Kurt as far as the boat goes. Although Susy can see that he is getting increasingly more worried about finding Tiny in the way he clenches his jaws and tries to spy through the rain into the disturbed surroundings. That's why she lets Goliath stay on deck, safe, though she still glances at him through the window every twenty seconds. Kurt is in control, and they need all eyes available to find Tiny.

"How does he know where to go?" Susy asks, curious. There are no road signs on the ocean, nothing to tell you where to go. If Tiny doesn't know where to go, then how do they know they are looking in the right spot?

"I don't know," Kurt says, and Susy's heart sinks.

She checks on Goliath, then goes back to her post.

"I just know that he does," Kurt continues. "He's got some sort of inner navigation like a migrating bird, or a whale. His body just knows how to stay on route."

A little stone, but still a stone, drops from her heart. She imagines Tiny out there, his face in the water, waves tossing him around, and from somewhere within him a ping emits, dark and deep, and it travels through the water hundreds of miles in each direction, until it hits something and bounces back, now a slightly weaker signal. And that same strange place within Tiny accepts the ping, decodes it and leaves a little bit of information behind before sending out another. Ping. Ping. Ping. It makes Susy feel a little better, and she checks on Goliath again.

---

Tiny usually goes to that place in his mind where nothing exists. It's like a locked room, deep inside his head, where thoughts aren't allowed to enter. But since memories are thoughts and he's promised Goliath to remember what he sees, he leaves the door open. It's not easy.

As he swims through the waves, following the movement of the water, up and down, being part of it rather than floating on it like Bertha, his inner door swings on its hinges, opening and closing.

Every now and then Tiny wakes with a jerk when the door shuts, and he remembers again to look at the things he encounters. Then the rhythm returns, one arm forward, wave lifting up, other arm forward, riding down wave, and the door slams shut again. Though the wind may whip across his back, and howl as if trying to scream his skin off, Tiny isn't aware of the violence. He is just part of the ocean.

Susy has to put the binoculars down every now and then or she starts feeling queasy from all the motion. Suddenly, the door opens and a pale-green Harry stumbles in, dripping wet.

"Neeb to blow by dose," he says, and grabs a box of tissues.

Then everything happens at once. Or, at least, so it seems.

The very first thing that happens is that Harry blows his nose. It's loud and strong and Susy thinks it will never end.

The second thing that happens is that Susy asks, after the blow finally dies out and they can hear again, "Where's Goliath?".

The third thing that happens is that Harry points to the front of the boat and says "he's right there", and there is something about the situation, or the way his words come out, that raise the hairs on Susy's neck. Or, maybe it's her subconscious that picks up on the fourth thing before her eyes and brain can even register it.

The fourth thing that happens started in a far-away place, in a far-away time. There's actually no saying where and when it started, but it doesn't matter. What matters is the fact that a giant wave heads right for them.

Harry's mind registers it first. Still pointing at Goliath, all he says is, "Oh God."

The next moment the wave becomes visible. It's a wave three times as big as any other wave that came before, and it rises out of the water like a wall surfing on top of another wave.

The fifth thing that happens is that Susy sees the wave in the corner of her eye, and, without hesitating one millisecond, she reaches for the door.

The sixth thing that happens is that Kurt's mind quickly calculates the size of the big wave, decides that Bertha can handle it and reaches for the throttle and adjusts the speed accordingly, because there is no way around it: the wave is going to crash right over them.

And the seventh and last thing that happens, when everything seems to happen at once, is that Susy yells "watch out!", but by then the wave is already over them.

Goliath is like a pit bull where he sits, refusing to let go of the binoculars, even though his fingers are numb from the cold rain and his shoulders ache. "Red buoy, red buoy," he repeats to himself, scanning the rough sea through the narrow scope. "Red buoy, red...". Out of nowhere the view in his binoculars is blocked. He brings them down to clean the lenses, muttering, "stupid rain...", and the moment he does a wall of water falls right over him. It's instant chaos.

Everything goes black and there's a loud screaming right in his ear, as if a scared cat has been locked in a barrel of water and is fighting for its life, bubbling, scratching, and the barrel is *inside* his ear.

Goliath feels himself being lifted, spun around, shaken, turned upside down, tumbled, banged against something hard, crushed, smothered and twisted until all air is removed from his lungs. It happens in an instant. It's a whirlwind of motion, and when he feels that familiar burning sensation in his chest he draws a breath and realizes that the screaming is not from a cat trapped in a barrel, but from him.

The view has changed completely. The air is filled with smoke and it stings his eyes and chest. He bobs up and down, uncontrollably, and before him the view of the ocean is gone and instead a great big wall has descended right in front of him. This might be it, Goliath thinks, the end, *the real end*, as he tries to make out the letters that dance on the other side of a cloud of diabolical fumes. He tries to breathe but the air is sour, saturated with fire and brimstone, as if he's trapped in the center of an apocalypse. The letters dance in front of him and through his tears, choking on the smoke and feeling sick to his stomach, he finally makes out what they say. Hell.

Then, before the thought of spending eternity in a smoky hell has sunk in, everything flips around again and he is yanked out of the soot and smudge through an arch in the sky, and when he lands with a thud he is right back where he started. Almost. He's on the back part of the deck, with Susy and Kurt kneeling around him, peering at him with wild eyes. But what really convinces Goliath that he's no longer in hell is the sight of Harry being sick over the railing.

———————————

Later, on the bridge, wrapped in three blankets and cradling a big cup of hot chocolate that slowly warms up his icy fingers, Goliath hears what happened.

"It was a big wave," Kurt explains. "Not the biggest, as far as big waves go, but big enough to sweep anything on deck with it."

"Not a big one?" Susy asks.

"It's all relative. The really big ones can sink an entire container ship."

Goliath wishes he could have seen it from the bridge, rising out of the ocean and coming at them at a light speed, hitting the bow, then falling over him, picking him up and washing him across deck and over the back railing where he was caught on a rope and dragged behind Bertha, right in her exhaust fumes.

Goliath can almost see it in front of him, as he takes a sip of the hot liquid. Outside the storm is still howling, stronger than ever.

"Why didn't I sink?" Goliath asks, thinking about that morning at the pool.

Susy flashes Kurt a glance, and although Goliath notices, he doesn't think it means anything. "You were very lucky, honey."

Kurt looks away.

"What do you mean lucky?"

"Well...," Susy squirms. Goliath notices that too. "You were caught on a piece of rope with a buoy that kept you afloat. Thank God."

Susy's eyes are wet. She sees Goliath noticing her tears, and before he can ask anything else she says it.

"We don't know for sure it's Tiny's." Her voice comes out weak and frail.

Kurt wipes the corners of his eyes with the part of his arm

that has the tattoo of a hula dancer.

"Kurt says it's possible he has several red buoys. Right?"

Kurt nods, but doesn't say anything more, and he doesn't turn around.

Goliath feels his stomach tighten and he can't get another sip of hot chocolate down, no matter how cold he feels.

---

It's a rough night, so rough that Goliath straps his wheelchair to the wall to keep it from rolling and turning. Nobody gets any sleep, and hardly a word is spoken. All of them are on the bridge, with the green light from the instrument panel giving everyone a weird alien glow. The only sound is the occasional sneeze from Harry. At least he's stopped vomiting.

Every now and then Susy comes over to adjust the blanket around Goliath's shoulders, while Bertha takes them on a ride through the raging storm, made worse because it's completely dark. Imagine going down a road in a car at night and suddenly you drop down a steep hill you didn't see coming. Your stomach does back flips until you hit bottom, and there you get a glimpse of it: A solid wall right in front of the window, yet somehow you don't smash into it. You manage to climb back up and before your stomach has adjusted to the new direction, you drop again.

It's a jarring ride and Bertha creaks and groans, but keeps going. This is an adventure, for sure, Goliath thinks, and even though he's so worried about Tiny that his stomach hurts, part of him thinks of Bertha in heaven, happy to be living.

Nobody looks through the binoculars anymore. It's too dark to see, and even if you could, there's no red buoy to look for. It's lying on deck.

Goliath feels like he is caught in a bad dream. The stillness inside the green light, a pen rolling back and forth over the map counter as Bertha dives and climbs, back and forth, up and down…it's unreal how the pen can move about calmly when outside the howling wind and the creaking hull makes it sound like the storm is trying to break the boat apart. None of it seems real. He closes his eyes, and without deciding to, or knowing how it begins, he starts to pray.

It's not any prayer he's been taught, like in Sunday school where they memorize things from the Bible. He just starts talking to God.

"Hi, God. Is that really your name, by the way? Or just a title? I've always heard people call you that, but isn't that like your title at work? Because that would be like calling Ben, our postman, 'postman'. Anyway, there might be an explanation for it, like you have a name but nobody knows it. Like Madonna. Honestly, calling you God makes me a bit uncomfortable. Can I just call you Jerry?

Anyway, Jerry, I'm not sure if you've noticed but we're in a bit of trouble here. We're on a boat in what Kurt calls a dagnabbit storm. Sorry, but that's what he calls it when my mom isn't around. Honestly, I don't really know if that's even a swear word?

Anyway, Kurt is a really good sailor and Bertha a good boat

so I think we'll be fine (if you have other information, please let me know asap). The problem is Tiny. Tiny is my best friend in the whole world (and that's saying a lot, Jerry, considering we're eight billion people down here. But I guess you know that already.) Right now he is out there, in the ocean, in the storm, for *me*.

Now, I know what you're going to ask. He didn't fall off the boat or anything. He *jumped* in, and swam ahead of us when we had some engine problems on account of Bertha being so old.

I know what you are thinking now. *Why did he do that? Jump in the ocean?* Well, it's kind of a long story and I don't know how much information you need. A lot of things happened at home and, anyway, we decided to swim across the Atlantic. We'll set a new world record, if we can make it. Tiny is the best swimmer I've ever seen. In fact, I bet Tiny is the best swimmer you've ever seen, Jerry, and you've probably seen them all. But it's really hog-faced out there now with the storm and all, and I'm really worried about Tiny. So I wanted to ask if you could get him back on board, or at least make sure that he is O.K.?

I don't have much money because all my savings went into this trip. And now that I think of it I don't even know if you need money because you could just invent whatever you want on the spot. Like, when you're hungry, you can just think 'ham sandwich' and a ham sandwich will appear in front of you.

What I'm saying is that I really need your help. And I'm sure you get a lot of calls from people asking for things, but Tiny is really, *really*, really special and if you get a chance to meet him, you'll understand.

I don't know if you keep a scorecard, or anything like that up there, but I'm pretty good. I mean, I'm not perfect and sometimes I just forget things like putting my dishes away (O.K., sometimes I just don't do it because it's really boring.) But I try to be a good person and...."

Maybe it's the way Bertha rocks and rolls, half of it is probably just from being exhausted from nearly drowning again, but Goliath falls asleep in the middle of his prayer. In his dream, he continues talking to God, or Jerry, pleading for Tiny's safe return.

---

It feels like he is flying. So big, so heavy on dry land, but here he moves gracefully. No matter what the water does, where it pulls or currents drag, he is in control. Because he is part water.

Tiny keeps opening the door to the room, even though it slams shut again and again. He prefers it in the room, but for Goliath's sake he stays on the outside. That's the reason he feels the muscles in his shoulders ache, and his thighs from all the kicking, and his chest from the non-stop breathing. 'Is this what it's like outside the room?' he thinks. Everything noticeable, magnified?

The thought occurs to him, though his mind is usually empty and calm when he is submerged, that perhaps leaving the buoy behind wasn't such a good idea.

And then he feels something grab hold of his feet. It clumps them together, nearly immobilizing him. Trash. The ocean is filled with trash. Plastic tarps, rope, junk and garbage, even old refrigerators.

He stops swimming, bends forward in order to reach down and free his feet. Not moving means not floating, and he starts a slow decent towards the bottom, and around him the sea gets more dark and more compact for every foot he sinks. And now he's sure of it. He could have used that buoy.

---

The next morning, when Goliath wakes up, everything is different. The bridge is filled with soft honey-colored sunlight, and for a brief moment, as he opens his eyes and stretches his arms over his head, shedding the layers of blankets, Goliath has no memory of the storm. Everything is serene and quiet. The bridge is empty, and particles of dust slowly float through the air. Then he sees the rope that secures his wheelchair to the wall, and he remembers. Tiny.

Susy and Kurt are on deck, each with a pair of binoculars, scanning the water. It's a glorious day. The sea has died down, and now gently laps against Bertha, apologizing for last night's outburst.

"Find him?" Goliath asks, his breath in his throat.

"Not yet," Kurt replies, his jaws working overtime.

"You go get dressed, honey," Susy says.

Goliath realizes that he isn't wearing any clothes. Just a blanket. The clothes from last night are in a wet pile on the bridge, and so he hurries to his room, his mind racing with different what ifs. What if they don't find Tiny today either? What if they never find him? What if he's....? Goliath pushes that particular thought to the furthest corner of his mind. It's too big, too dark, too scary. It might help if he whistles, he thinks. It's impossible to be scared or worried if you whistle.

He uses the rope and pulley to get below deck, and rolls through Bertha's belly to get to their room, whistling all the way. The brightness of the morning sun has blinded him and the room seems darker than usual. He rolls to the closet, gets out a t-shirt and pants and rolls to his bunk.

It's always easier for Goliath to get dressed on his back so he eases himself out of his wheelchair like he's done thousands of times before and lies back into the pile of old blankets. Suddenly the pile heaves. In the moment it takes Goliath to fly out of bed, legs or no legs, his only thought is "Bear! How did a bear get onto the boat? And how did it get into my bed?" And then the giant bear turns around, his long hair parting over his nose, and...

"Hey," the bear says, yawning.

It's Tiny.

"Tiny!"

Tiny doesn't waste a second to start recounting the things he's seen. "I saw a clam the color of wood and a red fish that looks like a dragon and a couple of seals and..."

Goliath interrupts him with a big hug. With his eyes closed he mumbles a silent, "Thank you, Jerry."

"Ehm, ok...," Tiny says, surprised and a bit uncomfortable. "Who's Jerry?"

"Nevermind. I'm just happy that you are all right."

Tiny doesn't understand what's going on. "I'm all right."

"Everyone was worried about you in the storm."

"What storm?" Tiny asks.

Goliath looks at him like he's crazy. "What storm? I mean, the one…" but Goliath stops there. He reminds himself that he will never fully understand his big friend. Unless he can *be* him and *feel* and *experience* exactly what he does, part of him will always be a mystery.

"So, you want to hear?"

"What?" Goliath says, then remembers. "Oh…yes! Tell me."

"So there was this fish that looks like a shovel, the bottom part of a shovel, the shovel part, and it had spikes on its head."

"A tiny lumpsucker." Goliath will claim that one even though he didn't see it himself. Since he told Tiny to look on account of him, he's pretty sure he can count it.

"Really, it's called Tiny too?"

"Funny, right? What else?"

"Let's see…" and Tiny sorts through the images he stored for Goliath outside the room.

Later, because they get so wrapped up in talking about life below the surface, they go up on deck, like it was any other day, and they nearly give Susy and Kurt a heart attack. A good kind of heart attack, because they are so relieved to see Tiny that

Goliath feels just a little bit bad for not letting them know right away. Just a little bit. Because it's impossible to feel bad on a day like this.

Kurt is so relieved that his eyes won't stop tearing up. Crying makes him uncomfortable so he spends the morning checking up on Bertha, making sure she didn't sustain any damages in the storm.

Goliath, Tiny and Harry are all sitting around the breakfast table outside, as Susy comes out with a huge tray filled with food. It looks like it's enough to feed an entire diner, and she begins putting down plates of pancakes, fried eggs, sausages, roasted potatoes and oatmeal for Goliath and Tiny.

There's an almost inaudible grunt from Harry, who has stopped being sick and is back to being a man of steel, and a very hungry one at that. Susy keeps putting down bowls in front of Goliath and Tiny only, along with  glasses of orange juice and milk and a heaping basked of freshly baked muffins.

The two boys eat like hungry wolves, the energy spent by both of them during the storm having left deep holes in their bellies. Harry casts longing glances at them as they stuff their faces. He can hear his stomach grumble.

Finally, Susy returns with a tray. She looks at Harry and smiles. There are eggs, sausages, potatoes, orange juice and a fresh cup of coffee, still steaming hot.

Susy puts the coffee down in front of him. "Sugar?" she asks in her sweetest voice.

"Yes, please," he says, and Susy pours a big scoop into it.

She even stirs it for him. "There you go," she says.

Harry grabs the cup, puts it to his lips and takes a sip, but immediately spits it out. "Holy mother of Mary! It's not sugar! It's salt!"

Susy gives him a wicked smile. "Two eggs," and she holds out the plate of eggs and flips it. The eggs land right in Harry's lap.

"What are you...aaaaah!" He doesn't have time to finish because Susy continues with the sausages and potatoes. "This is not..." Harry sputters, and Susy lifts the glass of orange juice and pours it right over his head. He feels it trickle down his shirt. "Is this some kind of..."

Susy beats him to it. Her smile is gone and her eyes have turned black. Through gritting teeth, she spits her next words. "If you ever let your silly rules come between me and my boys again I will throw you in the ocean when you sleep and let the sharks eat you." She stares at him. "Do you understand?"

Harry doesn't say anything. His eyelids suddenly start blinking, up and down, up and down. Susy takes that as a yes.

But she's not done yet. She grabs the official rulebook from Harry's jacket pocket and throws it into the ocean, where it sinks.

Goliath and Tiny can't believe their eyes. With their mouths full of food they try to giggle, but only manage to cough. They cough so violently that bits of egg and potato fly from their mouths.

"All right, show's over," Susy says patting their backs. Suddenly the anger is gone from her face. She is serene, almost a little embarrassed by her outburst. She makes sure Goliath and Tiny can breathe then quickly goes inside.

Goliath heaves, his throat burning from coughing so hard. But it's nothing compared to what Harry feels. His pride stings more than Goliath's throat, and in an attempt to regain some of his composure he brushes his orange juice sticky hair to the side, clears his throat, and in his most calm and polite voice he points towards the muffins. "May I?"

Goliath feels sorry for him. "Sure," he says, pushing the basket Harry's way.

Although, neither Goliath's throat nor Harry's pride makes as big an impression as what Tiny is feeling. It's his heart. It feels like it's on fire. Even in the chaos he heard Susy's words loud and clear. 'My boys.' That's what she said, 'My boys.' He's one of her boys.

## 53.3159° N, 13.3545° W, North Atlantic Ocean
## 11:15 PM, Thursday, May 19, 1988

Just like the storm passing and leaving behind it a period of good weather that stretches into the next storm, up and down in nature's never ending rhythm, so is also life onboard adapting to a similar rhythm. Tiny gets in the water late in the day, thirteen hours from when he last came swam. Harry doesn't say a word.

There are a few reasons. One, his official Guinness World Record rulebook is at the bottom of the ocean. Also, even if Harry did still have his rulebook he wouldn't have mentioned that Tiny started one hour late, or that Tiny got in the water without him.

The thing is, Harry is ashamed. Deeply and thoroughly ashamed. He can't understand how this happened. How he, the man of steel from Abbeyknockmoy, became such a finger pointing, rule abiding, know it all.

A bore, is what Mary used to call him when he quoted records from the vast library in his head. There was a time when she admired this skill he had, for a few golden weeks in the beginning of their relationship, before that quickly dissipated. *Harry, you are such a bore.*

It's not because he worked for Guinness. Plenty of non-boring people did, like Trevor, who always had a good record joke up his sleeve. It was just something Mary liked to call him. "Stop that, you bore," or "Pick up your socks, you bore." Harry heard it so much that a few months into their relationship he wasn't only convinced that Mary thought he was a bore, he felt like one. And that's when he started to act like a bore.

Because he didn't have any control at home. There, Mary ran the show, and Harry desperately tried to gain control over the one area he could: his job.

He began by organizing his desk. Once every pen was sharpened and every paper filed, he poured energy into his tasks. He used his official rulebook more than anyone else. In fact, he used it so much that his colleagues started calling him Rulebook Harry, and he quickly became the most disliked controller at the entire Guinness Book of World Records. Then it happened. Mary left him for a French juggler named Jean-Pierre that could keep three oranges, two bowling pins and a double edged sword in the air, all at once. Harry couldn't even keep one ball in the air for more than a couple of seconds.

One would think that after being freed of Mary, Harry could now go back to his old, happy self. But it was too late. The bore had stuck. Like a suntan that refused to go away.

Harry hadn't given it much thought. He was used to being Rulebook Harry. Then Susy brusquely pointed it out with the help of some fried eggs and a glass of orange juice. If that big boy had drowned, or the small one had been washed away... Harry shudders. It would have been entirely his fault. Because of his silly rules. And because of Jean-Pierre and his stupid juggling. And because Mary had made him believe he was a bore. And because he *was* a bore.

Harry glances over the railing, as if to see that the ocean is still there, before scurrying inside again. He went to apologize, but as soon as he saw Goliath sitting there, and Tiny swimming alongside the boat, all courage left him. How do you even begin to tell a kid in a wheelchair that you nearly killed him because you are a bore?

---

Susy was fussing so much over Tiny that he felt embarrassed the entire morning. He understands that everyone was worried, especially since they thought that he might be dead. He's never seen Kurt so emotional before. At first he thought he'd done something wrong. If they only knew what it felt like in the water, how everything felt safe there, like a life rolled in bubble wrap. When Kurt gave him an unusually long and hard hug, and Susy kept putting plates of food in front of him, touching his arm with every word she uttered, he knew they weren't mad. It was the opposite. They were happy he was there.

Goliath, who was expecting adventure, being a pretty seasoned explorer and all, even he was feeling tired. Nearly drowning for a second time takes a lot out of you, then add riding out a storm and convincing God to save your best friend. So for now, Goliath is happy to just sit on deck and listen to the steady hum from old Bertha, and the sounds of Tiny's arms hitting the water.

But the calm doesn't last long. It is Tiny who first sees them, since he is the one under water, and, well, that's where whales live.

He is swimming, happily lost inside the room of no thought, the endless rhythm of moving arms happening all by itself, when his eyes register something big. Something *really* big.

When a regular person is in the ocean and something humongous enters their vision, their body automatically wakes them up. Because it might be something coming to eat them. But Tiny isn't a regular person. He is yanked from the room of no thought not because he is afraid, but because he is surprised to see a sandbank this far out at sea.

They are three, huge torpedo shaped bodies gliding but a few feet below him, each one bigger than the other.

It takes Tiny a couple of seconds for reality to kick in. Tiny has three worlds in total. The one out of water, which is the hardest one to be in, but that one has Kurt, Goliath and cheese sandwiches. Which are nice things. The second one is in the room of no thought. The third one is where he is now, under water, wide awake and face to face with a family of whales.

Tiny stops swimming. The whales stop gliding. The four of them are suspended in salt water, not moving, just looking at each other. Slowly, the biggest whale glides towards Tiny. He comes within inches of him, but Tiny doesn't move. The big whale is a truly massive creature, an island of rubbery flesh, covered in barnacles, and just before its nose, the size of a Volkswagen, is right up against Tiny's chest, it stops. This ancient creature curls its upper lip and Tiny's heart nearly stops. Not because the mouth inches away from him is large enough to swallow him whole, but because when Tiny looks into its almond shaped eyes, he sees himself.

The whale has *his* eyes, or perhaps it's Tiny that has whale eyes. Innocent and all-knowing at once, the clear whale eye is surrounded by fleshy folds that look like smooth plastic putty, and the one thing Tiny immediately notices is that in that deep pool of wisdom there is not a single trace of evil or maliciousness. Only pure love.

There's something about seeing yourself stare back at you that makes Tiny unable to tear his gaze from the large mammal, and through the shimmering surface water it feels like he is staring into a mirror.

A wave of vibrations suddenly hit Tiny. It rings through him, setting every cell in motion, before exiting out through his back. Did the whale burp? That's when he hears the *ping*. Although it's not very loud, but deep and clear, it seems like the loudest thing in the world. As if someone struck a gong inside his head. Every part of him vibrates and maybe that's why he answers the way he does. The way his *body* does.

Somewhere behind his stomach, a muscle contracts sharply, and this time a sudden eruption of vibrations leave *his* body, moving in a forward direction. The *ping* follows.

Everything takes a moment to settle, then there's a new

set of vibrations, and a *ping* comes from the whale. Tiny can't explain how, but something in his mind uses these vibrations to create the word "friends", and, again without thinking, the space behind his stomach contracts and the following *ping* forms the word "yes". It's in the midst of other *pings* and contractions, that Tiny understands. They are communicating. Tiny is speaking whale.

They talk about where they are from - the whales are from everywhere, just like the water in the ocean - but after a few pings back and forth Tiny understands that just recently they are coming from a place the big whale calls Pyramid Grave, because an underwater mountain shaped like a pyramid slopes so far down into the depth of the sea it is like a grave.

They exchange names, just like when people meet. Papa whale is called Physeter, mama whale Ambergris and baby whale Cachalot. Cachalot has never seen a human before, and slowly swims around Tiny, curiously bumping into him with his snout. Physeter, on the other hand has seen humans before, but never this close. Only as small dots lining the decks on ships far away, or, as all whales have learned to avoid, big, unscrupulous fishing fleets. Humans usually mean danger. But with Tiny it's different. Tiny can speak their language and when he does his vibrations carry none of the human darkness, only purity. It is like he is one of them.

---

Above the surface Goliath notices the moment Tiny stops swimming. It's like something suddenly goes missing. *The sound,* Goliath thinks and looks up from his book. *I can't hear*

*Tiny's arms hitting the water.*

He leans over the railing, trying to see into the water. At first he can't find Tiny because he is several feet under water. Eventually he spots the tips of his long hair floating on the surface, like fine kelp.

He hollers up to the bridge, signaling Kurt to stop. Susy is out on deck even before Bertha has come to a standstill.

"What's wrong?" She asks.

"Dunno. Tiny stopped."

They look at Tiny's floating hair, and if they really focus they can see Tiny below the surface, gently moving his arms.

"Is he OK?"

"I think so," Goliath says, because it doesn't look like Tiny is struggling or anything.

"Maybe he's tired of lying down?" He offers, because sometimes when he sleeps too much he gets really tired of lying down.

Harry chooses his words carefully, still ashamed of himself for putting them in danger. "What if he's stuck?" he says, trying to show that he does care.

While Goliath stares at him as if his eyes themselves were capable of saying *dodo*, Susy thinks Harry's got a point.

"Maybe we should throw something in for him?"

Kurt, who has come down, is one step ahead of her. He takes off his shirt, kicks off his shoes and begins to wiggle himself out of his pants. He's going to jump into the water. Goliath has never seen Kurt without a shirt before and the tattoos on his shoulders and chest, with scenes of mermaids and sea monsters and pirate ships come alive as Kurt balances on the railing.

But before Kurt can jump in Tiny pops his head out of the water. "Physeter and Cachalot want to know if you'd like to meet them."

Kurt briefly loses his balance, nearly falling into the water. He circles his arms and without an inch to spare manages to get back down on deck again.

"Meet who?" Goliath asks curiously.

Physeter rises out of the water, his head big enough to dwarf Bertha, and as he lets out a breath that shoots a plume of water sky high, Goliath thinks he is about to faint. A blue whale, *Balaenoptera musculus*, right here, in front of him! Drops of whale water rain over the deck and a fine mist covers everything. A blue whale! Right there in front of him! Goliath thinks his heart can't beat any faster when Ambergris and Cachalot break the surface. Goliath stares. Three whales? THREE WHALES?! He even says it out loud. "Three whales!" People live their entire lives not even seeing one whale.

"This is Physeter and this is Ambergris and this Cachalot." Tiny says, pointing at each of the whales in the family.

"Holy mackerel!" Kurt says.

Harry is so awestruck he can only mumble. "This must be some sort of record..."

Susy thinks she's dreaming, but like any mother, thinks of

safety first. "Aren't they dangerous?"

Goliath has a better question. A question that would be the first thing anyone would want to know. "H...ho...how do you know their names?"

Tiny doesn't know how to answer the question. How does he know anyone's name? It's so obvious. "Well...they told me," he says.

They are in the middle of the ocean, the four of them on deck with mouths wide open (*Close your mouth*, Susy used to say to Goliath when he was younger, *or a bird might think he lives there*), while Tiny is in the water, surrounded by three blue whales, each bigger than the next, like Russian nesting dolls. It shouldn't be possible. Except it is. Goliath pinches himself but the whales are still there.

Life is wonderful and fantastic. A place where miracles happen around every corner. Things you don't understand at first, things that seem negative, horrible even, but then, as time passes you can see they are part of something bigger. Like falling into a swimming pool and nearly drowning. And then, here he is. In front of the biggest mammals in the world. *Life can't get any more fantastic than this*, Goliath thinks.

But he's wrong.

"You want to ride one?" Tiny asks.

Even though Goliath hears the words his mouth says, "What?"

"I don't think that's..." Susy starts, looking very worried.

But she is interrupted by a "Yes!" from Goliath.

"...a good idea."

In fact, he shouts it, several times. "Yes! Yes! Yes!" Then he seems to think of something. "But... are you sure it's OK? I mean, with them?"

"Let me ask again," Tiny says. He draws a big breath, filling his chest with air, and it looks as if he's about to sneeze. Instead, he *pings*.

He listens for a ping back, then turns to Goliath and says, "They say it's OK".

Goliath doesn't know what to be most excited about. The fact that he is about to ride a whale or that Tiny just talked to them. HE TALKED TO A WHALE!

There is a flurry of activity where Susy, wanting to talk him out of it, helps getting Goliath into a neoprene diving suit to keep him warm, and a life jacket to keep him afloat, in case he falls in the water. She has to fight hard with herself. Her motherly instinct wants to say "No! It's too dangerous!" But she is also so curious about seeing the joy in her son's eyes as he rides a whale. In the end, her curiosity wins.

"I'm ready," Goliath says, all suited up.

His little heart beats so fast that he is sweating under the warm neoprene suit. His mind is racing. It pulls out all the facts he has about blue whales. Facts like their hearts are the size of a car, and weighs more than one-thousand three hundred pounds, and the arteries leading to the heart are so big that a human could swim through them, and they beat only eight to ten times per minute, compared to a human's heart that beats sixty to eighty times a minute.

Kurt lowers him over the railing where Tiny's outstretched arms grab him, holding him over the surface. He kicks his way through the water, to Physeter, the biggest of the three whales, and sets Goliath down on his head.

Goliath has to pull himself up, using the large, knotty barnacles as grips. Finally he makes it to the top of the head where there is a flat surface right above and behind the massive mouth, in line with the whale's eyes.

Susy watches in agony. *What if he slips and falls into the ocean? Or worse, into the whale's big gape? What if the whale decides to dive?*

Goliath isn't worried. He is too busy being amazed at the touch of the leathery whale skin, and a few feet below him, Physeter's eyes. They look just like elephant eyes, Goliath thinks.

Susy is getting cold feet, and is about to call it off. First this dangerous trip across the Atlantic that she was talked into, and now riding a wild animal? What kind of mother is she? She opens her mouth when Goliath turns to her and waves.

"I'm ready!"

His face is beaming. His smile is impossibly wide and stretches from one ear to the other, and his eyes are so alive it seems they have been replaced with ocean water. Susy bites her tongue. She couldn't bear to take this joy from him.

Only now does Goliath see it. It's right there, between his legs.

He's almost sitting on it - the blowhole! It's an opening the size of Goliath's head, going right into the whale, and it is covered with a thin, sheet of skin. When a whale empties its lungs, it can shoot a mist of water tens of feet up in the air.

Goliath gently rubs Physeter's head around the blowhole with the palms of his hand. It feels thick and slick with wetness.

"He likes that," Tiny says.

Goliath continues to rub the head, a bit harder this time. Suddenly a waft of warm air shoots out from the opened blowhole, and it hits him right in the face.

"Whoa!" Goliath grimaces. "Did he just burp in my face?"

"I told you he liked it." Tiny says, and disappears under the surface. Physeter starts moving.

It's a lot different from Bertha moving. Physeter is *alive*. They begin gliding slowly through the water, Ambergris and Cachalot following behind. It is a bit like going on a boat at first, but then Physeter begins moving up and down, gently rolling forward and it feels like Goliath is riding on a giant wheel.

"Follow us!" Goliath calls out and Kurt picks up his jaw and hurries up to the bridge.

"That's the darndest thing I've ever seen at sea. A lad riding a whale!"

Goliath has the sun and the wind in his face and he feels Physeter shift slightly as the giant tail pushes them forward. He can't help but reach his arms out to the side and scream.

"Yeaaaaaahhhhhh!"

It feels like he is flying more than swimming. Not just like a passenger - it feels as if he's become an animal himself.

Cachalot and Ambergris are staying close, also rolling forward, up and down, up and down. Tiny is next to him, moving in the same way. The thought comes to him naturally. *There aren't just three whales in the water. There are four. Tiny is a whale, and I, I am an albatross!*

Goliath turns to wave at his mom on deck. Bertha is steaming along after them but Kurt doesn't want to get too close to the whales. Most whales actually have scars on their bodies from being run over by boat propellers at some point in their lives, and Kurt does not want to risk that.

Susy waves back and Goliath laughs and waves again. Susy waves more energetically, and Goliath waves again. Then Susy waves a third time, using both her arms, and it looks like she's screaming, not just waving. Goliath can't hear a thing with the wind in his ears and the excitement in his heart. He turns around (as much as he can) and finally he gets a clear view. And then he goes down into the water.

Susy sees the ship heading right for the whales. It came from out of nowhere. Spotting a ship isn't a big deal, even in the middle of the ocean, but when she grabbed the binoculars to take a closer look she saw a completely black ship with a strange, pointy bow, and no name visible even though Kurt has told her that all ships must have a name. There were men on deck, all wearing the same black overalls and knitted hats, and it was when she saw the gun slung over the shoulder of one of the men that her heart started racing. A few seconds later the ship had already come much closer and that's when it became clear. It wasn't just a pointy bow. It was a harpoon.

*It's starting to become a habit*, Goliath thinks as again everything around him is a liquid mass of water. The swirling of bubbles block his view but he feels himself go down, as Physeter's body has turned diagonally, and is heading straight towards the bottom. It happens so fast that he doesn't think of releasing the leathery hump until they've already gone under. This time, luckily, it's over just as quickly.

He feels Tiny grab him around the waist and, as Physeter continues his dive, Goliath's hand slips off the knob, and before he knows it he's breaking the surface again.

He spits out a mouthful of salty water, and rubs his stinging eyes.

"Bad men," Tiny says into his ear.

That's when Goliath hears it. Not just one boat, but two.

Kurt and Harry grab Goliath as Tiny holds him up, and carefully set him down on deck.

Susy has anger in her voice. "Are you trying to give me a heart attack?" She wraps him in a towel and begins roughly patting his body, even though he's still wearing a wetsuit.

Goliath can tell she's not angry, just scared. "I'm OK mom. Where did the whales go?" He cranes his neck to see.

"Don't worry about them right now."

But that's exactly what Goliath does. Worry. *Bad men*. There was something in Tiny's voice, something he's only heard that one other time, when they were attacked by Billy the Buffoon. Fear.

"Ahoy!" A voice calls.

Tiny climbs over the railing just as the black whaling ship glides up next to them. From its deck, towering high above, a man with short, blonde hair and icy blue eyes looks down at them. He's flanked on two sides by gruff looking sailors with faces that seem to have forgotten how to smile.

Kurt speaks calmly, but Goliath can tell from the tempo and softness that he is choosing his words carefully. "What can we help you with?"

"Well," the man, who Goliath dubs Captain Ice, says, something sinister in his eyes, "What *can* you help us with?"

Kurt's voice remains calm. "If you're having engine problems I'd be happy to radio for help."

Captain Ice considers them from above for a moment with his steely hard eyes. Without warning he spits, and the glob lands on deck, right between Goliath and Tiny. Tiny doesn't say a word, and probably wouldn't have even if it had landed right on him. He stands, dripping wet, looking at his feet.

Goliath scans the ocean around them. There's no sign of the whales. He notices Tiny doing that thing again, taking a deep breath into the back of his stomach, and there's that soundless jerk with his chest.

"What's going on?" Goliath whispers.

His next question is about to be 'where are the whales?', but Captain Ice beats him to it.

"You didn't happen to see where those whales went, did you?"

Even though they are in a smaller boat, and there are only five of them and these men have guns and harpoons, and they are caught in the middle of nowhere, Kurt gets something defiant in his voice when he answers. "What whales would that be?"

A seagull flies by. It's a rare sight this far out at sea. Captain Ice nods to one of his men, who raises his shotgun. The loud blast has everyone on Bertha twitch, and before the rolling sound wave has died out in the distance, the dead seagull falls to the water between the two boats.

The silence is different now, filled with a tense worry. Captain Ice speaks. "Perhaps the big fella knows?"

Tiny stands still, head down.

"What do you say, big guy. You seen any whales?"

"Don't say anything," Goliath whispers to Tiny.

His voice comes out very weak, almost impossible to hear even for Goliath. "Under."

Goliath tries not to move his mouth as he whispers. "What?"

"Hiding under us."

The whales are taking cover under Bertha, Goliath realizes, at the same time he realizes it's not just water that drips from Tiny.

It's sweat. He's so nervous he is sweating bullets.

"Is he stupid or something?" The men around Captain Ice laugh.

Susy isn't laughing. Her eyes go dark. "You listen to me you big bully..."

Captain Ice raises his voice. "Quiet!" It rings across the water like the gunshot. "You tell that retard to speak or we'll come down there and make him."

Tiny doesn't move. Nobody moves in a very long time.

"Don't say anything," Goliath whispers again, even though he knows Tiny wouldn't give up the whales in a million years.

Then there's a voice right behind them. "Don't talk to the lady that way." It's Harry. "And don't you talk to the boy that way either."

Harry steps from the doorway carrying a large axe. His eyes are dark, darker than Susy's even. "And if any of you as much as set a foot on this boat, you'll lose it."

There's a moment when time seems to stand still. Harry stares at Captain Ice and his men, like a stubborn pitbull, refusing to back down. Tiny can't stop sweating from the pressure of keeping his valuable secret, and Goliath can hear his own heartbeat. Then, suddenly, it's over.

Captain Ice spits one more time on Bertha's deck, and yells the orders. "Let's go."

They watch as the black whaler revs its engine and speeds away. Just as quickly as it appeared, it is gone.

Breaths that have been held are released and everyone draws a sigh of relief. Susy turns to Goliath and Tiny. "Are you OK?"

"Yeah," Goliath says.

Tiny finally looks up. "He says he's sorry."

"Who?"

"Physeter. For diving. But he saw the bad men."

Susy looks confounded, and who wouldn't be if whales just talked to you through a boy. But enough strange things have happened by then that this seems acceptable.

"Tell them I understand." Then she adds. "And thank them for the ride."

There's motion in the water. Physeter slowly emerges, water draining off his giant head, and he looks at them with his elephant eye.

"Oh, look! They're back!" Goliath's excitement knows no bounds.

"They say thank you," Tiny says.

"Tell them we'll always be friends," Goliath says to Tiny, his eyes glued to the magnificent beast of a whale.

"They say they will never forget us."

Goliath wants more. This is a conversation he never wants to end. "Tell them to go with us to Boston."

There's a pause as Tiny *pings* them.

"They can't. They have something they have to do."

"OK, but ask them about how deep they've been."

"Deep?"

"Yeah, when they dive."

"Really deep when they hunt giant squid."

There's no stopping Goliath's questions.

"What about...."

After another ten questions Tiny senses that Physeter is getting anxious to leave. "They have to go now."

Goliath reluctantly stops, and together they wave as the three whales slowly glide into the wide open ocean. They head in the opposite direction of the whaler, and Goliath prays that whaler will never find them.

When the whales are but flecks on the horizon Kurt heads back to the bridge, and Tiny and Goliath go inside to change.

Excitement still flooding his veins, Goliath can't stop asking questions. "How does it feel to talk to them? Is it an actual ping? Did they tell you any secrets?"

Susy starts after them but stops. She turns and goes back towards Harry. He's still clutching the axe. It's just hanging from his hand, like he's forgotten that it's there.

She puts her hands on his and gently unbends his fingers, loosening his grip. Carefully she takes the axe from him and sets it in a plastic bin.

"Thank you," she says and smiles warmly at him for the first time.

Harry looks lost. "Oh...I don't..."

She leans forward and gives him a quick kiss on the cheek, then heads towards the door. "Dinner in thirty."

She leaves Harry just standing there, unsure if he's more stunned that he stood up against those armed whale hunters, or that Susy kissed him.

"Oh boy," is all he can say.

---

It's a new day and Tiny is swimming. Bertha is puttering along as usual, and Kurt should be at the helm, as usual, except he isn't. Instead he is rummaging through the cabinet under the control panel. Then he finds what he's looking for. He blows a layer of dust from it, hits it against his fist a few times to restore its shape, and hands it to Harry. "Every ship needs a first mate."

Harry understands that this is the finest compliment he can get from Kurt, and he accepts the worn captain's hat and puts it on his head.

"Thank you," he mumbles.

Goliath watches as Susy brings Harry a cup of coffee with a wide smile, and Harry almost knocks it over, and in the process his pen rolls off the table and he and Susy both bend forward to get it, and collide. They rub their heads at the same time and Susy reaches for some napkins to wipe up the coffee, but instead nearly pushes the cup over again. Harry is quick, saving most of it, but still some of it splashes out and burns their hands. So they each hold one hand on their foreheads, and one in their mouths to ease the pain. Goliath sighs. His mom and Harry are acting like awkward teenagers around each other. Until yesterday Harry was a giant dodo, and now...well, he did stand up for them. Goliath isn't sure what that other feeling inside him is, the one that spins around somewhere in the pit of his stomach, when a deep, long hoot interrupts his thoughts.

"Can you get Tiny up?" Kurt says as he slows Bertha down to a crawl, his voice serious.

They have to lean forward to be able to see its deck through the bridge window. It's towering over them, a wall of steel. A humongous freighter.

Her name is Marie-Claire and she's carrying five thousand tons of bananas, heading for France.

"Iz engine troublez," the captain, Captain Rousseau, tells Kurt. Unlike Captain Ice, they can all tell right away that Rosseau is a kind and gentle man.

Captain Rousseau immediately invites them all on board. They tether Bertha to a rope, and then ride up an electric elevator that goes along the side of the Marie-Claire.

Kurt heads straight to the engine room with the machinist, and the two of them speak the language only engineers understand,

"The G-hammer cranked?"

"Oui, to the ninth vector."

"Kermit threads serviced?"

"Oui, last month in Colombia."

Meanwhile, Captain Rosseau offers to give them a tour of a different place - the banana room.

Imagine you are at a sports stadium watching your favorite team, and all around you are thousands of seats filled with screaming fans, as far as your eye can see. Then imagine the stadium is filled with bananas instead of people. In a giant hall below deck there are more bananas than they have ever seen in their lives. More bananas then they ever thought existed! Bananas fill containers stacked in row after row and they must have had more bananas than expected, because they ran out of containers to store them in, and here and there are huge piles of bananas on the floor.

"Wow," they say, as they walk between the piles.

If they didn't know they were on a ship in the middle of the ocean they would think they were in the South American jungle somewhere.

"Pleeze, eat the bananaz," Captain Rousseau offers.

He doesn't have to tell Goliath and Tiny twice. Tiny grabs a whole stalk and puts it on Goliath's lap as they take off amongst the piles and containers. They quickly disappear deeper into the ship, like the two explorers they are, leaving a trail of banana peels behind them.

"I have to go check somezing," Captain Rousseau says, and lifts his hat. He leaves Susy and Harry alone in the giant banana hall. They are slightly uncomfortable being alone. Because there is only so long one can stand silently and look at bananas, and even though he didn't know it at the time, because this is what he's wanted to do ever since he first saw her, Harry extends his arm towards Susy and says, "Care for a stroll?"

Perhaps Susy also had always wanted to get to know Harry from the start, or maybe it was just the way he so chivalrously stood up for them, that makes her accept his proposal. In fact, there is nothing she'd rather do right now than go for a banana walk with Harry. So they walk arm in arm down an aisle flanked by containers, mesmerized by the fact that they are actually walking through a banana plantation in the middle of the ocean.

Goliath and Tiny are in the middle of an adventure of their own. They would probably not even call going on a walk, arm in arm, much of an adventure, at least not compared to what they are in the midst of doing.

Down a long corridor lined on both sides with containers stacked to the ceiling, creating an enormous maze, they come upon a pile to end all banana piles. It's a heaping heap of green banana stalks. By now the newness of bananas has started to wear off, mostly because they've each eaten one banana too many, but the sheer size of the mound makes them stop. Goliath's eye spots something further up the pile.

"What was that?"

"What?" Tiny says, because while Goliath can look at any piece of land, and no matter the distance, pick out any animal, no matter how small, Tiny is more observant when it comes to things inside his head. Kurt sometimes calls him a dreamer.

"I saw something move up there," Goliath says, unbuckling his seat belt. Without hesitation he begins crawling up the pile of bananas. Tiny stays where he is because he isn't exactly adventurous when it comes to heights. Besides, he would probably just crush the bananas.

Goliath pulls himself higher and higher, and it really is like conquering a mountain. The bananas are like handles, and the fact that they are a bit sticky just means Goliath has a better grip. Soon he's so high he's half way up to the ceiling.

He looks down at Tiny, who, funnily enough, looks tiny next to the giant pile.

"Don't fall," Tiny calls up to him, and Goliath thinks that sometimes Tiny is just like his mother. Why would he fall, when he's perfectly in balance holding the ban...

Suddenly the banana he's holding comes lose and he feels himself start to fall backwards. The way it happens is the same way people usually describe something bad happening. That one second, right before a catastrophe occurs when you have time to think 'oh no, this is going to end badly'. That's exactly what Goliath is thinking as he feels himself slide down the steep slope of green bananas. He flails his arms, still clutching a banana in one hand, an image of the hard floor flashing through his mind. At the last second his free hand somehow manages to find a new banana, and luck of all lucks, it doesn't come lose as he grabs on to it.

He's in a bit of an awkward position, nearly upside down, but he's safe.

"Do you want me to come and get you?" Tiny says, about

to climb up the pile.

Goliath uses all his arm strength, which is pretty much the only strength he's got, and he slowly turns himself around. "Nah, I'm OK." That was a close one. One more thing to add to the avoid-because-it's-too-risky-list, right after sitting in the bow during a storm with giant waves.

"I'll be right down," he says, when something catches his eyes as he peers through the cavities between the stalks. He can swear he saw something crawling in there.

He puts his face up against the hole and spies into the center of the pile. He can't believe his eyes. Inside the pile of green bananas are Harry and his mom. And they are kissing.

For a few moments his mind is numb. How did they get inside the banana pile? Then his mind recovers from the shock and he understands. He's looking *through* the pile, and across the hall, to where Harry and his mom are standing behind a container. It's almost funny that he would think for a moment that they would fit inside the banana pile. The kissing part isn't so funny, though. It's not funny at all.

He doesn't mention it to Tiny when he comes down, one banana at the time.

"Find anything?"

"Nah," Goliath answers as he eases himself into the wheelchair. His hands are sticky against the rubber wheels.

"What do you think it was?"

"Probably just a mouse," Goliath answers, and gives his

chair a good push. The banana grip really gives him speed. Tiny catches up with just a few lunging steps.

Inside Goliath's head there is still the image of his mom and Harry kissing, so his observation skills are a bit dulled. Only when the black thing on Tiny's back moves does he do a double-take, and looks closer.

It's a tarantula.

"Don't move." Goliath says, wondering if he should tell Tiny he's got one of the world's biggest spiders on his back, but he's afraid that Tiny will freak out, and that would be the last he ever sees of that spider. So he tries to keep the conversation flowing.

"Ehm...I wonder if we'll be on TV when we get to Boston. What do you think?"

"Dunno."

"Ehm...Ever had pizza with clams?"

"Gross."

He continues with his questions all the way back through the beginning of the banana maze. However much he really doesn't want to talk to Harry, especially now, let alone ask him a favor, he has no choice. Because Susy *hates* spiders.

"Psst..."

"Yeah?"

Goliath nods towards Tiny's back, and the big, hairy spider.

"Put it in this," Goliath whispers, handing Harry an empty glass jar he's found on the floor.

To Harry's credit he responds with quite the cool. He takes the jar from Goliath, places it over the Tarantula, and with one elegant flick of the wrist, the spider is off Tiny's back. It's so skillfully done Tiny doesn't even notice. Although Goliath would never admit that, even in a million years.

---

The next day they are back on Bertha. There's a big pile of bananas on deck - a present from Captain Rousseau. Although, bananas are the last thing anyone wants to eat now. The night before they had dinner on the banana ship and everything they ate had banana in it: banana pasta with banana ketchup, banana soup, grilled banana, deep fried banana and banana pudding. On top of it all Susy made crepes with banana filling. Everyone in the French crew thought they were amazing.

"Sis was superb."

"Magnifique."

"Tres bien, Mademoiselle Susy."

"Are you sure you are not French?" they asked, because they could not believe that a non-Frenchman could make crepes that good. Susy just shrugged. She never did tell them about Francoise secret recipe.

Today they are all banana'ed out. Not one more banana. They leave them in a big pile on deck because there is nowhere else to store them, and while Tiny is swimming, Goliath is sitting in their sweet scent, admiring his tarantula. He's named her Chiquita.

"There are over seven hundred different kinds of tarantulas. What we have here is a red-rump tarantula." He's talking to himself. Susy and Harry are probably off kissing somewhere, and he would rather not think about that. Sure, he wants his mom to be happy, but what's wrong with just the two of them? They've been perfectly happy for as long as he can remember. And with Harry the dodo? No.

Kurt pops his head out the side window. "Radio."

"No thanks," Goliath says. He doesn't feel like music right now.

"No, the radio wants to speak to you," Kurt says, and holds out the microphone.

"To me?" Goliath is so surprised by this that he puts down the jar with Chiquita on deck, and quickly rolls towards the door.

A *real radio station?* Goliath thinks. *Wow!*

Meanwhile, a short, stubby wave makes Bertha jerk, knocking the jar over and popping the lid, and had anyone been there to see it they'd have seen Chiquita scurrying across deck, disappearing into the darkness inside the door.

"Hello?" Goliath says, his mouth close to the microphone. "Yes, this is Goliath."

He listens intently to the voice on the other side of the line. "I suppose so." He puts the mike down momentarily, and whispers to Susy, who is apparently done kissing for the day. "It's BBC Radio. I'm being interviewed." And then he's back at the microphone.

"OK, I'm ready." He listens to the question. "That's right, we're swimming across the Atlantic. Break the world record. Well, Tiny is. T-I-N-Y. Twelve. Dunno. Kurt does. He's the captain. Sure."

He hands the mike to Susy. "They want to talk to you."

"Me?"    She takes the mike hesitantly. "Yes, I am his mother. Not Tiny's. Technically. I might as well be as much as I feed him. He's a sweetheart. "

Suddenly Goliath remembers Chiquita, and hurries down to the deck, where he finds the empty jar.

"Oh, no!" He says out loud, but just as nobody was there to see Chiquita escape, nobody is there to hear him say it.

———————————

The next couple of days are the same. Tiny swims, Goliath and Susy do several more radio interviews, and Chiquita remains gone. Goliath doesn't tell anyone, not even Tiny, even though it makes him feel a little bit bad to keep a secret from him. He especially doesn't tell his mom. Nobody really wants to come near the jar anyway, so it works out well for a while. Just to be on the safe side he puts a black rag at the bottom of it, so from a distance it looks sort of like a spider.

"Everything is connected," Kurt always says, "Like a fishing net nobody sees." Goliath has heard him use that, and a lot of other sayings, many times, but he has never really thought much about them until now. Because that saying is basically what finds his father. Or, rather, it's what makes his father find him.

It starts with the banana boat. Every Frenchman at the party is so impressed with their adventure. They have never heard of anything so extraordinary.

"Incroyable."

"Fantastique."

"You sure Tiny is not French?"

Another person who also finds it 'incroyable' is Captain Rousseau. In fact, he finds it so 'incroyable' that he phones his cousin who works for the biggest newspaper in France, and that newspaper is read by a few people in England, and one of those people work for BBC Radio. And when the BBC airs their story about the boys who voyage across the Atlantic, set between a segment about the regional scone competition in Bristol (won by a Margaret Schlepp) and a show called *Gardening with Hortensia* (the show's host is named after a flower) interest for the boys starts brewing. Soon the local stations in Ireland pick it up, and men who have once sailed with Kurt, or have eaten at Susy's diner, elbow their friends and say, "I've sailed with him," or, "She's served me coffee." Then more newspapers and radio shows get a hold of it, and the news becomes what dry grass is to a fire, and Boom! just like that people all over the world knows about the two boys setting a new world record by swimming across the Atlantic. Incroyable.

This net, somehow, is big enough to catch Goliath's father. And he sends word that he is on his way to see them, like some knight in shining armor galloping through the ocean, leaving a wild trail of froth and ocean spray behind him. Goliath can't stop thinking about him. He thinks about him so much he completely forgets about everything else.

Harry happens to walk up to him while Tiny is swimming, he sees the jar that no longer contains Chiquita, and only a black rag. Harry looks at the jar, then at Goliath, who shortly after decides he's not quite a dodo, even though he kissed his mom. Harry could have put up a big stink, but all he says is, "don't tell your mom."

At night Goliath talks Tiny's ears off about his father, telling stories about where he's been, and his reasons for staying away, and if Tiny thinks it's all a lot of horse manure, as Kurt sometimes says about stories he hears on the news, he sure is kind enough to not say a word about it. He just fills in with an occasional 'wow'.

Goliath is happy get out all the stories he's had in his head for so long. It was starting to get crowded in there. Even to him it sometimes felt it wasn't true that his father was in India, working for a maharaja, or running a ski camp in Nepal, or growing pineapples in Brazil. The memories, or fantasies, were starting to fade, like old photographs, but now they were coming to life in all their glory again, bubbling out of Goliath like colorful confetti.

Every night Tiny falls asleep to Goliath's stories, and there are no longer any questions about life at sea. Tiny doesn't think much of it because Goliath always talks a lot. As a matter of fact, Tiny usually feels tired after dinner, and listening to Goliath is like listening to the radio - it just goes on and on, even if you don't say anything yourself.

They are about a quarter of the way across the Atlantic now

and Tiny has never swam this far, or for this long time, ever before. He feels fine but the fact that he is staying in his secret room with no thought so much turns him into a bit of a clam. Everything happens on the inside, so he doesn't need to talk. Every night as he climbs over the railing after the day's swim his body is weary, but it's the kind of weary that disappears after dinner and a good night's sleep, and not the kind that chips away at you, day after day, chip by chip, until the engine is full of sand and won't start again.

Tiny wakes up every morning feeling strong, and he welcomes getting into the water again. He's heard about the interviews and Susy says they all want to interview him. But what would he say? What do clams say? Bubble, bubble? That wouldn't be a very interesting interview. Swimming is his thing, not talking. So that's what he will do.

Susy is thinking about Goliath's father, too, but in a different way. She thinks, for example, why now? Why would that moustache-wearing, irresponsible no-good, afraid-of-commitment, call-yourself-a-father, suddenly come back now? And out here, in the middle of the ocean? She is left with a strange feeling in her chest that has her toss and turn at night. It's annoying because before she slept like a sea star.

Most of all she worries for Goliath. She's never seen him this excited before, except when he was riding Physeter, and she tries to calm him down. Not because she doesn't want him to be happy - of course she wants him to be happy - but because of the height his excitement has taken him and how hard the landing will be if he falls. But maybe, she thinks, maybe Goliath's dad has finally come to his senses? Maybe that moustache-wearing, irresponsible, no-good, afraid-of-commitment, call-yourself-a-father has finally come to his senses. So she keeps her mouth shut and continues to toss and turn at night.

It's noon the next day when a boat no bigger than a fleck of dirt appears on the horizon. It's Goliath, of course, that spots it before anyone else, having scanned the East for days on end. After ten minutes the boat is getting close. Goliath can hear the roar of the engines and watches the hull as it skates across the water, the bow bobbing up and down on the surface like a waiving hand.

*What's the first thing he should say?* Goliath wonders. "Hey," or something more direct that gets straight to the point maybe, like "Are you staying?" But then that might offend him. Although he *did* leave them. Maybe he'll just wait with the questions until they get to know each other. Maybe "how was India?" is a good one to start with. Someone on the motorboat pulls on the throttle and now it's only Bertha and Tiny that he can hear. *I wonder if he still has the moustache,* Goliath thinks, as the motorboat turns sideways to gently meet them, and Kurt softly halts Bertha.

A man with glasses and a suit comes out of the motorboat and puts fenders down with a hurried motion, and then disappears back inside again. There is movement behind the glass, but it's too fuzzy to make anything out. *Oh, here he comes, here he comes,* Goliath thinks, excited, and then Susy steps into his line of sight. She's getting on the motorboat! Goliath can't believe it. What if my dad is in a wheelchair too, and that's why he can't come out on deck? Wouldn't that be almost...funny?

He rolls across deck, towards the motorboat. OK, how do I

get over the railing without the help of Tiny? Tiny's swimming ahead because he doesn't like starting and stopping, and Kurt's up on the bridge and Harry seems to have gone up in smoke.

Where are people when I need them!

Goliath is trying to pull himself over the railing when Susy comes back outside.

"Mom, I need your help with this. Hey did you see...." His words trail off. She looks weird. Like she's seen a really bad or scary movie, while eating too much popcorn.

"Honey...," She begins and it's all that it takes, that one word, for Goliath to know his dad isn't on the boat. As if everything is rehearsed and timed perfectly, a big-bellied man wearing a Hawaiian shirt and a white hat pushes Susy out of the way, and climbs aboard Bertha.

"Where is he?" The man says. He looks around. "Tiny?!" He calls out louder.

Even though he's five hundred feet ahead of them, deep inside his room of no thought, Tiny is yanked out of his peace so hard that he returns all the way back to his childhood. Because the voice that rumbles through the air and cuts through the water belongs to his father.

———————————

Tiny is terrified as he climbs over the railing on to the deck. Goliath knows that glassy stare by now, eyes directed straight at his feet, and if it wasn't for the water running down his body he's sure Tiny would be sweating bullets again.

Paddy, or Saint Paddy as they call him at the local pub, the agent tells them, even though Goliath hasn't heard of any saint that wants to cut off his son's hand and sell them to the highest bidder, waddles up to Tiny, walking as if he was paddling a canoe or pulling himself along on a rope. He gives him a big hug. It's not a loving hug by any means, more like a violent patting, the way he crashes into Tiny with his big belly, then slaps his back with both hands like Tiny was an old pillow he was shaking out.

It's over in a few seconds. Paddy takes a few steps back. He squints his eyes and looks at Tiny, who is still staring at his feet.

"My...," Paddy begins, "...boy," and it's clear they are hard words for him to utter. Then there is silence. Awkward silence. Not for long, though, because the agent fills in the gaps, which Goliath soon learns, is what agents do. They talk.

"We are very happy to be here, both me and your, ehm... father. Wow, what an accomplishment. People are really interested in knowing more, being part of all this. We can sell it. We can sell *you*. We're gaining exposure by the hour and now is the time. A book deal, a movie deal, speedos, action figures, anything you can think of. We can sell it. We can sell *you*. It's Tiny, right? Right. Tiny, we can sell YOU. This, what you are doing on this...ehm, trawler, it's so hot right now and we..."

"She's not a trawler," Kurt says.

The agent stops talking, but just for a second. "It's not? I thought...Well, it doesn't matter," he says and continues, as if agents have special lungs that don't need to stop for air. "We can even sell trawlers with the help of Tiny. It's going to be huge. With my help this can be huge. Catalogues, radio, online, you name it. Maybe even Dancing With the Stars, why not, right?"

Paddy clears his throat, and motions with his hand for the agent to hurry up. He seems to have forgotten all about Tiny already, tapping at his phone instead of trying to talk with his son whom he hasn't seen for years. "No reception out here, huh?" He says to no one in particular.

"We use bottles," Goliath says.

"Huh?" Paddy gruffs without taking his eyes off the screen.

"An empty bottle, you write a note, and put a cork in it. Throw it in the water and wait."

Paddy stares at Goliath, a toad-like smirk across his face. *Maybe he's thinking about what he can get for my legs,* Goliath thinks.

"Funny, kid," Paddy says and turns to the agent. "Can we wrap this up?"

"Absolutely. As I was saying, there are real possibilities here, a once-in-a- lifetime opportunity, and we need to make sure our asset is protected."

"Asset?" Susy's standing with her hands on her hips.

"She's mad," Goliath whispers to Tiny, who finally looks up.

The agent looks flustered, which is what happens when Susy puts her hands on her hips like that. It's like his mom has a superpower too.

"I mean, well, yes, asset, but also opportunity, whatever you want to call it. Good for you, good for us."

"I want to call them boys because that is what they are. Young boys," Susy says, still using her superpower.

Paddy, who doesn't seem to have the patience of a saint either, snaps in an irritated voice, "Listen, you two can call it what you want. As long as you sign the papers so we can get out of here."

"What papers?" Susy asks.

"I was afraid of this," Kurt mumbles.

The agent looks at Tiny and Goliath. "Is there somewhere we can speak in private?"

All the adults look at them, as if suddenly they realize that they are aliens from another planet.

"Follow me," Kurt says, and the adults disappear into the cabin.

As soon as they are gone, Goliath is ready. "Come on!" he says, rolling towards the second door.

Tiny is frozen. But Goliath is an expert on persuasion and doesn't give up.

"I said, come on!" And Tiny finally thaws.

———————————

Goliath and Tiny peek from behind the wall that separates the sleeping and eating quarters. Kurt, Susy, Paddy and the agent are sitting around the table, focusing on a piece of paper.

"What if I refuse to sign it?" Kurt says.

"Then we wouldn't have a choice but to take legal action," the agent says.

Susy is confused. "Legal action?"

"Listen, he's my son," Paddy interrupts. "Just because he happened to live with you doesn't mean you can take all the profit."

"Profit? We're not doing this for profit!" Kurt slams his fist into the table. "You haven't given a rat's ass about Tiny since he had the guts to leave your abusive home." Kurt is so angry he spits as he speaks. "Why, I oughta…"

Paddy seems unaffected by the outburst. "Ought to what? Like I said, he's my son, legally."

Kurt's jaw muscles work as he grinds his teeth. How much better this world would be without people like Paddy, he thinks, and how much better he would feel if it was Paddy he was grinding between his teeth.

"They are fighting over something," Goliath whispers to Tiny, from their hidden spot.

"I'm not going back. To him," Tiny says.

"Just sign it and we'll leave you to finish the record and get Graham his treatment," the agent says.

Susy can't hide the contempt in her voice. "It's Goliath."

"What? Oh, yes, Goliath." He holds out a pen. "Sign right here."

"Oh no," Goliath says.

"What? Tiny looks scared. "I told you I am not going with them."

"Don't worry. They'll have to get through me to get to you." They have to get through a bird-sized boy in a wheelchair, to get to the giant boy, big enough for everyone to fear.

Even though it's the last thing he wants to do, Kurt takes the pen, and signs on the dotted line. As soon as he's done he gets up and lets out a raspy gasp, and he and Susy storm out.

"Oh no," Goliath says again.

"What? Am I going?"

Paddy holds the contract up and looks at it, his eyes shimmering with greed.

"Congrats," the agent says. "You are now the legal owner of Tiny's world record brand."

There's a tear in Paddy's eye. The agent immediately thinks what anyone in his situation would think, and tries to help. "You know, if you really want him to live with you again we can go to court and file..."

But Paddy doesn't care about Tiny. "Bah, I don't want that freak in my house again," he says, and gets up.

Tiny breathes a sigh of relief. In spite of the fact that his own father just called him a freak that he doesn't want to be near, it is the best thing Tiny has ever heard.

"Oh no," Goliath says for a third time.

Tiny doesn't understand. He just said they wouldn't take him, so what could be wrong? "What is it?"

Goliath nods. "Chiquita," He says.

Tiny peeks around the wall. They have found the black tarantula.

"Let's get off this barge before we start to smell like fish," Paddy says, starting up the stairs, Chiquita clinging to his back like she was part of a Halloween costume.

Goliath and Tiny hurry up on deck, through the back door, and reach the top just in time to see Paddy and the agent huffing and puffing their way to the motorboat. Paddy is climbing over the railing when Goliath calls out.

"Hey, Mr. Paddy the Saint."

"Huh?" Paddy turns around halfway, straddling the railings between the two boats.

"You have a *Brachypelma vagans* on your shoulder."

Susy and Harry come out on deck and they also see the big spider. Susy covers her mouth so as not to let out a shriek.

"A what?" Paddy says, and turns his head as far as it goes to one side, and when he does he comes face to face with Chiquita.

"Ahhhhh!" he screams and begins violently brushing his shoulder in panic, his body swinging dangerously on top of the railing. "Ahhhhh! Get it off me!"

Kurt watches from the bridge and decides it's a good time to fire up the engine. Bertha starts with a subdued putter, then immediately starts gliding away from the motorboat. Paddy, who has one foot on each boat, is slowly moving into a split, still flaying his arms trying to get Chiquita off his back.

"Is it gone? Is it?"

"Mind the gap," the agent says, but it's too late.

The gap opens quicker than Paddy can come down in a split, and with a roar he falls into the ocean between the two boats. "Nooooo!"

They run to the railing to see if he needs help. Paddy is fine. He is angry, spitting water and clutching the wet contract in one hand, but fine. So they leave him where he is and watch as the agent throws a roped ladder into the water.

Goliath misses most of it because he is carefully moving up on Chiquita, who has been flung onto Bertha, and now balances precariously on the railing.

"Gotcha!" He says as he covers her with the glass jar. He flips it elegantly and secures the lid.

Kurt snickers to himself up on the bridge, and gives Bertha more gas. Slowly they begin to pull away, so they don't have to hear the swearing Paddy as he climbs up the ladder.

"You better get back to swimming boy, and break that world record, or I will chop off those hands for real this time!"

Things on Bertha quickly get back to normal as Tiny starts swimming again. Nobody mentions the contract, or what it means and soon it's as if it never happened.

Susy gives Goliath a stern reminder that if Chiquita is to be on board (and she'd rather not have her there at all), he must make sure the lid is securely fastened at all times, or she will get off at the nearest harbor.

Even though there aren't any harbors near where they are, he promises to never let her out of sight. In fact, he is so busy keeping his eyes on Chiquita that for the whole day he forgets about being disappointed about his father not coming back. It's after dinner, when night falls, that he remembers. At least Tiny has a dad, even if he wants to cut his hands off. Goliath's dad doesn't even bother wanting to make a few bucks on my body parts.

Goliath tries to figure out why his father doesn't like him, for hours, until a restless sleep finally overtakes him. In his dreams everybody - Tiny, his mom, Harry and Kurt, even himself – has a moustache.

———————————

The next day isn't much better.

Although Susy sits with him on deck when Tiny is swimming, and she answers every question Goliath asks about his father (or at least tries to because she doesn't know where he is or if he's really working for a Maharadja, or even if he still has a moustache), once Goliath has run out of questions he still feels weird. Like he's angry at something but doesn't know what.

Is he angry because Tiny's father showed up and not his father? Does that then mean that he is angry at Tiny's father, or at his own father? Or is he angry with his mother, who once had her father but lost him, like one loses a glove? Or is he angry at his wheelchair, because without it, well, who knows? Or is he angry because...wait...that might be it. He's angry with himself. Not for being Goliath, and not for having Duchenne muscular dystrophy, and not even for being in a wheelchair. He is angry with himself for hoping. For hoping and believing that things were about to change when..., when nothing really changes. It's like life came down and punched him right in the face, as if saying, that was a dumb thing to do, but you only have yourself to blame for hoping. I *hope* you learned your lesson.

While Goliath suffers from what adults would call "growing up a bit", Susy and Harry, who really have nothing else to do, enjoy each other's company. They sit on a bench in the stern and play cards. They invite Goliath to play with them several times, but he turns them down. He's busy growing up.

Every time they finish a set, Susy and Harry move a little closer, as if each card granted them another inch. Soon they are flush up against each other, and Harry puts his arm around Susy's shoulder.

Goliath can't bear to look at them. There's nothing worse than happy people when you are feeling down. So Goliath rolls to his room and closes the door. There. Feeling sad about oneself takes a certain amount of solitude. Laughter, card playing and handholding can ruin it all.

He scoots into bed and starts reading *Moby Dick*. It's a

great work of literature, and by great Goliath means "big". The book is so big it's heavy to hold up when you are lying on your back. He looks at his arms. They are pretty strong, from all the wheeling. They are actually the only part of his body that he can trust.

"Hey arms, you are pretty strong," He says to his arms. Then he quickly realizes his mistake. He can't give himself compliments and be in a bad mood at the same time, so he puts down the book and gets out his periscope instead.

Periscopes are what submarines use to look at stuff above the surface, while most of the submarine is under the surface. What Goliath refers to as his periscope is a stick with a pocket mirror taped to one end of it. If he raises it to the window that sits right under the ceiling, and angles it just so, he can see Tiny swimming from bed.

One arm goes up, over and forward, then the next arm does the same, then back to the first, and so on. It's a captivating rhythm, especially if you are looking at it through a tiny mirror. Arm, arm, twist, turn, breathe, arm, arm, twist turn, on and on, and before Goliath has realized it he has fallen asleep.

He dreams about a pirate ship with rows of black canons along the side, like dark, hungry mouths. When he walks the deck and corridors he finds no pirates on board, and no matter how many doors he opens he can't find a single soul. It's like a ghost ship drifting through the ocean.

He comes to a door that says 'Powder Keg Room', and gets the feeling someone might be on the other side of it. The door is locked, though, so he picks up a hatchet with a sharp, soot black blade, and just as he is about to swing it and knock down the door, he wakes with a jerk.

He can see from the light through the window that it's getting dusky and grey outside. He must have slept for hours. He lifts the periscope and checks on Tiny. Still swimming, but Goliath knows from the fading light that he's about to wind down for the day.

He takes the periscope down and yawns. What was that? An image flashes through his mind. Is he still dreaming? He gets the stick back up and even though the mirror is so small that the world is shrunken to the size of his palm, in the distance behind Tiny, who has just stopped swimming and glares towards it in the same way Goliath now does, is the black whaling ship. Bertha suddenly shudders as her engine is turned off, as if it's some sort of sign.

Even though nobody mentions the whaling ship during dinner, how it's moored just around the corner from them, at least by middle of the ocean standards, nobody has failed to notice it there, either, sticking out like a sore thumb from an otherwise empty landscape. It makes conversation more tense than usual. It's what they call an elephant in the room, Goliath thinks, because the elephant is right there, eating heaping spoonful's of ravioli, but nobody mentions that it's sort of weird that an elephant is sitting at the dinner table eating ravioli.

After dinner Kurt joins Susy and Harry in their never-ending card game, and Tiny and Goliath are left to themselves. They don't talk about it, but they can feel it in the room, that unspoken thing that floats around, taking up space.

It's Goliath that finally says it. Partly because he's wide awake from napping for several hours during the day, but mostly because he has that inner fire that makes him want to stand up to bullies and oppressors, just like that time they were egged. Before they know how, they have managed to gather all materials needed, and are just waiting for the adults to go to bed.

It's after midnight when the last lights go off, and silence fills Bertha's every corner. Except the corner where Goliath and Tiny crouch on deck, whispering to each other.

"You got the rope?" Goliath asks, even though the moonlight illuminates the night enough for Goliath to clearly see it hanging from Tiny's shoulder.

"Yes."

"You're supposed to say check."

"Ok."

"Rope?"

"Check."

"Bananas?"

"Check."

"OK, let's go," Goliath says and Tiny lifts him up and puts him on his back, where Goliath holds on to his shoulders. Just like on Physeter.

Goliath is wearing his rain jacket and rubber boots.

"You sure you don't want the wetsuit?" Tiny says, looking concerned.

"It's such a hassle getting it on that I'll risk waking everyone. I'll be fine."

"Check," Tiny says, and while nearly as big as a whale, albeit a small one, he moves gracefully across deck with a coil of rope around one shoulder, a sack of bananas in one hand, and Goliath on his back. He climbs over the railing and into the water without a sound.

Tiny swims as carefully as he can, so as not to splash Goliath. Luckily the water is calm, and with the moon shining brightly it's easy to see where they are going.

The whaler is anchored a fifteen minute swim away. It lies dark and ominous without a single light on deck or in its windows, blending perfectly into the surrounding darkness. Just like a ghost ship. If it wasn't for the silver glare from the moonlight they wouldn't have been able to find it.

Like the captain on a ship Goliath directs Tiny. "More left. Full speed ahead. Mind the wave," and despite dragging the bananas in one hand, Tiny makes good time. It isn't long before the black hull towers over them.

It's a spooky feeling, being this close to a ship filled with men with guns that want to kill whales. Goliath feels his heart beat and realizes that anyone on deck that looks down would be able to see them. What if they accidentally bumped into the hull, and a sailor got up to check on the sound?

Goliath suddenly feels very cold, even though he's just a little bit wet. "Let's go to the back," he whispers as low as he can, and Tiny carefully moves his arm though the water, alongside the whaler.

At the back of the ship there is a small landing. Tiny backs against it so Goliath can ease himself onto it. He's now sitting just above the surface with his rubber boots dangling in the water.

&

"OK, now put a couple of bananas in each hole."

"Check," Tiny says, and Goliath doesn't bother to correct him.

"And wrap the rope around several times."

Tiny takes a deep breath, preparing to dive down into the dark water.

"Wait!" Goliath just thought of something.

Tiny doesn't move.

"We need a sign in case something goes wrong. If I do this," Goliath uses his hand to lift up one of his rubber boots from the water, "then don't come up just yet."

"Check." Tiny draws another breath, and disappears under the surface.

With Tiny gone Goliath suddenly feels utterly alone. It's dark and he's still feeling cold, and just the thought of Tiny never coming back up chills him even further. What would he do then? A kid that can't walk or swim, trapped on a small platform just above the surface of the cold sea, at the back of a whaler filled with gun carrying hunters.

He looks around and there's...nothing. No land to step on even if he could step. Only moonlit water, and where it ends, impenetrable darkness. He's so alone he might as well be on the moon. Until he's not alone any more.

He hears the match being struck before he sees anything. Then, moments later, it falls like a shooting star through the night, and lands right in front of him. The flame goes out with a brief hiss as it hits the water.

When Goliath looks up he can actually see a man leaning forward with his arms on the railing, smoking a cigarette. Goliath doesn't breathe. If the man looks straight down he will surely see him.

Goliath concentrates on not moving. It's pretty hard, even for someone that has trouble moving. It's like telling yourself to go to sleep when you are not sleepy. The opposite happens. All of a sudden his nose starts itching, and then his arm, and soon his whole body itches. He feels acutely uncomfortable and tries to prop himself up to a better position. Gently, he uses his hands to scoot against the hull, but since he doesn't have any control over his legs they just drag along with what his body does, and his boots send a ripple through the water.

His boots! With the help of his arms he lifts both his legs out of the water, just enough to get them above the surface. Then what isn't supposed to happen, happens. One boot slides off his noodle leg, and drops into the water with a soft splash.

Goliath holds his breath. He presses his back into the hull as hard as he can, hoping to make himself invisible. But his boot isn't. It bobs on the surface in front of him, slowly moving away from the landing, out into the open.

He senses that the man is looking straight down at him. It's hard to see in the dark, and he doesn't dare turn his face and look up. Otherwise why would he be leaning over the railing like that, motionless?

Goliath decides to blow his own cover, because it's silly to pretend when he's clearly already been spotted. Busted. His mom and Kurt won't be happy with them. But at least he can get off this landing and dry off. He draws a deep breath. "I can explain everything."

There's nothing.

"Hello?"

The shadowy figure above blows out a cloud of smoke, and then drops the glowing cigarette butt in the water right in front of Goliath. Just like the butt disappears, so does the man, for when Goliath looks up, the railing is empty.

He lets out a sigh of relief. That was a close call. It's time to get out of there. Where is Tiny? He scans the water but there's nothing but just that: water. He must be done by now, Goliath thinks. Where is he? Then it hits him. The boot. It's the boot!

The boot is bobbing on the surface, out of reach from him. Tiny is very literal. If they have agreed on two boots in the water under the landing, then Tiny will not come up until he sees two boots under the landing.

He waits another minute, which feels like an hour when you are cold and waiting for someone to come up from the deep, black water. Goliath knows it's possible he could wait for hours, because Tiny would not let him down. Sometimes he is just too darn dependable.

The only problem is that Goliath doesn't have hours to

spare. He is now seriously cold, with his naked foot dragging in the water, chilling the rest of him even more with every second that passes. He knows what he has to do. He doesn't want to, but he has no choice. He says a Hail Mary and pushes himself off the landing.

The water feels freezing at first, as it quickly seeps under his raincoat, and within seconds his entire body is wet. He swims towards the boot, and just as he grabs it Tiny rises under him, lifting him out of the water.

"Did you fall?" He asks.

"My boot did. How did it go?"

"I did it, but..." Tiny looks unsure.

"But what?"

"I'm afraid they will get angry."

"Would you rather they keep killing whales? Besides, you shouldn't be afraid of anyone. Now let's go back, I'm freezing."

On the swim back Goliath gets so cold he can't stop shaking. He holds on to Tiny's head, while his teeth clap together so violently that for a moment he's afraid they will all shatter and fall out like cubes of ice.

Tiny quietly carries him down to bed and Goliath pulls all the blankets he can find to cover himself with. He still feels icy cold but, nevertheless, under his tall pile of blankets it doesn't take long until he falls asleep. Mission accomplished.

Captain Ice stands straight as a pin. He's sipping from a cup of coffee and gazes out over the ocean. His icy, blue eyes trail the horizon, while exploring the even further reaching horizon in his mind. He's got a feeling, and when he's got a feeling, something always happens. It never fails and that's why most of the crew are afraid of him. Not just because of the rumor that he once threw a man overboard for forgetting to wear black - the only accepted and violently enforced dress code - or the terrifying tale that he once sawed his own finger off just to see if he could do it without making a sound.

"Sir...?" A man in his mid-twenties, clean shaven like no other sailor, and obviously dressed in black, carefully holds out a piece of paper. "Uhm...here is the report. Three grays sighted at thirty-two degrees South."

Once again Captain Ice's hunch was right. Whales were stirring the ocean surface, and the surface of his mind. He has a sixth sense. That's why they call him Captain Hundreds. Not so he could hear it, of course, nobody was foolish enough to do that. But Captain Ice knew everything that happened on his whaler, every word spoken and every thought. Captain Hundreds. He'd let that one slide. In fact, he didn't mind that nickname one bit. Because it was true. He *had* killed hundreds of whales.

"Prepare to depart in five," he says without taking his eyes off the horizon. Captain Hundreds.

Goliath can hardly open his eyes. At first he thinks he's forgotten to take his hat off and it has slid down over his face during the night. But when he tries to remove it his hands only touch his skin. And oh, boy, is it hot.

The fever has made his eyes so puffy that when he eventually manages to crank his eyelids open and take a look at himself in the pocket mirror, he think he's looking at a chipmunk.

"Holy smokes," Goliath says with a raspy voice.

Tiny looks down from above. "Oh..." Is all he says as he sees his friend.

"Yeah..."

"Are you OK?"

"Apart from looking like a chipmunk?"

"Yes."

"No. My head and throat really hurt, and I'm so hot that I'm sweating, but I still feel cold. It's weird."

There's a knock on the door. Moments later Susy pops her head in.

"You boys up?" She sees Goliath. "Oh, honey." She comes in and puts her hand on his forehead. "You are burning up," she says as she begins to peel off layers from his pile of blankets.

"Stop, I'm cold!"

Susy is relentless. "You need to get that temperature down, young man," And she keeps peeling the blankets off him.

Five minutes later, Goliath is on deck, dressed in his down jacket. He put his foot down about it, and if it's hard to imagine someone in a wheelchair putting his foot down, just imagine how hard it is to convince a very determined Goliath about the opposite. But Susy knows how to handle him and now there he sits, on deck, wrapped in his jacket, looking and feeling miserable.

"Just ten minutes to get some fresh air. You can go back to bed after breakfast," Susy says and goes inside.

Goliath and Tiny sit side by side, waiting for the hot chocolate. They look at the whaler through binoculars. Goliath struggles to open his eyes enough to see anything, but when he finally does, there it is. The all- black ghost ship.

It looks different during the day. Slightly less evil. At this hour people are out on deck, scurrying back and forth as if they were in a hurry.

It seems last night was just a dream, something that took place in another world. Another time, even. If it hadn't been for Goliath's fever reminding him of the reality of getting wet and cold, he might have believed it really was a dream. But if there was one thing that made his fever feel a little bit better, it was the fact that they would be watching these sea bullies get what they deserved.

---

Captain Ice is not a man easily surprised - he is usually the one doing the surprising - but today he is surprised when he presses the yellow engine button on the dashboard, and nothing happens. His ship has never failed him before, and it is a strange coincidence that it does so now, just as they have reports of whales nearby.

He presses the button again. Nothing. Something must be blocking the intake. He presses it again. That something better get out of the way, he thinks, because nothing stops Captain Ice from adding to his hundreds. Perhaps one day they will even call him Captain Thousands.

But the engine refuses to turn and Captain Ice, clearly irritated, pulls out a large knife. All the men around him quickly disappear like smoke on a windy day. He puts the knife up against the control panel, threatening it. "Nobody stops me, not even you."

It seems to work. Sort of. When he presses the yellow button again the engine rumbles to life, because even it dares not oppose the mighty captain. But almost as if saying *I told you so*, the engine begins misfiring, then coughing, before it dies.

Captain Ice lifts the receiver; gripping it so hard his knuckles whiten. But his voice is under control.

"Machine room, what seems to be the problem?"

He listens and his knuckles change from white to red as he squeezes the receiver even harder.

"Bananas?"

The clean-shaven young man comes in and he doesn't seem to have sense enough to be afraid. So while the other men press up against the wall, or hide behind a corner, he delivers the second bad news of the day.

"Uhm, Captain, there's a rope caught around the propeller."

Suddenly the receiver can't take it anymore and the sound as it cracks makes everyone shudder.

———————————

Susy comes out, carrying a tray, just as Goliath and Tiny, mesmerized by what they see through their binoculars, snicker among themselves.

"That's it, the rope caught."

"You think they're angry?"

"Who's angry?" Susy asks, and looks at the black ship in the distance.

The boys take down their binoculars.

"Nobody," Goliath says, and accepts a cup from his mother.

Tiny gulps his down as if it was a glass of water on a summer day, and gets up.

"I'm going in," he says and one could very well think it was eighty degrees and summer by the beach, and not in the geographical middle of the Atlantic Ocean, by the ease with which he pulls off his T-shirt and jumps in the water.

Kurt, always on time, always alert, immediately starts Bertha, and they begin chugging towards the second half towards Boston, one arm at the time.

Susy looks at Goliath. "You really don't look well, honey. Let's take you back to bed."

"Duh," is all Goliath can think, but he doesn't say it. He's actually glad he was up to see the stupid whaler break down. Besides, he's too feverish to even be a smarty-pants.

---

Captain Ice is still clutching the cracked receiver, as he watches Bertha steam away from them. On his vast, inner horizon he sees two kids, one small and one giant, moving towards his ship. And just as he knows where whales hide under the surface he knows that these boys are responsible for the sabotage. Outraged, he keeps it all in. He can't spare any more receivers. Instead, he swears that he will get back at them. No matter what. With one, quick movement he sinks the knife info the wood surrounding the control panel, where it trembles for a moment, just like the men on his ship.

---

Goliath tries to stay up, if only for the fact that it's too much trouble to get back down, undress, and get in bed. So he watches Tiny swim while Susy watches *him*, constantly sticking a thermometer in his mouth to check his temperature. It climbs steadily, in tune with the sun, and by midday Susy gets Harry's help to carry him downstairs.

By then Goliath is somewhere halfway between waking and sleeping, and through his swollen eyes he thinks he sees a moustache on the man carrying him.

"You came," he says through his fever haze.

"Shhh," Susy says, "Try to get some rest." But Goliath is trapped in that space between realities.

"Where have you been?" he asks Harry.

Harry seems confused. But only for a moment. "I went to get milk."

It takes longer than in a waking state for the words to sink in and their meaning to settle, but after a brief pause Goliath responds. "It must be sour by now."

"How's that?"

"You've been gone for years."

"Oh, well..." Harry says the first thing that enters his mind, "I went away with a circus."

Susy raises her eyebrows, and Harry shrugs.

After a pause comes Goliath's amazement. "Wow, the circus. Where did you go?"

Harry doesn't know where it comes from but the stories bubble up in him without effort. "Romania. You see, I toured with the gypsies."

They reach Goliath's bed where they carefully remove his jacket, and cover him with blankets.

"Gypsies?" Goliath now speaks from behind closed eyes.

"Yes, they were tattooed from toe to fingertip and they taught me a magic dance." Susy takes Goliath's temperature again so when he speaks his words have to fight the thermometer.

"Owat kind ov magik?"

Susy reads the temperature and shakes her head. It's high. She opens a window and removes one of Goliath's blankets. He begins to protest but then Harry gets his attention.

"Well, every time I did this dance it would take me to a new place. The first time I was quite surprised when it happened.

I was in a village square in the Romanian countryside and did the movements just like my gypsy friends had shown me - toe heel, toe heel, clap, dip down and spring up, twist to the left and tap my heels together. It made my head spin and when I could finally refocus I couldn't believe my eyes. Gone was the village square and I found myself in an entirely different place. At first I didn't recognize it, but when I looked around I saw in the distance something I recognized. The Eiffel Tower. Somehow…don't ask me how, the magic dance had taken me to Paris."

Goliath's lips move softly, but no words come over them. He has fallen asleep.

"Thank you," Susy whispers and squeezes Harry's shoulder.

All through the night Susy and Harry stay with Goliath. Tiny goes to bed in Kurt's room, after checking in on Goliath. But there's been no improvement with his fever. Instead it has climbed even higher and now stubbornly hovers at a hundred and three.

Every now and then Goliath says something, as if waking from a deep sleep, and then falls back into the abyss just as fast again. And Harry continues his story, answering any questions Goliath has.

Harry goes all over the world with the magic dance, and meets incredible people that teach him new tricks. For instance, a man in Nepal teaches him how to see through walls, and a woman in India teaches him to be invisible.

Every now and then Goliath says "wow," before he falls back into slumber again, until his dream mind has processed the information and prompts another question. Just as often Harry and Susy nod off, and they wake with a jerk as Goliath speaks, and Harry continues the story of the amazing travels as Goliath's moustache wearing dad, while Susy takes his temperature again, until they both nod off and do it all over.

By morning everyone is really tired. Susy has managed to close her eyes just a few moments at a time, and now she can't tell if she's dreaming or awake. She puts her hand on Goliath's forehead - he's burning hot. The temperature has climbed even higher during the night and she is beginning to get really worried. She leaves Harry to watch over Goliath and goes up to see Kurt.

"Tiny doesn't feel like swimming today," Kurt says.

"You feeling sick too?" Susy looks at Tiny, who's sitting on the upper cot, his legs dangling down.

"No," Tiny says and shakes his head. "I don't want to go until Goliath is better."

Susy squeezes his big toe, and turns to Kurt. She lowers her voice so only he can hear.

"What if we have to take him to the hospital?"

"Is it that bad?"

"Not quite yet, but it's getting close."

Kurt scratches his head. To anyone else he would have said it, but not to Susy. There are no gas stations in the middle of the ocean. And no hospitals.

"I could call the coast guard, but it will take days for anyone to get to us."

Susy nods. Suddenly she feels so tired. She knew it was a bad idea to take Goliath into the middle of the ocean. He's just too delicate and weak to handle the wind, the temperature, and the...Something about the other day clicks into place in her mind, and she turns to Tiny.

"What did the two of you do the other night?"

Tiny, who's never been able to lie, looks down at his knees, as if they will help keep him out of trouble. But Susy is not letting him off the hook that easy.

"You can tell me."

It doesn't take much pressure for Tiny to confess.

"We went to the black ship..."

Susy's words come out harder than planned. "You did *what*!?"

It's the lack of sleep combined with the worry that makes Susy's voice sharp for the first time.

"We swam there and Goliath got wet..."

Tiny just wants to tell her everything and maybe she can figure out how to make Goliath better, but she doesn't give him a chance.

"You...you...," Susy doesn't think clearly, and the moment she uses the word she instantly regrets it, "you IDIOTS!"

The damage is done. She sees it hit Tiny like a sledgehammer. That one word, flung from her mouth, is actually so powerful that Tiny grabs his chest.

But she's got too much on her mind to worry about everyone else's feelings right now. Goliath is sick and if he doesn't get better, he could die.

"Sorry...," Tiny says, as Susy hurries out.

Suddenly, he feels heavy as a rock. Like he would literally sink to the bottom of the ocean if he jumped into the water right now.

What if Goliath dies? Then it would be his fault. He'd be a real freak, a monster, just like everybody's always said.

"She's just worried about Goliath, that's all," Kurt says and pats Tiny's knee.

Kurt's touch makes Tiny realize that he has really let down the only people he loves.

It all comes over him, like a bucket of ice water. Suddenly it's too much to bear and he jumps down from his cot. "Some air," is all he says as he disappears through the door, and up to the deck, where he doesn't take more than one deep breath before diving head first into the waves.

Susy feels bad for how she handled that. She should never have taken her anger out on Tiny like that. She's just worried and tired, and can't help but feel like a bad mother.

She replaces the cool, wet towel on Goliath's forehead with a new one.

"Would you mind?" She asks Harry, who despite being red-eyed and weary, cheerfully puts his hand on the towel. When it really matters, it seems Harry doesn't mind much.

"I just have to do something," Susy says and leaves, hoping that Tiny will accept her apology.

Susy checks his room but neither Tiny nor Kurt are there. She checks the kitchen, then walks once around deck, on her way to the bridge. There's no Tiny anywhere.

Kurt stands bent over the map, calculating the fastest route towards the nearest hospital.

"How's it looking?"

"Not great. We're five days and nights at full speed to nearest land. How's Goliath?"

"Same. Fever still high." She looks around the deck again. "Have you seen Tiny?"

"He was getting some air. He's not on deck?"

"I looked everywhere."

Kurt looks up. He scans the water around them.

Susy gets it. "He wouldn't...?"

"I hope not. But he was pretty upset, and the water is the only place he feels safe."

---

Tiny doesn't feel safe. He is swimming straight down, vertically, deeper and deeper into the cold darkness, as if he wants to burrow into the center of the earth. The pressure is getting stronger for every few feet he sinks, squeezing his ribcage together in a wise tight grip. He refuses to give up. He moves his big hands and his big feet through the dark water, going further, and further down, not even thinking about how he has to save enough air to get back up to the surface again. There are no gas stations at the bottom of the ocean, or oxygen tanks.

But it doesn't cross Tiny's mind. He just wants to go deeper and deeper, his muscles fighting the pressure, pushing back against the millions of gallons of water surrounding him on all sides, water that is usually his friend, but that wouldn't think twice to crush him.

There it is, a pea-sized burning sensation in the pit of his stomach, the very first sign he soon needs to draw a new breath. He's felt it before, although never at this depth, because he's never been at this depth before. But he ignores it.

His hands pull harder, using the water like a rope, the burning growing to the size of a lime. It's completely dark now. Even if he looks up there is nothing but total blackness. What is up? What is down? Tiny trusts his internal compass and keeps going down.

The lime is now an orange. He can feel it as if it was a body part, pulsating, glowing with a sour heat. He has no choice; he must get down to the bottom. For Goliath's sake, he must fight the ocean, the pressure, and the desire for air. He must fight death.

He goes harder and harder, his legs pushing water out of the way, sending him forward. Then, finally, he feels it. Sand. Muddy, soft, slippery sand.

Both his hands sink into it, and he pulls himself along the bottom. Like a crab he scrambles sideways, blind to everything but the feeling of sand, feeling his way forward, touching, searching, hoping, while the orange swells to the size of a melon.

---

The situation with Goliath is unchanged. His fever is now a dangerous one hundred and four, and Susy is beyond worried.

"He'll be fine," Harry says calmly, and takes another sip from his coffee.

There is something comforting just hearing the words, even though Susy knows Harry is just trying to make her feel better. But hope...everyone needs hope. Without it nothing would be possible.

"You think so?"

"I know so. He's got a strong heart," Harry says and taps his own chest. "I should know, being a man of steel from Abbeyknockmoy."

Susy manages a smile. But it's short-lived. She's also worried about Tiny. Alone out there again, and it's all her fault. "And what about Tiny?"

"He'll be fine too," Harry says with the same confidence. "But, just in case, I'll go look for him."

After Harry is gone, the room suddenly seems so empty, even though Goliath is right there. Susy can't help but feel as if she's in the middle of the ocean, all by herself, and there's nowhere to go. She feels so lonely she starts to cry.

Big tears roll down her cheeks in a matter of seconds.

She cries over her worry for Goliath, and she cries over her worry for Tiny, and for the sadness of Goliath's father, and for all the times she hasn't been a good mother, and she cries for the choices she regrets, and the dreams that never came true. She cries so much that her tears wet her legs right into her skin, and even drips into her shoes. She lets it all out, and finally, when there are no more tears left to spill, she wipes her eyes with her sweater. Even her hair is wet, it seems, and when she opens her eyes there stands Tiny, water dripping onto her head from his outstretched hand.

"Here," he says and gives her a handful of an odd looking seaweed.

---

Kurt has heard of it before, but he's never actually seen it. *Sailors grace*, or *feverlily*, is what they call it.

He lets it steep for three minutes in hot water before he brings the cup down. Susy rouses Goliath from his deep hibernation, holding the cup against his lips.

"Drink this, honey."

She doesn't know how but she gets nearly half the cup into him before his mouth finally clasps shut.

Tiny hasn't said another word. He watches from just outside the room. Everybody waits and eventually Harry nods off. Susy is also feeling awfully tired and is just about to fall asleep when she hears the voice she couldn't live without. Slightly weaker, but there's no mistaking. Goliath is awake.

"Mom, Dad wasn't a tiger hunter in India. He was a gypsy dancer."

---

Tiny stands in the aft, coiling and uncoiling a rope, over and over again. He's still unsure about what Susy thinks of him after all this, if she's angry because he was irresponsible. He was, because Goliath is like a little bird and he's seen with his own eyes what happens to little birds that fall out of a tree. He should have known better. If only thinking about what might happen was his strong suit.

Tiny starts uncoiling the rope pile again as Susy approaches. Suddenly he feels very shy, but he's made up his mind. He'll face it head on and speak up. "I'm sorry for being irrespons..."

Susy hugs him hard. Harder than what Tiny would have imagined Susy to be able to hug, and whatever else he was about to say is knocked right out of him, and is lost in the wind.

But Susy isn't lost. She knows exactly what she wants to say. "Tiny," she begins. "I am so sorry and ashamed for what I called you. I was just so worried about Goliath. The truth is - I don't want you to ever forget this - I think you are the bravest, kindest and most amazing boy I have ever met. And no matter what happens, Kurt, Goliath and I, will always be your family."

Tiny has never received so much praise before in his life, and had so much not happened lately, things that had opened his eyes to the world, both good and bad, he would have kept staring down at his toes without being able to say a word.

Now he doesn't.

He looks at Susy. He even dares a smile. "What about Harry?"

Susy didn't see that coming. For a moment she's a bit flustered and doesn't know quite how to respond. "Well...we'll have to see...I mean..." She fumbles with her words and then realizes something. "Does Goliath know?"

"I think so. I mean, he hasn't said anything but it's hard because it's about his dad."

Susy considers Tiny with surprise. It's like she's seeing him in a new light. He knows more than what he lets on. She feels dumb for not realizing that Tiny notices everything that happens. *What is going on inside that big head of his I'll never know*, she thinks, and gives him another big hug. She starts back down, but stops and turns to Tiny.

"Please don't go on any more nightly adventures, the two of you, no matter what Goliath says, alright?"

"Yes, ma'am. I mean, no, ma'am," and he goes back to coiling the rope because he can't believe what he just did. This was about as forward as he's ever been with anyone in his whole life.

---

Even though they are in the middle of the Atlantic, and closer to the Arctic than when they started, a sudden heat wave has them all down to T-shirts and shorts. Everyone thinks is great, except Kurt.

"El Niño," he mutters.

"Who?" Goliath, who is nearly back to normal and patrols deck with his binoculars and animal books, asks.

But Kurt doesn't want to explain it further. "Bah," is all he says, and goes back up to the bridge where he sits in front of a fan.

Tiny swims as usual and when he comes up for a drink Susy notices that his back is a shrimpy red from the sun. She suggests he wait a couple of hours until the sun gets weaker before going in again, and Harry, who was once such a stickler with his official rules, agrees.

"Great idea," he says, and places another piece down of a giant puzzle of the pyramids.

So Kurt puts Bertha on a couple of hours break, and goes to his bunk to take a nap himself, or a siesta, which is what he learned to do when he was on a ship that carried oranges from Spain, and suddenly - in his own words - "everyone on board were sleeping like babies...and it was in the middle of the day!"

Goliath and Tiny have a water spitting competition where they try to squirt a mouthful of water into a bottle placed several feet away. Even though Goliath is smaller and sits much lower, he beats Tiny nearly every time.

"It's in the tongue," Goliath says as he offers some expert advice, and they go again and again until Kurt wakes up from his siesta, and leans out the window.

"I hope that's not our drinking water." And Goliath and Tiny swallow their mouthfuls and shake their heads 'no'. And without saying it out loud they mouth the words as Kurt says them.

"Because there are no grocery stores in the middle of the ocean."

---

It's after dinner when Tiny gets back in the water again. The sun is setting, and it casts the sky in a pink hue.

It's a totally new experience for Tiny, the ocean being a different place to swim in at night, with different sounds, different creatures awake, and different light. Yes, there is light in the ocean at night.

At first he trudges through a darkness that is more like a shiny gold from the reflection of the moon. But it's not long before he enters a belt of phosphorus plankton.

They float just below the surface and when Tiny glides into them, stirring up their tranquil existence, they release electric charges that set them aglow. The ocean becomes a neon green soup and Tiny has never seen anything like it before. It's like an aquatic disco, or swimming through the sky in a lightning storm.

Before his amazement has settled much a school of glowing shrimp sweep by below him. The total mass of them - there must be millions - make it look as if a pink submarine is lighting up the entire subterranean world. If he wasn't sure of it before, he sure is sure of it now: for as long as he lives he will never witness anything as beautiful on land.

The night swimming is a new experience for everyone. On board, Goliath, Susy, Harry and occasionally Kurt, who runs up and down to the bridge to give Bertha some adjustments every now and then, sit on deck and enjoy the warm night breeze. Above them the tiki torches add color splashes in the night, and to everyone's surprise and delight, Kurt gets a fire going in the portable fire pit in the middle of deck.

"If there's one thing we have, it's water to put out a fire," he says, then adds to Goliath, "but I'm trusting you to keep an eye on it."

And that he does. In fact, Goliath can hardly keep his eyes off it. The soft rocking of the boat moves the starry skies behind the orange flames, filling the air with a scent of ocean and forest alike. There's something about it that makes Goliath realize that when you least expect it, the world will hit you with all the beauty it's got.

---

The next morning Goliath and Tiny are awoken by a strange sound. It's a long, drawnout and shrill shriek, and whatever it is, it's nothing either of them have ever heard before.

They hurry out of bed, their minds and imaginations racing. Is it Harry playing the old trumpet? Or, is it some sort of bird they didn't know existed? Or, is it aliens visiting from another planet?

The shriek trumpets again. Goliath doesn't even have time to get into his wheelchair. He has to get up on deck right this second.

"Just carry me!"

Tiny doesn't hesitate for a second, and soon they stand on deck, next to a sleepy looking Kurt rubbing his eyes. But he isn't rubbing his eyes just because he's sleepy. He's rubbing them because he thinks he must be dreaming.

Before them, bobbing up and down in the water like two grey beach balls, two very loud beach balls, are a pair of elephants.

"After fifty years at sea I thought I'd seen it all when you rode that whale. But I sure have never seen an elephant in the middle of the ocean before!"

Goliath is hanging from Tiny's arms like a ragdoll, and he's speechless. Unless you count "wow" as speech.

"Wow, wow, wow, wow. WOW!"

"I thought you boys were saluting me with the trumpet again," Harry says, still wearing his pajamas.

The elephants are splashing each other with water and are clearly having a good time.

"Oh. My. God," Susy says, pulling her robe tight and fastening it with a knot. "Is this...normal?"

Kurt, for once, has nothing witty to say. "I don't know what's normal any longer. I mean, we are twelve hundred miles from the nearest..."

"Nautilus, Philomena!"

They turn around, and right on the opposite side of Bertha, a big ship is anchored.

A man with an elegant moustache looks down at them from deck, and below him, big block letters spell out 'Anatolios Sea Circus'.

"Ahoy!" The man who must be no other than Anatolios himself, says, and waves.

"Ahoy..." Susy says and waves back, while Goliath still can't speak.

"Wow, wow, wow, wow....wow."

Anatolios is just as warm hearted and boisterous as you'd expect a Greek with a floating circus would be. "We have always been seafarers. Just think of the Odyssey," he says, and he tells them the story of how he came upon such an unusual occupation, while showing them around the ship.

"When I was a little boy a circus came to town, and my grandfather, a fisherman, took me to see the tigers and the elephants, the daredevil trapeze artists, the Spanish horses and the clumsy clown, and I never forgot that feeling of magic. But I'm Greek so I can't be on land too long, so what to do?" He looks at them as if it's an actual question.

"Ehm..." They scramble for an answer but Anatolios has all the answers already.

"So I started a floating circus." He slaps his hands together, as if saying, *problem solved*.

It's not like any other ship they've ever seen. Then again, they've never seen a floating circus before.

The midsection holds a big circus tent with a ring and everything, and in the aft Anatolios keeps the stables that house Nautilus and Philomena, two snow white horses from Castille named Doris and Rosa, and a retired lion named Billy - retired because he lost his teeth and no audience would be afraid of a toothless lion.

"Can I touch him?" Goliath asks.

"Absolutisimo", Anatolios says and opens Billy's cage without hesitation.

Susy is not sure it's such a good idea for Goliath to go into a lion cage, especially not after surviving that fever, and diving with the whales, and so on. But before she can protest Goliath has already rolled into the cage.

He goes right up to where Billy lies sleeping on the floor.

"Wake up, Billy," Anatolios says, and gently tugs Billy's tail.

It's a tired lion that opens his eyes and after a few yawns, stands up.

"Meet my new friends," Anatolios says, and pushes Goliath even closer. He whispers to him, "he can't see that well."

Susy is watching in horror from outside the cage as Billy puts his nose on Goliath's chest, sniffing him. He may be old but he's still huge compared to her little boy.

Suddenly Billy opens his gape wide, and swallows Goliath's entire head.

"Is OK, is OK," Anatolios says to Susy who has come running into the cage. "He thinks it's show." He does a gesture with his hands close to Billy's eyes, and he let's go of Goliath's head.

Goliath, however, now covered in slimy lion saliva, doesn't seem upset at all. He seems to think that being covered in lion saliva is the greatest thing that ever happened to him.

He wipes off the slime from his glasses, takes up his notebook, and writes, *Lion*, right after *Elephant*. "Wow, wow, wow," he mumbles.

They leave Billy the Lion and continue on their tour of the floating circus. Wherever they go they come across circus workers that are either building, adjusting or repairing something. They nod and smile mysteriously at them as they pass, but never say a word.

"Why do they all look the same?" Goliath whispers to Susy, but apparently not low enough, for Anatolios picks up on it.

"They are Papuans, the wonderfullest people in the world, after Greeks. Mystical, strong, pure hearted, loyal. The animals love them because they trust them. Just like you," He says and points at Tiny.

"Huh?" Tiny says, a bit startled as he didn't expect to suddenly be the center of attention.

"Good heart," Anatolios says, and taps his finger against Tiny's massive chest, and as if sensing that equality is very important at a certain age, he taps Goliath's head, and says "Good head," before continuing the tour the only way a Greek circus director can: loud, joyful, with endless stories and a booming laughter.

Eventually they all enjoy a lunch of spanakopita, which nobody learns how to pronounce, but everybody enjoys nevertheless.

"I have no idea how to say it," Kurt says and takes another bite, "But my mouth doesn't seem to care."

The resident strongman, and a bearded lady who must have gotten all the strongman's hair because his head is all bare, have lunch with them. All the chairs are taken, and as Tiny is looking for somewhere to sit down, he spots what looks to be a big log. With his spanakopita in one hand, he uses his other hand to simply pull the log closer to the table, while the Strongman eyes him. He is mighty impressed with Tiny's physique, and can't believe how he just moved what wasn't a log at all, but a steel beam, as if it was made out of paper. He tries to persuade Tiny to lift some of the heavy weights he uses to awe audiences in ports all over the world. But Tiny isn't interested, or is just too shy to try.

Once they have all eaten four spanakopita each (but still haven't learned how to pronounce it), Kurt declares that it's time for them to get going. With all the stops and extra days he is getting increasingly worried that they won't have enough fuel to get to Boston.

After giving everyone a hug, Anatolios sees them off from deck. He even gets Nautilus to fanfare them as they leave. Susy is blowing kisses as they depart, because that's what they do in Greece, and everybody else is waving and cheering, wondering, as Bertha takes them further and further away, if Anatolios and his animals weren't just a dream, or at least a mirage, for it was almost too magical to be true.

Perhaps it really did happen because the next day, as Tiny swims and Goliath sits on deck recounting his list of animals observed, which has gone through a significant growth these last weeks and is now starting to look like something a real explorer would be proud of (all that is really missing is a crocodile and a snow leopard) he sees in the distance a boat no bigger than a fleck of dirt.

He brings his binoculars out and the fleck becomes a speck, and soon the speck grows to a lump and Goliath thinks, *Anatolios must have forgotten to tell us something really important! Perhaps Nautilus and Philomena have learned a new trick, or perhaps the strongman thinks he can lift more than Tiny?* But when the lump turns into the size of a coin, everything that is good disappears, and he starts screaming to Tiny.

"Go faster! They're back, go faster!"

Tiny pauses for a second and looks up, then quickly puts his head back down and starts stroking as hard as he can.

Kurt sees Tiny pull away from Bertha, and increases the speed.

"Now what is that lad doing?" He mutters.

"We have visitors," Harry says, looking back through the side window, at the coal black whaler storming their way.

Captain Ice is at the helm, but he isn't manning the controls. Instead he's got his binoculars locked on Bertha, a cold smile curling his lips gently upward. "They are running," he says to no one but himself, even though several other people are on the bridge. "But there's nowhere to hide," and his lips curl even higher.

He brings the binoculars down and barks out an order. "Get the harpoons ready."

"Yes, sir!" A sailor says, hurrying outside.

"Whales?" The clean-shaven, young man with more courage than the rest, asks. He's got the same blue eyes as Captain Ice.

"What?"

"Arming the harpoon. Have you spotted the whales?"

"Just one," Captain Ice says, studying Bertha in the distance.

The young man looks at the old fishing boat with concern.

"Dad..."

Captain Ice turns around, quick as a cobra, and his words come out with more poison than a snakebite.

"I've told you not to call me that on board."

The young man looks down for a moment, ashamed, and then faces his father again.

"Captain, is that really necessary?"

Captain Ice now studies him, as if trying to find anything in his face to disprove that it really is his son standing in front of him. His words come out without emotion. "Revenge is never necessary. But it is fun."

With that he pushes the boy to the side, and barks out more orders to his men.

Susy has to yell at Tiny several times before he interrupts his powerful strokes and pops his head up. Harry watches the whaler get closer and closer, while Goliath looks disappointed.

"We could have outrun them."

Tiny climbs onboard. He looks scared.

"Are you OK?" Susy asks.

"Are they coming?"

"It's going to be fine," She says.

Tiny still looks scared because he knows something Susy doesn't. "They are angry."

Goliath looks at Tiny and shakes his head, mouthing the word 'no'. This time Susy catches them. She won't allow another incident on this trip. She turns to Tiny because she knows he will tell her the truth.

"Did you two do something to that ship?"

Tiny swallows hard. There's no way he can lie. "Yes."

Goliath shakes his head. "It wasn't that bad, I promise."

Harry isn't taking his eyes from the fast approaching whaler. "It looks like they are manning the harpoon."

"What?" Susy says and grabs the binoculars. "Oh my Lord, it looks like a warship!" She turns to the boys. "What did you do?"

Goliath shrugs and gives her his most innocent face, while

Tiny can't help but stare at the pile of bananas.

"These?" Susy asks. "You used *these* to sabotage their ship?"

Tiny looks at the coiled ropes.

"And a rope?"

*That's it*, Goliath thinks. Tiny is officially the worst liar in the history of liars.

Kurt comes out on deck wearing an old World War I helmet and carrying a gun that seems to be just as old.

"Whoa, what are you doing?" Susy is officially freaking out.

"There's no way we can outrun them," Kurt says. "Here, grab the hatchet." He hands it to Harry.

"But...but..." Susy doesn't know what to say, or do.

"We have to defend ourselves," Harry says.

Goliath doesn't seem too worried. "Is there a gun for me?"

"No!" Susy's voice is shrill. She can't believe what is happening. First they live through storms, and accidents, and a fever and now they are being attacked by...by whaling pirates?!

Goliath can tell from his mother's voice that there is no talking her into him getting a gun, so he hurries down to his room to get his slingshot. When he comes back Kurt is handing Tiny a plank.

"What do you do when someone attacks you?"

"Uhm...I run." Tiny says, and it's true, he's run away from so many things in his life that if he didn't happen to have webbed fingers and toes he'd probably be a runner instead of a swimmer.

Kurt grunts and shakes his head. He never could convince Tiny to stand up for himself.

Even though it's a serious matter, a very small part of Kurt seems to look forward to a battle. There is just something about his face when he says, "You fight back," and thrusts the plank onto Tiny.

From inside the whaler, Captain Ice's son scans the horizon. He sees five people standing on deck, facing them, and they are all holding some sort of make shift weapon in their hands. "It looks like an army of scarecrows," he mumbles to himself, while his father is busy yelling at his men to prepare the harpoon. Even though the five scarecrows are outgunned and outmanned, there is something in the way they stand, defiantly, that makes him...worried.

---

They stand side by side and watch the whaler thunder towards them. They can hear the wild roaring from its engine.

"This is crazy," Susy says, and Harry thinks she has a point. What are three adults and two kids going to do about a whole ship filled with men with guns?

"Perhaps when they see us they'll be so scared they turn around?" Goliath suggests.

Harry doesn't have the heart to tell him that not even a group of nuns would be scared of them.

"Maybe..." he says, just to make Goliath feel good, and he barely has time to finish before the whaler does a sharp turn, and heads away from them.

Captain Ice's son has taken over the controls. Captain Ice rushes inside, angry and convinced that the young man sabotaging his revenge is absolutely not his son. What son would go against his father's will like that? He is just about to grab his shoulder and shake some sense into him when the young man speaks.

"They're back. The whales are back."

Captain Ice halts his hand midair. It sits there for a moment, trembling with a rage that may just have found an outlet. *What did he say? Whales?*

"Right there," The young man points at the group of three whales, south of the old fishing boat. It's Physeter, Ambergris and Cachalot. "If we get the whales we get both revenge, and make money."

Captain Ice can't believe his ears. It's the perfect revenge. And who came up with it? His son. Yes, he's sure now. It's his own flesh and blood standing there, and his hand comes down softly upon his shoulder.

---

With their hearts in their throats they watch the whaler make a sharp turn, shortly before they are about to get rammed.

"What in the..." Kurt mumbles, as surprised as everyone else.

Everyone except for Goliath. He jumps up and down in his seat with excitement. "Yay! We scared them off!"

Susy is dumbfounded. "I can't believe it."

Harry, who is still watching through the binoculars, suspects something isn't right. And as soon as he sees the plume of water his suspicion is confirmed.

"They are going after the whales!" he says, and starts running towards the cabin.

Kurt has Bertha speeding towards the whales. Well, speeding isn't the word anyone would use to describe it, but he has Bertha going at full throttle. She chugs along as fast as she can, while Goliath, Tiny and Susy watch in horror from deck.

The whaler circles an area where they think the whales will surface to get air after hiding under water for a while. A grown up whale can hold its breath for ninety minutes, but a baby whale has to breathe every three to five minutes.

"Get away from them!" Goliath shouts.

The whaler pays them no attention, and continues to prowl the water, the harpoon locked and loaded and ready to fire at the next whale that breaks the surface.

Kurt tries to steer Bertha in the path of the whaler, blocking its way like a linebacker in American football.

"Sons of seaslugs," he mutters under his breath, while Harry follows the whalers every move.

"Going left. Turning right. Back again. Faster. Going around." Harry acts like his eyes and ears.

If they can just stay on their tail they will disturb them enough for the whales to make a getaway.

But an old fishing vessel like Bertha is no match for the fast and modern whaler.

"The little one is bound to come up for air anytime soon," The wily-eyed harpooner with a big scar running down his left cheek, tells his mate, a bleak and scared looking fellow who, if he had a choice, would probably rather be assigned kitchen duty, than having to aim that razor sharp silver spear, at the bubbly and toy-like whale. But there's no disobeying a direct order. Unless of course you want to swim home.

"Over there!"

The wily-eyed harpooner turns the cold, black metal stand the harpoon is attached to, and his mate has no choice but to follow along.

The moment Cachalot breaks the surface, Tiny spots him.

"There," He says and looks at a spot on the ocean about 90 degrees from Bertha and the whaler. Moments later, someone on the whaler has gotten the command and its engine roars as it heads for the young whale.

Cachalot instinctively knows that he is in danger, and only takes a small sip of air, before he again is forced to dive down and hide in the depths of the sea.

"He got away," Goliath says elated.

Tiny knows something the others don't, and while he sheds his towel and steps out of his slippers, he can feel the ever increasing heartbeats of Cachalot, as he tries to use every ounce of oxygen he's got.

"Don't!" Susy screams.

It's too late. She can only watch in horror as Tiny disappears into the ocean.

---

At a depth of thirty-five feet Tiny finds the whale family. They are not surprised to see him. They have sensed his presence all day.

Tiny hovers in front of them. The ping Ambergris sends is stronger and sharper than before. *Why are your kind trying to hurt us?*

Tiny doesn't think, at least not like a human, and his body pings back. *I'm not one of them.*

Physeter sends a softer ping in return. It's not just directed at Tiny, but at all of them. There is something woeful about it. *It is the way of the world.*

But Tiny doesn't like that world and if he had to choose one it would be this one, the one below the surface. *I won't let them hurt you.*

*He has to breathe again soon, his lungs are still small.*

Tiny wishes he had the power to stop the whalers. Perhaps a sharp mind that could come up with a plan would have helped now. But all he has is this big, stupid body. Big, stupid body... *I have an idea.*

"There it is!" The wily-eyed harpooner again leans into the harpoon to swivel it around, and his mate who seems to weigh hardly nothing, swivels with it.

"Fire at will!" Captain Ice's voice sounds cold and unemotional in the speaker.

The harpooner looks into the sight and tries to zero in on the baby whale. It's hard when everything is moving, but after settling in he finally has him in the crosshairs.

"Don't shoot," His mate suddenly says, and puts his hand in front of the sight.

"What in the....!" The harpooner is about to yell something mean and cruel to his mate, when he sees it.

"The boy."

Tiny is right in front of the whale, treading water, and making himself as big as possible in order to protect Cachalot from any harpoon shots.

On Bertha emotions are running high. Goliath screams at the whalers. "Don't point that thing at my friend!" He loads his slingshot with a pebble and releases it towards the whaler. But the pebble only bounces of its hull without doing any damage.

"Don't make things worse!" Susy says and takes the slingshot from him.

"But Mom!"

"No buts!" She turns to Tiny. "Tiny, get out of there!"

———————————

Captain Ice listens in the receiver up on the bridge. "What *about* the boy?" He doesn't think twice before he answers his own question. "I guess if he insists, shoot him." He turns to his son. "Those fingers might fetch a pretty penny on the black market."

There are no words coming through the receiver, only the steady rasps of breathing. Someone on the other end is clearly thinking hard.

But Captain Ice waits for no one. "That's an order!"

There's still only breathing, as if the harpooner is wrestling with his decision.

"I said, that is a direct order!" Captain Ice yells.

Finally a weak and unsure voice responds. "Yessir."

"Don't do it," The mate pleads with him, and again puts his hand over the sight.

"You heard the captain. Now get out of my way."

"You can't shoot the boy!"

"Don't worry, I'll just get the whale."

Still, the mate refuses to remove his hand from the sight.

The harpooner looks at him gravely. "I said, get out of my way."

The mate looks scared. And he *is* scared. More afraid than he's ever been before in his life. But he still can't let them shoot at the whale with the boy there. What if they miss?

"No," he says.

"We are whale hunters. That's what we do. We hunt whales and when we find them, we kill them."

The mate seems about to start crying. He finally removes his hand.

"Thataboy," The harpooner says, and zeroes in on Cachalot. "Now hold it steady." His finger squeezes the trigger, slowly, and just as the shot is about to go off and the harpoon catapulted from his chamber, the mate gives it a firm push.

BOOM! Everybody jumps from the loud explosion, and just two feet from Tiny the surface erupts in a cascade where the harpoon disappears into the water.

"You fool!" The harpooner says, knowing his mate just sealed his fate.

"You'll pay for this."

"I don't care. I'm not killing any more whales...and I'm certainly not killing any humans!"

Suddenly a pebble hits the harpooner square in the head. "Ouch!"

Across the stretch of water Susy is shooting at them with the slingshot.

"You stay away from my boy!"

Another pebble hits the window behind them, and cracks it.

"You hear me? Stay away from him, I said!" Susy is so angry her voice breaks, while she loads pebble after pebble that Goliath hands her.

"Wait," Goliath says, after the fifth pebble. "Where did they go?"

Once again the surface is empty, and both Tiny and Cachalot are gone.

---

They meet again, face to face, at thirty-five feet.

*We can try again,* Tiny pings. *We just need a little more time.*

None of the whales ping back.

*Maybe I can make them go one way, and you can go the other?*

There's still no ping coming back. Tiny wonders what's wrong when suddenly Physeter glides forward and gently puts his massive nose right up against his chest.

*There is only one way to save my family.*

Tiny senses that something out of his control is about to happen. Somehow the nose on his chest makes him unable to ping. It's like a hand silencing his mouth.

*It is the whales' way.*

Tiny understands. He wants to scream, convince them of another plan, anything but this, but his pings are gone.

*One leaves space for another.* And just like that the big nose pulls away from his chest, and before he knows it, it rises towards the surface.

---

Captain Ice is holding the mate over the railing. "I'm throwing you to the sharks, you no good traitor!"

A huge, submarine shaped body breaks the surface, and rises out of the water. It lets out a giant breath, and a plume of vapor shoots past them, reaching a hundred feet up in the air.

Captain Ice freezes. "The harpoon," He whispers, and lets go of the mate, who falls into the ocean. Captain Ice pushes the harpooner out of the way, and takes hold of the black weapon. He aims it at Physeter, who lies still, blocking the path towards Ambergris and Cachalot.

Captain Ice's mouth turns upward, not into a smile, but into a grin. He silently mouths one word, and puts his finger on the trigger. "Gotcha."

---

Tiny knows what he has to do but he can't seem to move. Things have already been decided upon. It started thousands of years ago, nature's way, the whale's way, the world's way, and he's just one part of it. One tiny part.

He hears the subdued boom and feels it vibrate through the water, and before the blood begins to color it red, he does what he was born to do.

*Go!* He pings, and begins to swim.

Susy puts her hand over Goliath's eyes and shuts hers when the harpoon is fired into Physeter's magnificent body. He thrashes his big tail, slapping it against the surface, and the entire whaler is covered in water.

A second harpoon is loaded and a new shot rings out. BOOM!

Goliath sees it all in sound and he starts to cry behind his mother's hand.

Physeter blows out a powerful breath through his hole, and Goliath can still feel it under his hands, the rubbery skin, so alive, elastic and ancient.

The third harpoon is fired. BOOM! and Goliath brings his hands up and covers his ears. He focuses on the feeling of floating through the ocean atop that big head and brain, five times the size of a humans, containing all the collected wisdom of the sea, and he presses so hard the only thing he can hear is his own pulse.

Not until they are a mile away do they dare come up to the surface to breath. Their lungs are burning and they can't go any further. But they are out of danger. He did it. He delivered them to safety, like a shepherd of the ocean.

Tiny's heart beats hard and he draws big breaths. No pings are needed now. They know what is done, and they have to keep going. Nature makes no excuses, and demands no apologies. The rain does not tell the sun it's sorry. They are all part of the same circle. Every drop part of the same ocean.

Tiny watches them go. They tumble forward majestically and fluidly, towards a safer place, if they can find one, and a long life as the wisdom keepers of the ocean.

When they are finally out of sight Tiny turns and starts back towards Bertha with a black hole in his heart.

---

"It's over," Susy says, her stomach churning.

She pushes Goliath to the other side of deck, away from the grisly scene. He presses his hands down over his ears, and keeps his eyes tightly clamped shut. He doesn't see Kurt or Harry struggle to pull the mate onboard or how, when they finally manage, they sink to the floor, their backs against the railing. As if all air has gone out of them. Not because they are tired, but because their hearts are so filled with sorrow and despair, they suddenly weigh twice as much.

"I tried to stop it," The mate says.

"I know, I saw it," Harry says, and pats his knee.

Goliath suddenly removes his hands from his ears and opens his eyes. His cheeks are red and streaked from tears. He looks at them, his mouth ajar, as if he's listening. Can they not hear it? It's there, in the distance. Not a sound but...like something that hits you in the back of your stomach.

"He's angry."

They all look at him. They don't get it. Goliath feels very cold now, and he knows why. He's scared.

"Tiny. He's very angry."

Then they hear the screaming.

---

Physeter is tied to the side of the whaler, blood running from deep gashes in his side. Tiny tastes the blood five hundred feet away, and it ignites something in him. It might as well be his blood that's been spilled, and the world that was once white, always peaceful, always avoiding fights and trouble, always running away, now turns black. Tiny feels it surge through every part of his body. He's never felt like this before. It's a raging, rushing, pumping, overpowering anger. He wants to destroy them.

He glides through the water, stealthy, deadly like a shark locked on a target, and as he gets closer all he sees is red. He doesn't look right at him, but he knows he is dead. He can feel it. There's an emptiness where there was once a boundless energy, and with a few explosive strokes he leaps out of the water with a blood chilling shout, a primal scream that's as much part of nature as the ocean. He clings to the side of the whaler, holding on to the minimal seams and rivets in the black steel. Somehow he scales it up to the anchor hanging down from the port hole, and to the people on board that watch him he couldn't look more intimidating. It's as if a sea monster has leaped from the ocean, and onto their ship.

Tiny's eyes are completely black. He grabs the big anchor with both hands, the muscles in his shoulders and arms bulging, and it's like he is no longer there. Gone is the timid, shy and gentle giant. What hangs from the bow of the big whaler is nothing other than completely wild, and untamable.

On Bertha everybody watches in silence. Too much has happened in a short span of time, that they have lost the power to react. All they can do is watch, as events unfold before them. Destiny. There is nothing they *can* do. The old Tiny is gone and the new Tiny has only one thought in his head. He wants to sink them.

Tiny leans his big head back and lets out a guttural shriek. He starts pushing with his legs against the hull, pulling the heavy anchor with him, and then, like riding a swing, he quickly bends his legs and lets the anchor drop right back down, where it crashes into the hull with a heavy thud.

The anchor, which weighs twelve hundred pounds, feels like cotton in Tiny's hands. His legs, telephone-pole thick thighs and calves, explode against the hull as he swings the anchor out and up into the air again, as if it was nothing. When the pendulum swings back he aims the tip of the anchor at one spot on the hull where the paint has already chipped off and a small dent is formed, and he rides his iron swing like a kamikaze pilot into that very same spot. It's a direct hit and the inside of the ship rings out as a giant gong.

Again and again Tiny slams the anchor into the hull, and on deck the crew is scurrying around like nervous rats. Captain Ice is shouting out orders but in the chaos nobody seems to know what to do. They've never had a raging giant trying to knock a hole in their ship before. Tiny hits the ship again and again, the muscles in his body like the muscles of a whale, thick, stable and inexhaustible, the rage in his eyes undiminished. A small hole has opened up in the reinforced steel hull, and for every hit the hole becomes a little bigger.

Captain Ice is trying to gain control, but his crew seems unable to get Tiny off the anchor. They try everything. They pour a bucket of water on him, but Tiny hardly notices it. Then they try using a long stick to poke him with, but Tiny just grabs the end of it, and with one twist of his wrist, he snaps it in two.

Again and again he slams into the ship, the taste of whale blood still in his mouth. He wants to rip this ship to pieces, pulverize it, eradicate it from the planet, along with all evil, all killing, all sadness, bullies, garbage and greed. He hits the hull again and knocks a hole big enough to get his hands into. Sitting on the anchor he grabs one edge of the jagged steel and begins yanking on it like a madman. Neither Captain Ice nor his crew can believe their eyes as Tiny, in his glorious rage, finds the superhuman strength to slowly rip the steel apart with his bare hands.

This sends the crew into an even bigger flurry, and Captain Ice is going berserk. The wild animal that was once a shy boy is trying to rip their ship to pieces!

On Bertha everyone is watching as the whale crew bust open a crate.

"We have to do something," Susy says.

"To save them?" Kurt asks.

Harry is watching with binoculars. "They are getting a net out."

The crew work quickly to untangle it, and then attach it to

a crane to hoist it up until it hangs right above Tiny, who has now peeled off half a panel of hardened, ship grade steel, and there seems to be no weakening of his strength.

Captain Ice gives the order and the net drops. It lands right on Tiny. Now, hardened steel is one thing, but a net, with its flexing rope, is a difficult enemy, regardless of how strong you are. Tiny quickly gets tangled in the mass, and when Captain Ice gives the order to pull the net up, Tiny lets out another shriek.

Goliath has only heard that kind of shriek at one place before. At the zoo. It's the scream of a captured, wild animal.

"Oh no," Kurt says, and everybody assumes he is talking about Tiny being caught.

Nobody turns around, and when Captain Ice picks up a rifle and aims it the squirming Tiny, hanging but a few feet above deck, and Kurt speaks a second time, still nobody turns around. "By the holy mother of Ireland," he mumbles.

Too much is happening right in front of them, but if they only would turn around they would see the biggest rogue wave Kurt has ever seen in his entire life, building at the horizon.

Waves the size of a fifteen-story building are extremely rare, but every two hundred years or so, somewhere in the world, they are born through a perfect combination of wind, weather patterns, and underwater earthquakes. It would be a miracle to witness such a rare occurrence, except that everyone that ever has is now dead, at the bottom of the ocean.

"We've got a problem," Kurt says.

"You can say that again." Harry says, still following Captain Ice's every move through the binoculars.

"Mom, is he going to shoot Tiny?"

"No, honey." Susy answers with all the confidence she can muster. But the truth is she isn't very confident about anything anymore. If they can only get Tiny out of the net and get on with the last part of their trip, then everything might work out after all.

Kurt, who knows something nobody else knows at this very moment, knows they must act fast. He calculates the rogue wave to hit them in about one minute.

"Hey!" His voice rings out loud and clear between the two ships. As if captains of the sea have a special language heard only by them, Captain Ice looks up.

Kurt doesn't say anything. He doesn't need to. He points towards the incoming disaster behind them.

Captain Ice follows the direction of his finger until he sees it. He looks at it for a few seconds, with furrowed brows, as if he doesn't quite understand what it is.

Finally Kurt speaks. "She's bigger than anything I've ever seen."

Captain Ice knows as well as Kurt that their chances are miniscule, and despite Tiny, and the whale tied to the side of his ship, and his burning anger and lust for revenge, his years of experience at sea make him realize that he must let all of that go if he is to stand a chance to survive the most violent natural phenomenon he's ever witnessed.

He throws the gun on deck and starts barking out orders.

"Turn around! On the double if you want to live! Full speed ahead!"

It seems to take only but a few seconds before the whaler is speeding away from them, in the opposite direction of the rogue wave, and with Physeter still tied to its one side, giving them a slight tilt.

"He's trying to outrun it," Kurt says with resignation.

"What about Tiny?" Goliath asks with his heart in his throat, but nobody seems to have an answer for him.

Harry will be damned if they are just going to sit there and wait to die. "Everybody inside!" he yells, and grabs Goliath.

They run as fast as they can and get to the bridge with thirty seconds to spare. Thirty seconds to impact. Goliath can see the wall of water and he knows it's real because they all say it is, except it doesn't look real. It's just a wall and walls are not supposed to be on the ocean. They are not supposed to be moving forward like this wall is. When Kurt slams the throttle full speed ahead, steering Bertha right towards it, instead of turning around and going in the other direction, Goliath is sure he's dreaming. Who would drive a boat straight towards a moving wall?

Susy also can't believe what she's seeing. It feels as if she's been through a washing machine lately, with one thing after another turning her world upside down. And even though she clearly sees the incoming rogue wave, feeling the deepest fear for her and Goliath's lives, for everyone's lives, her voice somehow comes out calm and clear. It's as if her voice is trying to convince her that everything is going to be alright. But what do voices know?

"Why are we going straight towards it?"

It's a logical question, even for a voice. Perhaps the only logical question when in twenty seconds they will be face to face with that black fluid that seems to have solidified into a giant slab of alabaster.

"You can't outrun it."

Kurt seems unnaturally calm too, and that, if the rogue wave wasn't enough, makes Harry realize that they really are in great danger. Because that's how people react in real danger. If it's normal to freak out over simple danger, like seeing a spider, or getting scared when someone jumps out of the closet, it's just as normal that people keep their cool in real dangerous situations. Because your body knows that's the only way to survive. Faced with something so big you can't see any way out of it, all you can do is accept it, and calmly wait for it to come.

"The only way through one of these monsters is to face her head on," Kurt says, and that alone takes another ten seconds out of their last seconds alive.

Ten seconds to go, Goliath thinks, because he's always been good at math.

He thinks about how it all started, that day at the pool when he fell in and Tiny saved him. It could have been a catastrophe, he could have died. But he didn't. Instead he made a best friend, which lead him to an adventure of a lifetime.

He feels Susy take his hand, then Harry taking his other. Five seconds. So this is going to be alright too. They are getting through this catastrophe, and Tiny will get through it wherever he is, and they'll continue on their journey because that's what an adventure really is. It's life with a bunch of things happening and you keep going even though you never know what's around the corner.

On the 12th of May, twenty-one days from Boston, the dark wall of water hits them at a speed of twenty-three miles per second, and everything goes black.

---

Only God sees clearly through the dark night, when everyone else fumbles in blindness, lost in the unlit corners of life. Only God - or Jerry - can watch through his lens as worldly events unfold like movies on a screen. Only Jerry sees the biggest rogue wave to rise out of the North Atlantic since 1806, later nicknamed *Napoleon* by weathermen and meteorologists because it galloped across the ocean wildly like a thousand man mounted army, and only Jerry sees the lone former fishing vessel named Bertha, like a tiny speck of dust on a large silver shield, struggle full speed ahead, right towards this formidable army. Only Jerry, who's seen it all, every detail of every detail in the world, is filled with something that can only be described as awe, for the courage displayed below him. And perhaps it touches something in his heart that hasn't been touched in a long time, among all the wars and diseases and suffering that spreads throughout his kingdom, and perhaps that's why he reaches a Godly finger down from the heavens and draws around Bertha a golden circle of protection, from bow to stern. When the mighty aquatic army has closed the distance between them, without slowing down, or its anger fading, and the fishing vessel hits the very bottom of the steep wall, momentarily beginning an impossible climb, and a pending annihilation from being crushed under the brute force of many thousands of tons of water, an opening, no bigger than a slit, appears in the wall, and the fishing vessel is sucked inside it, and disappears. And God, or Jerry, smiles, as he retracts his glowing finger back up into the heavens.

---

Captain Ice mans the controls himself, pushing the whaler to its limits. The net, with Tiny trapped inside, sways wildly across deck during the bumpy ride, while behind them the galloping army of water is closing in, its hoofs kicking up a dark, frothy rumble.

"It's gaining on us, Captain!" The crew is frozen from fear.

His son is so scared he forgets to use proper titles. "Dad, do something!"

Captain Ice can't hear them. He can only hear his own heart beating, counting down the seconds, like a clock on New Year's Eve.

Tiny watches them from inside the net and he sees the panic and fear on their faces through the glass. He's seen it before, in the ocean, in hunted animals' eyes, the panic when they try to flee, and the fear when they realize that they can't. *You are the whales now,* Tiny thinks, and just like that his anger leaves him.

Up above Jerry watches them too. He watches his army, and it's his not because he controls it, but because he is the creator of everything, including every drop of water, and every wave. And he sees it charging across the Atlantic, closing the distance to what is running from it by the second.

There is no awe to be felt for one who runs away, unless it is to save another, and he extends no fingers and draws no glowing, protective circle. Instead, the circle of life will have to work itself out, as it always has, and always will. So he leans back, perhaps attends to other matters in the world, and lets the ocean have its revenge.

On the twelfth of May, twenty-one days out of Boston, Napoleon's army catches up with them at a speed of twenty-three miles per second, and they are never seen again.

---

Once again Goliath finds himself under water. But this time it's different. He can actually breathe.

When the slit in the huge rogue wave opens up, and Bertha is sucked into it rather than being crushed at the bottom of the steep mountain, they find themselves under one hundred feet of water.

The pressure is enormous and the windows surrounding the bridge creek under the weight, threatening to shatter and fill the boat with water so quickly it would implode. But, somehow, the windows hold for the unearthly pressure and the five of them glide in silence through the deep blue sea, just like a whale.

Then, as if the oxygen trapped inside Bertha suddenly remembers that it ought to race for the surface, Bertha stops gliding forward and instead rises straight up, like a bubble released from the depths of the sea.

They burst through the water's surface like a cork, and the landing, after what feels like catching a fair amount of air, is more jarring than going into the wave. Everybody falls to the floor, along with everything else that isn't locked down. Cups, maps, jackets and boots fly out of cupboards, chests and closets, as Bertha again comes to rest on the now-placid ocean.

As Susy opens her eyes and regains her barings, she pulls a pile of clothes off of Goliath where he lies on the floor. He looks shocked. And no wonder. They just went through a wave they shouldn't have been able to survive. "Honey, are you hurt?"

Goliath looks around the room. It's a new day. It's even a new life.

Harry and Kurt pull themselves from the floor and rush over to help Goliath back into his wheelchair. "How do you feel, Buddy?" Harry says.

Goliath speaks slowly, his voice serious. "I can't feel my legs."

He looks at them with a deadpan expression. There's a moment when Susy doesn't know if she should laugh or cry, before they all understand. Goliath cracks a smile, and that's the signal. They all start laughing.

They laugh the tension away, until they remember that Tiny isn't with them.

Tiny doesn't panic when the wave hits. Suddenly the net is under water, and he tumbles around and around. Tiny relaxes and lets his body go limp. He knows he can't fight the force of the ocean, and lets the movement take him where it wants. Not until it stops tumbling does Tiny try to find the opening of the net, and when he does, he swims towards the surface.

He stays there for more than an hour, swimming back and forth, looking for anyone, anything. But there is no trace of the whaler, or any of the sailors. Though Tiny's heart was filled with rage, the ocean has washed it away, and he would selflessly save anyone he finds. The ocean has claimed its price, however, and after covering the area several times, he finally starts swimming in the direction of Bertha.

It takes an hour to reach her, and when he does they are waiting for him on deck. Susy hugs him hard, and he's starting to get used that feeling. The feeling of coming home. Then Harry and Kurt do the same, and it's all beginning to sink in. What they've been through. Where they've been. Heaven and hell.

The only person that doesn't seem to have been very worried is Goliath.

"I knew you would come back," He says.

"Me too." Tiny says.

It's not that Goliath really wasn't worried. It's just that suddenly, sitting there on deck after going right through that wave, breathing the ocean air, and knowing that only people that are alive can breathe, Goliath was just overcome with this feeling that everything was going to be alright. He didn't just feel it; he felt it so hard that he knew it. After all they've been through, there was no way on earth that Tiny wouldn't come back now.

There was something else too, something that made Goliath sure Tiny would come back - if there is one thing Tiny can do, regardless of rogue waves, whale hunters or storms, it is swim.

"Mom's making spaghetti and meatballs for dinner."

"Sounds good."

Things quickly goes back to normal aboard Bertha, with Tiny swimming every day, dinner in the evening, and him and Goliath talking in their bunks before they go to sleep. Still, something *has* changed. Not just with Tiny, who has withdrawn even more into himself, especially when swimming, where he rarely leaves his room of no thought. They don't talk about the whaler, or the men that were swallowed by the ocean. They don't talk about Physeter. However, each of them, in their own mind, remembers Physeter and the whaler every morning as they climb up the stairs to deck and they see the ocean. It reminds them of life, and death, that the two are forever intertwined, and that the reason they are there, crossing the Atlantic Ocean one stroke at a time, is life. Not only Goliath's life, and his treatment to have a longer, better one, but Kurt's life, which again has found meaning, and Tiny performing a once-in-a-lifetime feat, not to mention Susy and Harry finding a life together. It's a trip about and for life, and this day, nearing the end of May, three hundred miles from Boston, as they walk to deck and see the ocean the first thing in the morning, they remember Physeter, and the whaler, and they are happy to be alive.

## 43.0330° N, 63.5557° W, North Atlantic Ocean
## 09:27 AM, Saturday, July 2nd, 1988

It's the forty-eighth day of their long journey. They are now only seven days from Boston. Tiny can tell that they are nearing land by what he encounters: garbage. Plastic jugs, old fishing nets and soda cans serve as a bitter reminder to Tiny of life on land. It's not just from the garbage he encounters floating in the ocean. He also has to deal with garbage in the form of people.

In the middle of his swim he hears a boat coming, and looks up. He knows, his signals sharpened by the many weeks at sea, his body and his mind by now speaking more 'whale' than English, that something is coming.

It's not anything as bad as whale hunters. It's just life on land catching up with them. In a way, it's what they wanted from the start. Media attention, some recognition for their world record attempt, and hopefully that will be enough to pay for Goliath's treatment. Even though the boat that arrives delivers both those dreams, it comes with a price. That becomes obvious as soon as Paddy the Saint climbs aboard Bertha, along with the agent, a cameraman, and this time, a woman Tiny's never seen before.

Soon a flurry of activities begins, with photos of Tiny and Goliath of course, but also of everything else, even the fenders and the coiled rope, as if they had swam across the Atlantic as well.

The woman is a reporter for a big television news channel, and she is there to interview Tiny. But before they can begin, there's more paperwork.

"Let's get down to brass tacks," Paddy says, and puts a check on the table in front of everyone. "That will cover the boy's treatment, or if that doesn't work at least set him up with wheelchairs for the rest of his life. They even make 'em computerized these days and..."

"What do we have to give in return?" Kurt asks while Susy ogles the check in amazement, because he knows nobody does something for nothing, at least not Tiny's dad.

"Brass tacks, I like it," Paddy says. "Nothing. He just has to be himself. Just do some interviews, take some photos, be on some shows, maybe a small tour, those kind of things."

"That sounds incredible," Susy says and stares at the check.

"Just sign here," Paddy says, and pushes a contract towards Tiny.

Tiny doesn't look at his dad, and doesn't seem to know what to do.

"Right there." Paddy taps the dotted line.

Tiny looks at Susy for guidance. It's a tough decision, but she's also mesmerized by the check. "This would cover Goliath's treatment," she says, although the last thing she wants is to pressure Tiny to do something he doesn't want to. Well, the second last thing, because the last thing she wants is for Goliath to become worse. Even though she feels a little bit guilty, she adds, "And that's why we are here, right?"

That's enough for Tiny. It *is* why they are here, and he signs the dotted line with a big "T".

When it's time for the interview, the reporter, whose name is Wanda, speaks first to Goliath. He has plenty to say about everything from the raccoons in his backyard to the whales he rode in the ocean, and he spits it out so fast that Wanda has to ask him to slow down, several times.

With Tiny it's a bit...slower. A boy of a few words usually, he is too shy to say much more than yes or no to Wanda's questions. It doesn't help that Tiny's dad and the agent are there, trying to coax better and more elaborate answers out of him.

"Tell her how you train, boy. Show her your hands. See the webbed fingers, just like on a frog? One of a kind, that is. Very valuable. How tall are you, boy? Tell her about the wave."

At the end of it Tiny is so confused and stressed that he doesn't understand the simplest question. Wanda is visibly annoyed with the little information she has been able to gather from the world famous swimmer, but she does her best not to show it. She does feel worried about how it will go in the studio, with cameras and a live audience, but she figures Tiny will grow into it.

Tiny, who just wants back into the ocean, has no idea about being in a studio with cameras answering questions in front of a live audience, and if he did he would never have signed that contract. His dad pulls Wanda aside and tells her that he will personally guarantee that Tiny will be ready to be exploited. 'Exploited', is the word he uses. He'll make sure of it, or that boy can kiss his treatment goodbye.

Harry, watching from the stairs leading up to the bridge, doesn't like what he hears, and goes to find Susy. She is still eyeing the check.

"Can you believe it?" she says. "Fifty thousand dollars."

"We have to give it back," Harry says.

"What?" Susy can't believe her ears.

"They are planning to turn Tiny into a circus freak. If we accept this money we can't say no. He'll have to go to their shows and be put on display for the world to see."

Susy doesn't say anything for a whole minute. This money can save her son, and give him a better life. It's a once in a lifetime opportunity. She'll never be able to save this much as a waitress. She looks at the check. Deep inside she knows she can't accept it. She can't trade the life of one boy for another. She couldn't live with herself. Goliath wouldn't want it. They'll just have to figure something else out.

"Let's give it back," She sighs, and starts towards the door.

"It's not that easy," Harry says.

Susy stops and looks at him, quizzically.

"I thought you said..."

"It's too late to just give it back. He signed the contract. They have a legal right to exploit him. Unless..."

"Unless what?"

Harry puts a finger over his lips, and glances up the stairs. "This is what I'm thinking..."

---

Nobody waves as the boat with Tiny's dad speeds away. Tiny and Goliath are on deck watching it leave, and Tiny says something that is unusually forthright. "I wish I'd never have to see him again."

The irony isn't lost on Goliath, and he's not afraid to say it out loud. "It's funny that you can't wait for your dad to leave, and I can't wait for mine to come."

Tiny thinks about it. In a way it is funny. It's also not true. "Your dad isn't coming."

In the past Tiny would never have been so direct with anyone, not even with Kurt, but this trip has changed something in him. He's seeing certain things so clearly, as if they could be no other way. Goliath *is* his best friend, but best friends can get upset too, and Tiny worries that he's gone too far when Goliath doesn't say anything. Tiny is just about to say he's sorry when Goliath speaks.

"I know he's not." He says and throws his gum into the water.

"That's OK, though." Tiny says, not just like someone says

it to make a person feel better, but like he really means it, because he knows something you don't.

For the first time in his life, not just because of what Tiny said, but because of life, Goliath feels that it is OK. More than that, Goliath has thought about something for a while now but never felt there was a good moment to bring it up. Until now.

"You're not afraid anymore, are you?" he says, looking at his friend.

Tiny thinks back on his life so far and remembers the fear he always had, like a steady companion, and how the only thing he thought he could do about it was to run away. He's not running away anymore. The moment he broke through the hull to the whaler, he also broke through the hull surrounding his heart. There is nothing to be afraid of once you have been forced to face your worst nightmare. Most of it was in his head; his big head that sits perched atop that big body. Tiny doesn't have to run from anyone, ever again.

"I feel free when I swim. But now I also feel free when I don't."

"You're OK," Goliath says.

"You're OK too."

The two boys who've been through so much, despite their young age, look at the ocean they've almost crossed, and without saying it - sometimes words are not needed - they think that a true best friend is someone that helps you see your weakness, then helps you overcome it.

———————————————

Things are moving very quickly. The seven days left turn to five days, and then three, and although they've had plenty of time to think about it, they haven't thought of actually arriving in Boston. It was always about the swim, crossing the Atlantic and being on Bertha in the middle of the ocean. Now that things are drawing close to the finish line and calls over the radio come in several times a day with requests for interviews (all of which are answered with a 'maybe later', because Tiny is too busy swimming), it dawns on them that their adventure is coming to an end, and everyone gets a little stressed and starts scrubbing the deck, cleaning the kitchen and packing their bags.

There are boats on the water - every day they spot more and more boats - and while the middle of the ocean was like being on the moon, this close to land has them feel that they are back in civilization. It feels both good and annoying to have people around again, but here they are and this is what they set out to do.

The second to last day passes uneventful and at the end of the day they can see the blotchy shape of land in the distance.

Susy cooks a special dinner that night, and everything feels special. "Our last dinner on board."

Kurt has an old bottle of port wine that he claims is from the sunken ship of the pirate Captain Bluebeard, and he ceremoniously pours them each a small glass. Even Tiny and Goliath get a small glass of pirate port. Kurt lifts his in a toast.

"It ain't over until the fat lady sinks, but I still want to thank you all."

Everyone lifts their glasses, and they clang them together over the middle of the table.

"It's been an honor," Harry says. His voice takes on a bit of a more official tone. "And I'm happy to say that after tomorrow you will have earned an official Guinness World Record for the longest swim in the world."

He didn't have to do that. According to the official rules that are now at the bottom of the ocean, they did have a few times, with storms, sickness and rogue waves, where they went more than twelve hours between each daily swim, but Harry makes no mention of it. It's not lost on Goliath how Susy radiates when she looks at Harry.

"Still think he's a dodo?" Tiny whispers.

"Yeah," Goliath says. "But the good kind."

Susy gets tears in her eyes as she stands up to say a few words. "I just want to say that I love you all so much, and that even though it's been an adventure of a lifetime...I never want to go through this again."

They all laugh and settle back into eating, because they think that's the last of the speeches, when Tiny suddenly stands up.

He towers over the table and everybody goes quiet. There's still shyness there, but he looks up now, facing them all. Even his voice comes out strong and clear. "Kurt, I want to say thank you for taking care of me. When you get old I will take care of you."

Harry sits next to Kurt and Tiny rests his eyes on him now.

"Harry, thank you for not being a dodo, and we both think you are alright, and it seems Susy really likes you."

Tiny turns to Susy who has started tearing up again. Tiny suddenly looks a bit more shy, but he keeps going. "Susy, thank you for being so nice to me, and making me feel like you love me."

Susy's eyes now overflow with tears. "I do love you," she says, and even though Tiny hears it he can't interrupt his speech because he's been practicing for days under water. He turns to Goliath.

"Goliath, thank you for being my best friend. Even though I've never had one before I know I could never have a better one, and I will always be there to lift you when you need it."

There. He's done. He's said more things to more people at one time than he's ever done in his entire life, and he feels strange inside. Strange but good. Exhilarated, actually, as if he just jumped off a big cliff.

He sits down and when he sees them all looking at him, and he notices the tears in their eyes, even the shipmate that was thrown from the whaler has tears in his eyes, his shyness suddenly comes back, and the only place he can look is at his empty lasagna plate. This is what he stares at as he hears the claps. It starts in Goliath's corner and spreads around the table, and soon the entire dining room is filled with the pops of proud hands cheering for him. He looks up. Everything is in a haze. Now it's his turn to cry, but he makes himself look at them. His family.

---

It's the last day of the longest swim in the world. And it's a beautiful one, as if the morning and the sky know what day it is, and do their best to put on a show.

Tiny glides into the water after breakfast and Kurt toots Bertha's horn one last time to signal the start, and Tiny sets off.

It doesn't take long before they've got company. Boats of all sizes have come into Massachusetts Bay to witness the world record they've read about in newspapers and heard on the radio for weeks. Tiny's dad and the agent have kept busy, and pitched Tiny as the 'Irish Sea Monster'. There's even a blurry, close-up photo of his hand with the caption 'The Webbed-Fingered Creature'. Luckily no one on board knows about it. However, the ever increasing number of boats around them do, and they get closer and closer, snapping photos of the 'Irish Sea Monster', until Kurt has to use his radio to warn them about keeping a safe distance, else someone might run over Tiny by mistake.

It only gets worse the closer they get to Boston. They can see the skyline now, the tall buildings of the city towering in the distance. Even more boats are out, some from TV stations with large cameras on deck, and a news helicopter is buzzing overhead, reporting live on the event.

Goliath gets an old radio going and listens to the reports, amazed at what he hears. There are hundreds, if not thousands of people waiting at the dock! And it's because of them! They did this. They came up with the idea and how to make it happen. And they did make it happen! Big time!

Maybe too big time, because boats keep getting close to

where Tiny is swimming and Kurt has to blow his horn several times to warn them. Each time he does Tiny stops and looks up before continuing.

They are on the homestretch when it happens. They are only one mile from the harbor and Goliath can make out the crowds waiting for them in the distance, and hear their cheers, when out of nowhere a boat comes speeding towards them. There are hundreds of boats in the bay so one shouldn't stand out from another, but there is something about the way this particular boat heads in a direct line towards them. It's unwavering, like an arrow shot at a target, and it makes Goliath cringe. There are just too many things that are happening at once, and only when it gets closer, cutting straight through the inner circle of boats that surround them, heading straight for Tiny where he lies stroking, one arm, two, three, breathe, and Goliath gets a glimpse of the man at the helm, does he know something bad is about to happen - there's something about that moustache that is familiar.

The next thing he hears is the thud as the speedboat hits Tiny in the head. It's a dull and wet sound, like that of dropping a butchered chicken on the floor.

For a millisecond he meets the mustached man's eyes as the boat roars away, and it seems like - although it doesn't make any sense - like he winks at him.

Goliath doesn't even wait to think about it. He rolls his wheelchair as hard as his arms allow, and collides with the railing so violently that he flies out of his seat, and over the edge. He's already flying towards the surface as Susy yells out.

"No! It's not....!"

Goliath hits the water and begins to sink right away. He tries to look for Tiny in the dark water but he can't see anything. Just a whirlwind of bubbles. As he ascends towards the darkness, rushing away from the brighter surface above, his humor is the last thing to leave him, and he thinks, 'Great, what is this, like, the fourth time I'm drowning?' before darkness completely encapsulates him.

---

It's bright on the other side of life. As if heaven had a constant sunshine, right outside the window.

*I am dead,* Goliath thinks, as he opens his eyes. He feels that the world is moving under him, his body floating down a river. But then the lights above him would be stars, and they're not. They're rectangular beams that flash in a steady interval.

His body feels heavy and limp and he doesn't even bother trying to move it. Not that he has to because here in heaven - he's not one hundred percent sure he is in heaven yet, but he's definitely on his way, like on the highway to God or something like that - there are people, or angels probably, that lift him and put him down, and there's a hissing sound like there's a leak somewhere, and then everything goes black again.

"We are bypassing the waitlist and doing the procedure right now when his body temperature is low," one of the angels says.

*Wow, they speak English in heaven,* is all Goliath can think before he can't hear anything else.

Everything is white. The walls, his bed, even the clothes he's wearing. He notices more angels, all wearing white. They seem curious about him, the way they lean over the bed to peer at him, prodding him with their fingers as if they've never seen a boy from Galway, Ireland before. Goliath understands it must be because he is new. Even though he might be dead, *he* hasn't forgot his manners.

"Hello," he says. "I'm Goliath. I just died."

The angels seem to find this amusing, because they start chuckling and chattering in an angel language Goliath has never heard before.

"The procedure went well, Miss O'Callaghan," One angel says to someone across the room. The light over there is so bright Goliath can only make out the very outlines of their spirits.

"Is he awake?" A voice asks.

There's more jibber-jabber from the angels. Goliath hopes not everyone speaks like this in heaven, or he'll have a hard time making friends.

"He's still sedated, but he'll be coming around soon."

*It sure is stranger in heaven than I thought it would be,* Goliath thinks.

At one point the darkness lifts and Goliath floats to the ceiling. He sees himself lying in bed, wearing the white robe thing, but it's got a blue tent right over his chest. He sees the angels all standing around him, bending over into the tent.

*What's in there?* Goliath wonders.

"What happened to the other boy?"

"I'm not sure. I think he drowned."

*They are right about that,* Goliath thinks. *I drowned alright. It took four times, but eventually it worked. But what other boy are they talking about? They can't mean....Do they mean Tiny? Right, I dove in to get Tiny after the boat hit him. But I never saw him down there.*

"Some sort of record attempt."

*That's right, we did break a record. We swam across the Atlantic Ocean! But, what happened to Tiny? He must still be down there, on Earth.*

"Sad. Hand me a grip, would you?"

"He was some sort of giant."

*Was? Wait, Tiny is dead too? So he's here, in heaven, with me? That's...I guess that's going to be fun to be together forever. I just wish Tiny would have made it. Geez, Mom and Kurt must be so sad without us.*

"There, let's stitch him up and call it a day."

"Nurse, increase the gas, seems like he is waking up.

*Waking up? That's what they call sleeping here in heaven, floating in the air above yourself?* It sure is a strange place, Goliath thinks, as darkness sweeps in from the right, like a closing curtain, and erases the light.

Susy sits by the side of the hospital bed. She's waiting for Goliath to wake up. The doctor said his treatment went well, but you never know until you know.

Harry is down in the cafeteria getting coffee, and Kurt is taking a nap in a chair by the window. And Tiny...well, who could have even imagined such an ending? After that long journey, and in front of the cameras and everything it was just... Perfect.

"Mom?" Goliath peers at her from the bed. He looks like he's slept for four days, which he has.

"Oh my sweet boy, how are you feeling?"

"Mom, are you dead too?"

"What? No, I'm not..."

"Because me and Tiny are in heaven, and there are angels and..."

"You are not dead, lad. You are tougher than nails," Kurt says and peers at him with a warm smile.

Goliath looks surprised. "I'm not?"

"No, you had your treatment and the doctors say everything went alright." Susy beams with joy.

"What about the angels?"

"Well, sometimes angels come down to earth to help people," Susy says.

"But..." Goliath is confused. "But what about Tiny?"

"Oh, that lad's an angel alright," Kurt says.

Goliath can't believe his ears. *He's* not dead, but Tiny is? So now Tiny is in heaven, with no friends and people there speak a funny language that nobody understands? What happened? Everything is just so unreal. All he knows is that he was once a boy in Galway, and he fell in a pool, and... What if he died already, there in the pool, and all that happened after, all the people he met, like Tiny, Bertha, Kurt, and the things they did, like swimming across the Atlantic, was all just him being dead?

"Are you sure I'm not dead?"

Susy bends down over him as if giving him a hug, but instead she bites him in the nose.

"Ouch! That really hurt!" Goliath complains.

"Now, if you were dead would I be able to do that?" Susy asks, and Kurt chuckles.

She does have a point, Goliath thinks. But that also means... "But what about Tiny?"

Harry opens the door, holding two coffee cups. There must be a crowd outside because flashes go off, and there's the buzzing of voices. But Goliath only really hears Harry's.

"We are all so very sad about Tiny's death. That's all I have to say. Now please respect our privacy," And he closes the door and again brings silence to the room.

So, it's true. He, Goliath, the weak wheelchair-bound boy that wasn't expected to live past fifteen, somehow survived the wild adventures of the Atlantic Ocean while Tiny, the formidable giant, strong like ten grown men and with the heart of a saint, didn't? Goliath feels his tears well up. Water, he thinks, as he looks through the distorted view, I can't seem to escape it.

Wait...Doesn't that look like water, over there, going in under the closet? Or is that just my tears playing a trick on me? No, it really is. It looks like...someone with wet feet walked into the closet. "Mom," Goliath says, and points towards it.

As if on signal the door opens, and out steps Tiny. He's dripping wet, his long hair like a silvery mane, peering curiously at Goliath.

"Tiny!" Goliath screams.

"Shhhh...!" Harry and Susy say, at the same time.

But screaming is the only voice level Goliath has right now. "I thought you were dead!"

"Shhhh...! He officially is!" Harry and Susy whisper.

"But..."

The last piece of the puzzle falls in place. Where there was darkness, light shines in, illuminating everything.

---

When Goliath went overboard he was already in the water when Susy finished her sentence, "He's not really been hit! We're just pretending!"

When Harry told Susy they had to return the check he knew Tiny's father would never let Tiny out of the contract. The man who was willing to cut off his own son's hands, and sell them to the highest bidder, would not hesitate one second to exploit him in the media. Harry knew this. He also knew that the only way out of that predicament, the only sure way, was if Tiny "died".

So they came up with a plan to show the whole world, including Tiny's so- called father, that Tiny was dead. They arranged for a boat to drive really close to him and make it look like he'd been hit. They couldn't let Goliath know because of the hundreds of cameras directed their way, and it all had to look real or it would have been for nothing. Except, they didn't mean for Goliath to jump into the water and try to save Tiny.

"We should have told you," Harry says.

"Honey, we're so sorry," Susy says.

Goliath's head is spinning. "But...what about the man driving the boat? He had a moustache, and..."

"That was Anatolios. He said he winked at you," Susy continues.

"But...why is Tiny wet right now?"

"I went to the pool downstairs when you were sleeping. I put this on," Tiny shows him a white robe with a hood that hangs on the wall, "And I go out through the back."

"But...," Tiny tries to think of more questions. It's almost as if he can't believe everything is OK. That everything went according to plan. That they actually did it. They swam across the Atlantic Ocean. They broke the world record. They got his treatment. Tiny is alive.

"But..." There's one piece of the puzzle that's missing. It's right there. Goliath can feel it. It's like a crumb in your bed when you are trying to go to sleep.

"But..." It itches and scratches and is all uncomfortable against his skin.

"But..." And suddenly it comes to him. The big question neither of them has thought of.

"But how are we going to get back home?"

Everybody looks at each other. Nobody speaks.

"I mean, if Bertha is here, and all our stuff..."

"That is a good question," Susy says.

"I hadn't thought of that," Harry says, and scratches his head.

"Son of a gun," Kurt adds. Apparently he hadn't thought of that either.

"Maybe we can just keep going?" Tiny suggests.

Goliath isn't slow to agree. "Like swimming around the world? Cool!"

"No, no, no," Susy begins, but she's got no chance. Tiny and Goliath are already planning their next adventure.

"We can go to Hawaii!" Goliath says energetically, and no one could have guessed that he just woke up after being kept sedated for four days. "They have sea turtles!"

"OK," Tiny says, as if they were simply choosing what TV show to watch.

"Please stop them," Susy says to Harry.

Harry just shakes his head, and smiles. "It's impossible. These two have iron wills. Besides, swimming around the world would be a pretty good world record..."

"I know for a fact that Old Bertha wouldn't mind another adventure," Kurt says.

"Lord have mercy on me," Susy says and looks up at the ceiling, not knowing that Jerry is looking down at them.

He is smiling. Not because it's funny, but because they did it. They delivered a miracle - a message everyone in the world can see; *It doesn't matter if you are young or old, small or big. What matters is the strength of your spirit.* The world will never forget what those two boys from Galway, Ireland did. They proved that with enough spirit you can turn your weakness into your greatest strength.

2 3, 4, 6, 9